T0369535

At Your Service

C.M. Braithwaite

iUniverse, Inc.
Bloomington

At Your Service

iUniverse books may be ordered through booksellers or by contacting:

iUniverse
1663 Liberty Drive
Bloomington, IN 47403
www.iuniverse.com
1-800-Authors (1-800-288-4677)

ISBN: 978-1-4502-7108-0 (pbk)
ISBN: 978-1-4502-7109-7 (cloth)
ISBN: 978-1-4502-7110-3 (ebk)

Printed in the United States of America

iUniverse rev. date: 1/3/2011

Acknowledgments

I wish to thank my friends and family, who encouraged me to bring this story forth, especially Neibert, who read the first drafts and asked for more.

Special thanks to Judicial Security Inspector Leigh-Anne Rucker-Reid, who patiently answered my many questions concerning the US Marshals Service. Also to Stacey Steele, who provided valuable information on the fascinating world of flight attendants. Any misinformation in either area is to be laid at my door.

Thanks to my writing buddy, Cliff, who encouraged me when I was faltering and to Keith, who took the time to read this and make some great comments. Also to Aniquay, for the cover design.

Most especially, thanks be to God because I can do all things through Christ, who strengthens me. (Philippians 4:13)

Introduction

The US Marshals Service is the nation's oldest and most versatile federal law enforcement agency. The Marshals Service occupies a uniquely central position in the federal justice system. It is the enforcement arm of the federal courts, and as such, it is involved in virtually every federal law enforcement initiative.

More than 3,340 deputy US marshals and criminal investigators form the backbone of the agency. Apprehending federal fugitives, protecting the federal judiciary, operating the witness security program, transporting federal prisoners, and seizing property acquired by criminals through illegal activities are among their many duties.

The agency's tactical unit, the special operations group, is a rapidly deployable and highly trained force of law enforcement officers created in 1971. SOG is comprised of a small full-time cadre and eighty to one hundred volunteer deputy US marshals, who must meet high standards and complete rigorous training. SOG responds to hundreds of specialized missions each year—everything from high-threat trials to extreme hostage situations. Due to the extensive training of SOG members, the unit is often called upon to train military, federal, state, local, and foreign law enforcement groups in various tactical specialties.

He was so utterly, sinfully attractive!

As Serena continued to look at him, the air felt charged, electrified. Her glance dropped to his lips—he had such gorgeous, kissable lips—and she felt a sudden hunger to feel those lips pressed against her own. Without conscious thought, she ran her tongue over her upper lip and caught the bottom one between her teeth. She heard his sudden intake of breath and looked up again. His eyes locked unwaveringly on hers. She thought his eyes were gray, but they darkened now with the intensity of his expression until they blazed at her like twin coals of fire. The air between them shimmered with heat, a sense of expectancy. Serena felt she couldn't tear her gaze away if her life depended on it.

Prologue

A bead of sweat trickled through the curls on his head, rolled down his temple, and dropped onto his forearm. He didn't notice, as all his attention was riveted on the drama at the front of the bank. A thin young man, basketball cap pulled low down on his head, had his left arm locked around the neck of a young woman and his right held a Smith & Wesson semiautomatic pistol, which was jammed into the woman's right temple.

His woman.

He felt his gut clench tightly, and deep in his brain, in the part where he kept the horrors he encountered hidden, he could feel panic trying to claw its way out. Ruthlessly, he clamped down, sealing off the destructive feelings, forcing them back down into that black hole in his mind. He couldn't afford to panic. Panicking would not help anything. As he took a deep, steadying breath, he felt a reassuring calm steal over him; his brain felt clear and sharp as his analytical mind took over. He took a more intense look at the situation and weighed his options.

The deputy US marshals, who had been tracking the fugitive, had his two accomplices in custody and now had their weapons pointed at the fugitive and were yelling at him to release the woman and put his gun down. The fugitive and his hostage were in the recessed area in front of the door of the bank, and his right side was vulnerable.

That was the key. The fugitive was vulnerable on the right. He would attack him on that side and save his woman. He indicated to the deputy marshal in charge that he was going to come up on the fugitive's right flank. It was a token gesture of courtesy. He didn't know or care if the deputy was aware of his reputation, that he was not a stranger to hostage situations. It was his woman being held hostage, and he was damned if he was going to sit there and let others call the shots.

He moved away until he was completely out of the fugitive's line of sight and then started to inch his way toward the recessed area, praying as he had never prayed before—that the fugitive would stay where he was, that some trigger-happy deputy marshal wouldn't decide to be a hero, and, most of all, he prayed that the woman he loved would still be alive at the end of it all and he wouldn't have been the cause of her death. Because if he lost her, life would no longer have meaning. Unbidden but sharp and clear, the memory of their first meeting flashed into his mind.

Chapter 1

Deputy US Marshal Kyle Drummond lifted the binoculars to his eyes and focused on the car turning into the motel parking lot. The description tallied with the information the team of marshals had on what the fugitive was driving. He nudged his partner, Keith Thompson, and passed the binoculars to him. Picking up the radio, he called the team leader, Deputy Mark Jones of the Las Vegas Marshals Department.

"Got a visual on the vehicle. Suspect emerging, heading for the room."

He turned to Keith, who gave him a thumbs-up with the binoculars still glued to his face, and continued, "Affirmative. Suspect confirmed. It's Pete Jackson." His voice was tinged with satisfaction and relief.

Pete Jackson, wanted in Sans Souxi, one of the Caribbean islands, for the alleged murder of the local beauty queen and attempted murder of her fiancé, was believed to have fled to the United States. Their investigations had led Drummond and Thompson from Georgia to Las Vegas, but Jackson turned out to be skilled at evading capture and tested their capabilities.

However, as with most lawbreakers, he made a simple mistake. He paid for a motel room with a credit card, enabling the joint fugitive task force to track him down. Working together with detectives of the Las Vegas Police Department and deputy marshals from the Las Vegas office, they had the motel under surveillance for the past two days, and it looked like their information was finally going to pay off. Kyle, for one, was glad, as it was damned hot and uncomfortable in the SUV. Even though spring had barely begun, the heat was stifling in Las Vegas. Jones's voice sounded tinny as he replied.

"Okay, Drummond, you and Thompson take up preliminary positions. Rogers and I are on our way. Williams and Burke, remain where you are. Let's wrap this one up."

Kyle responded, replaced the radio on his belt, and slid out the door. Keith joined him, and they stood on either side of the door of the motel room, through which Jackson had disappeared. Jones and Rogers arrived, and Jones gave a quick nod to Thompson. The deputies burst into the room, weapons drawn, and surprised Jackson, who was sitting on the bed, drinking a beer.

"Federal agents! Hands in the air! Get those hands in the air!"

The four deputies converged on Jackson. Incredibly, his eyes cut to his weapon—a Smith & Wesson 9-mm handgun—which was lying on the nightstand.

"Don't you do it," Kyle said softly. Something in his voice made Jackson look up at him. What he saw on Kyle's face caused Jackson to freeze with his hand outstretched.

"Let me lay it out for you, yeah. You have four weapons pointed at you, held by four itchy trigger fingers. We also have on protective gear while you're in your nice little tourist shirt. If you think you're Billy the Kid and can take out all of us before we can get off one shot, you go ahead. But I tell you, I'd hate to see that pretty shirt all messed up, yeah."

Kyle stared down at Jackson, hoping to God the fool didn't go for the gun. Slowly, his eyes never leaving Kyle's face, Jackson's hands came up, and he rested them on top of his head. Keith stepped closer—staying out of the line of fire—and removed the Smith & Wesson.

"Face down on the floor," Jones told Jackson. Jackson

complied, and Jones quickly pulled down his hands and snapped on a pair of handcuffs. Kyle gave an inward sigh of relief as he holstered his weapon. Another successful fugitive apprehension. Now all that was left was to search the room and collect whatever evidence was there and, of course, the interminable paperwork. Thankfully, he and Keith could leave most of that with the Las Vegas Marshals' office.

The two Las Vegas deputies, Jones and Rogers, hauled Jackson to his feet and led him out of the room. Kyle heard the familiar sound of Keith choking back a laugh and looked across at him. Keith looked like he was about to burst.

"Billy the Kid? Itchy trigger fingers?" Keith gave up the battle and exploded with laughter. "C'mon, Drum, that the best you could do?" He held on to his stomach as another wave of laughter burst forth.

Kyle raised his hands in supplication. "It was this movie I was watching a couple nights ago. *Young Guns.* All that cowboy chatter stuck, okay?" Kyle protested mildly, beginning to chuckle himself. "At least it worked, didn't it? The fool stopped going for his gun."

"Yeah, he was probably so horrified at your C-movie acting skills, he thought it more merciful to surrender and spare us all." Another gale of laughter from Keith.

"Ah, just shut up, would you?" Kyle said, laughing in spite of himself. He'd forgotten how much Keith liked a good joke. He had to admit, it wasn't one of his finer moments, but like he told Keith, it had gotten the job done. Jackson had surrendered without incident.

He and Keith continued to search the room, Keith still chuckling every now and then. Once the complex extradition process was completed, the Sans Souxi Police Force would be notified and would escort Jackson back to Sans Souxi, where he would stand trial for murder and attempted murder. Although the investigations started in Georgia, for smoother processing, the extradition process would be handled through the Las Vegas Marshals' office, as the fugitive was apprehended in Las Vegas. If they worked swiftly, he and Keith might be able to catch a flight back to Georgia this evening.

Lady Luck smiled on Kyle. He and Keith completed their paperwork quickly and took their leave of Jones and the other Las Vegas deputy marshals as well as Williams and Burke, the police officers, who worked along with them on the task force. Now here he was, actually on board a Southern Air flight back to Georgia.

Kyle placed his hand on the back of his neck, gave it a firm squeeze, tilted his head back, and turned it slowly from side to side. He stretched his long legs out in front of him, as much as he could in the limited space on the aircraft. It had been one hell of a week, he had to admit.

Fugitives often thought they were hiding in plain sight, out in a busy city with crowds of people. And it was true in a sense. But the trouble with that theory was that what worked for them also worked for the LEO, the law enforcement officers. They could also blend in with the crowds. It worked better in the LEO's favor. If Jackson had been in a quiet neighborhood, the probability of spotting a strange vehicle was much greater than in a city.

Kyle looked across at Keith, who seemed a bit restless. He was twisting and fidgeting in his seat.

"Thommo, you're making me tired just watching you. You're like a dog chasing its own tail. Relax, bro," Kyle said as Keith continued to fidget.

"Can't seem to get comfortable. I hate airline seats. Seems there's never enough room." Keith scowled in frustration.

"If I can stretch out, you don't have a problem," Kyle said, leaning back.

"Yeah, yeah, we know you've got a couple inches on me, but I've got the build," Keith boasted, flexing his biceps and striking a pose like a contestant in a Mr. Olympia contest. In truth, his muscles were impressive, but Kyle was no slouch either, with his whipcord physique.

The passengers had not yet started boarding, and Keith took the opportunity to make a quick comment to Kyle.

"You know, for a minute back there, I swear Jackson was actually going to go for his gun. Until you made him think about it, cowboy." Keith chuckled.

"He certainly was loaded, wasn't he?" Keith said musingly, referring to the ten thousand dollars in US currency they had found in Jackson's bag.

"Getting ready to disappear. He was setting up false papers, had an address in his pocket of a known forger. Williams and Burke were very happy to get that information, yeah," Kyle said lazily.

Keith unbuckled his seat belt and stood up.

"I think I'll visit the john before this flight fills up. I don't intend to move once this bird gets up in the air."

His footsteps faded as he made his way to the back of the aircraft, and there was a soft click as the lavatory door closed.

Kyle closed his eyes and thought about the reason he was currently in Georgia on temporary duty. A member of the special operations group of the US Marshals Service, he had become injured during his last assignment, two weeks before his thirty-second birthday. Even though it was not life threatening, it was serious enough to have kept him out of the SOG until he had recovered fully. To be a member of the SOG, you needed to be at the top of your game.

Kyle alternated between assisting law enforcement officials with specific training needs and being a basic training instructor at FLETC, the Federal Law Enforcement Training Center at Glynco, in Georgia. He also handled routine marshal duties: working with Keith and other deputy marshals on fugitive arrests, escorting federal prisoners to court, and other similar duties. Although Keith empathized with him for the injury which kept him out of the SOG, Kyle knew his friend was nonetheless delighted he was going to be in Georgia for an extended period of time. Keith took it upon himself to devise training programs to get Kyle back into peak physical condition, although it was sometimes unclear at the end of some sessions on whom the workout had taken a greater toll.

The flight was now beginning to board. Even though they were not the federal air marshals with the flight, as deputy US marshals, he and Keith had chosen to board before the regular passengers and were seated near the back of the aircraft, in two aisle seats. The flight attendants were welcoming the passengers aboard with bright smiles, indicating when larger carry-on bags needed to be stowed in the overhead bins and generally directing the flow of traffic. It never ceased to amaze Kyle how many people tried to stuff overnight bags under the seats in front of them when there was clearly not enough space. He could see one passenger was about to argue with the flight attendant a few rows ahead of him.

"I'm sorry, ma'am, but you'll need to place your bag in the overhead bin," the flight attendant said politely but firmly. "Let me assist you."

Without seeming to do so, she adroitly took charge, quickly stowing the piece of luggage in the overhead bin.

"There we go, all set." She smiled cheerfully at the passenger, who sat down without another word.

Kyle had been observing the exchange, approving of how easily the flight attendant had taken charge of what had the potential to become a sticky situation. As she had reached up to place the bag in the bin, he had seen the play of muscles in her arms and had taken a more detailed inspection. He admired her trim build in the uniform, noting her firm legs and calves and nicely rounded rear end, thinking he had not noticed her when he had come on board.

She looked to be around five feet four or five. He thought there was a height requirement for flight attendants, as they had to be capable of working the emergency exits competently.

If so, she had probably barely made the grade. He was willing her to turn around so he could see her face when—as if in answer to his wish—she gave a half turn, glancing around as if to check how many more rows of seats remained. Her head flicked up, and her eyes made contact with his.

"Whoa!" Kyle felt like a fist had punched him in the gut. He stared into two warm chocolate brown eyes, set above a small nose and a pair of sweetly curving full lips that looked like they laughed a lot. The whole combination was framed by thick, curly, natural hair, which was pulled back at the sides and fell to shoulder length. He had a sudden vision of her hair totally free and falling onto his shoulder. He missed a breath. Her eyes widened for a moment as she looked at him, and then she came toward him, bending forward a little to speak to him in a low tone.

"Good evening, sir. Welcome on board. I'm sorry; I hadn't realized there was someone seated here. Is everything okay?"

"Yes, thank you, ma'am," Kyle responded. He extended his hand, and she grasped it firmly, giving it a quick pump. Her hand felt soft and warm nestling in his. Heat sparked between them. She had a slightly puzzled and dazed look on her face, as if she had felt it too and could not understand what it was.

"Glad to have you on board with us," she replied. "If there's anything you need, please, don't hesitate to let us know."

She gave him a quick but somewhat searching smile, as if looking for the answer to some question, turned smoothly, and headed up the aisle to continue with the business of seating passengers.

Kyle watched her every step of the way. He was suddenly feeling uncommonly warm, his jeans feeling much too tight. He was extremely grateful Keith had gotten up to use the lavatory a short while ago. Observant as he was, Keith would have noticed the unusual exchange between himself and the flight attendant and would have been teasing him mercilessly.

He wondered if she were as affected as he was by their brief exchange.

As she marched up the aisle of the aircraft, Serena Hopewell pasted a meaningless smile on her face, automatically assisting passengers to their seats as her heart continued to thump in her chest.

What the hell happened there just now? She was aware of the faint trembling of her limbs, of her accelerated heartbeat. Every sense seemed heightened and, yet, in a vacuum at the same time. She was aware of sounds—the chatter of the passengers, the voices of her fellow attendants, the thump and slide of bags being shoved into the overhead bins. The lights in the cabin seemed brighter; the colors of people's clothes and the fabric of the aircraft seats appeared sharper. She could smell a swirl of perfumes, colognes, hair sprays—all mixed with the slightly acrid smell of sweat. Yet they all seemed separate and apart, like someone else was going through this amazing experience, not her. And it was all tied to the man in seat 26C.

When she had looked around and her eyes made contact with his, the strangest thing happened. She felt an awareness flow between them, and they seemed to be in a cocoon. The rest of the world faded out, and she was held immobile by his intent, smoldering gaze until her feet drew her mindlessly forward toward him. When she took his hand to shake it, the awareness had centered on their hands clasped together. She felt a flash of heat—sharp, unexpected, but somehow pleasant. It burned through every pore, made its way straight through her stomach, and pooled lower in her pelvis, where it throbbed and pulled at her nerve endings. Totally unnerved, she had mumbled something, hoping she made sense, and fled up the aisle, away from the disturbing sensation.

Serena took a long, slow breath and exhaled it softly. Almost in a daze, she helped passengers find their seats as they continued to come aboard. She could feel his intense gaze boring into the small of her back. It was like a laser beam, a concentrated output of power. She was afraid to turn around. Her memory retained the brief impression she had garnered in that short sharp encounter and replayed it in her mind's eye in glorious detail.

He appeared tall; his legs were partially stretched out in the aisle, and his head topped the back of the seat just a bit. His polo shirt and black jeans fit snugly over what appeared to be a well-muscled body. His shoulders and chest were broad, not bulky and overdone like a bodybuilder's but well-defined; he probably worked out often and took care of himself. His fingers were long, his grip firm, his hand slightly rough and with a few calluses, indicating a man who was accustomed to the outdoors and not the soft pampered hands of an office worker. And his face!

Serena swallowed as a hot flush involuntarily washed over her own face. Good grief, surely she wasn't going through *the change* at twenty-eight! His face was a dream. Short curly hair, which was slightly longer in the back, capped off a well-shaped head. He had thick, silky lashes, the kind for which women spent a fortune on mascara, trying in vain to achieve. If he had a sister and she didn't have lashes like his, Serena could well believe his sister would forever be mad at him.

He had high cheekbones, separated by a firm, straight nose with slightly flared nostrils. His face was clean shaven, no mustache or beard marred the perfect lines of his face. His mouth. She shuddered again. Firm no-nonsense lips but, oh, they looked like they would be very good at kissing, very good indeed. *He* looked like he would be very good at kissing.

Serena felt another menopausal-type flush wash over her. His eyes were an unusual color—a very dark gray bordering on black, full of heat and fire and the promise of exciting things waiting to be discovered. His eyes compelled her, mesmerized her. She felt discombobulated when she looked into those eyes.

Serena became aware of a clicking sound close by—right in her face, in fact—and blinked out of her musings and back into the present. Angelie, the senior attendant, was standing with a slight frown on her face, apparently trying to get her attention.

"Serena! What is wrong with you? Pull yourself together. We've got a full flight. Could you get me some napkins from the back, please? Someone's spilled some soda."

The "already" was unspoken, but Serena could see it hovering on Angelie's tongue. Not twenty minutes into the flight and *already* some mopping up to be done. Serena flushed yet again, but this time it was because she was mortified to have been found so unfocused and inattentive in her duties.

"Sure, right away," she answered. She turned with fast-beating heart to make her way to the back of the cabin. To her immense relief, the sexy passenger in 26C had his eyes closed—those fabulous eyes—and his head tilted back and resting on the back of the seat. Exhaling a soft breath of relief, she made her way to the galley, sneaking a quick glance at him as she passed and praying he wouldn't suddenly open his eyes. Yep, his lashes were to die for. She had got it right the first time. She sighed again. It was going to be a very long flight indeed.

Chapter 2

Kyle felt intrigued by the flight attendant. What was it about her? On one level, he felt amazed at his behavior. He didn't date much or have long-term relationships. His job was everything to him; he loved it passionately, gave it his heart and soul. He had affairs, yes—he was a man, after all—but they never lasted long. One of the reasons for this was that when many of the women he dated found out he was a deputy US marshal, that information took center stage and he, Kyle the man, was shunted to the side. They liked the excitement, the danger, the supposed glamour. Whenever that happened, he gently eased out of the relationship.

Sometimes he wondered idly if there was a woman out there for whom he would ever feel more than a passing fancy. This was always a fleeting thought, like a feather blown by the breeze, lightly touching the surface before swirling away with the next draught of air. His work consumed him, gave him all the thrills and most of the pleasures he needed.

But now, this sudden physical attraction, here on an aircraft of all places. When he had looked into her eyes, he felt an instant connection, not to mention how his heart started to race. And when they shook hands and he was suffused by heat—what in the world was that! To say he was intrigued was putting it mildly. The fatigue he felt when he first boarded the flight vanished utterly. He *had* to get to know this woman. There were no ifs, ands, or maybes. It was imperative—suddenly the most important thing he would ever have to do in his life.

He smiled, fiercely glad he *was* on the flight and had the opportunity to study her for over three hours undisturbed. He wanted the chance to make eye contact again, perhaps touch her and see if he felt that sensation again, but she never seemed to look in his direction.

After studying her closely for a little while, Kyle decided she was trying very hard not to look at him. And if she was avoiding him when her job was to attend to passengers, that meant she was as affected as he was by their brief encounter. She was slightly shaken, he realized, feeling a rush of satisfaction it wasn't all on his side. He smiled again. As she was avoiding his eyes, it made it easier for him to study her in greater detail without giving offense, and what he saw pleased him.

A nice figure, trim waist and curvaceous hips. Slim, not fat at all—just with a little meat on her bones. The kind of woman a man liked to hold, cuddle up to on a cold night, and not feel bony protrusions digging into him and spoiling the mood. His kind of woman, he thought with satisfaction. Her skin had a vital, healthy glow, the kind which came from good living, a sensible diet and exercise, and not out of a bottle. It looked smooth and silky, and he ached to touch it, run his hands over it and savor the texture.

Kyle let out a breath slowly, quietly, trying not to disturb Keith, who had returned to his seat and settled himself as comfortably as he could. He was glancing through a *Men's Health* magazine a previous passenger had left in the pocket of the seat in front of him.

Her face was beautiful, with those lovely chocolate brown eyes and skin with the same healthy look. It seemed to be free of makeup but he figured—with a trace of cynicism—it was whatever women wore these days that made them appear they didn't have on any makeup. But perhaps it was more than that, he thought as he continued to study her unobtrusively.

Her face glowed with life, as if an inner light was shining through. Her lips had a light touch of a bronze-colored lipstick with red undertones. It suited her complexion and added the right amount of color—not too bright and garish, not too pale and washed out. And her hair. Again he noticed how it was thick and already starting to escape from the clips behind which she had ruthlessly tried to tame it into submission. He wondered if she were as wild as her hair and also needed to be tamed. He felt a flash of heat at the thought, another missed breath.

Chocolate Eyes was good at her job, he noticed, always with a smile for the passengers and a cheerful attitude as she attended to their needs. He wished he knew her name, but the level of chatter in the aircraft, muted though it was, and combined with the throb of the engines, made it impossible to hear if any of her fellow attendants called her by name. No matter, he decided, he'd find out soon enough. He leaned back in his seat and gave her his full, undivided attention, utterly and totally captivated.

Kyle closed his eyes but his senses were on full alert. He hoped if he appeared to be sleeping, Chocolate Eyes would come tripping down the aisle, where he was sitting, to get to the galley. She was carefully avoiding that area; it was usually one of the other flight attendants who came to the back to fetch whatever was needed as she remained at the front of the cabin. He knew her name now—Serena; he heard one of the other attendants address her a little sharply as she tried to get her attention. It seemed she was being asked to get something from the galley.

Kyle knew when she approached because he got a whiff of her perfume; the same scent had teased him when he spoke to her and shook her hand. It was a light floral scent, not overpowering or musky. It reminded him of sunny days and warm breezes. It was exactly right for her. He inhaled gently, enjoying the fragrance, steeling himself not to open his eyes and give her any cause for anxiety. He wanted her to prance up and down the aircraft, passing tantalizingly close to him, and she would only do so if she thought he was resting. He smiled to himself, enjoying the game.

As the flight droned on, the activity in the cabin slowed down as the passengers settled in; some were sleeping, a few others were chatting quietly with each other. Here and there, overhead reading lights dotted the panels, indicating where some passengers read magazines and novels or were engrossed with their laptops. Kyle kept his eyes closed whenever Serena came down to the back of the cabin, immediately opening them when the scent of her perfume drifted away. He occupied his time in this light-hearted manner, knowing there was nothing he could do during the flight. However, it would be a different story once they got on the ground.

The warning lights came on, and the senior attendant made the announcements for landing: instructing the passengers to return to their seats, turn off cell phones and put away electronic equipment, bring their seats upright, and have their tray tables secured. The other attendants, Serena included, made sweeps of the cabin: collecting garbage, ensuring hand luggage which had been in use was safely stowed in the space under the seat or back in the overhead bin. Kyle had opened his eyes but engaged Keith in conversation while he surreptitiously kept an eye on Serena, following her movements as she walked swiftly up and down the aisle. The aircraft touched down with a slight bump, and they were safely taxiing to the terminal.

Kyle waited impatiently for the passengers to deplane, wanting to get up front, to get close to the flight attendant, Serena. Although she had been up and down the aisle of the aircraft continuously since he closed his eyes and pretended to be asleep, she had only twice come down for a prolonged stay to the end of the aircraft, where he and Keith were seated. The first time, when they were distributing the in-flight beverage and snack of pretzels and, again, when he couldn't help himself—he so wanted to look at her—and indicated he would like another drink. She had seemed a little nervous, so he tried to be as non-threatening as possible, but he was determined he was going to talk to her tonight. He was glad Keith was in a quiet mood—which was unusual for him and especially given his earlier merriment over Kyle's cowboy dialogue—and did not feel the need for continuous conversation.

He allowed Keith to go ahead of him so he would be able to linger and have a few words with her without Keith crowding him at his back. Kyle was determined to make contact with Serena again. He stepped up and deliberately took her hand, giving her a slow smile as he thanked her for making his flight enjoyable. She gave him a wide-eyed look again and stammered out it was her pleasure.

"Uh, bro, anything you want to share here?" Keith asked Kyle as they stepped out into the walkway. Kyle knew he would not have missed the little exchange between the two of them. "Putting the moves on that flight attendant? I miss something on the flight?"

"Mind your own business, Milk, or I'll mind it for you, yeah," Kyle replied with his unhurried drawl as the two made their way quickly through the terminal. Keith responded with a laugh and appeared quite unfazed by the threat. Whenever Kyle called Keith by his nickname, it was usually accompanied with the promise of some dire action but which almost never materialized. Keith was so light skinned, Kyle had given him the nickname during basic training, but it was a nickname only he could use with impunity, as Keith did not suffer fools gladly. You did *not* call him Milk if you wanted to continue breathing normally.

"It's quite a while to baggage claim, so you might as well talk to me."

Kyle made no answer but continued to move with the flow of humanity, sidestepping and avoiding passengers bent on getting to their respective gates. They went down the escalator to the shuttle trains, came off at the baggage claim stop, and headed for the escalator to take them up and out the terminal building.

All the while, Keith was relentless, keeping up a steady barrage of questions, trying to get Kyle to answer. As they stepped off the top of the escalator, Kyle turned to Keith, interrupting him in full flow.

"Awrite, Thommo, I'm sticking around for a while. See you tomorrow at the office, yeah."

Keith gave a delighted laugh. "Oh, all right then. Drum on the prowl! Good luck, man. Hope you get her."

He clasped Kyle in a quick manly hug, and then turned and made his way to the exit with his overnight bag, chuckling all the way.

Kyle turned away with a frown and a slight feeling of distaste, somewhat irritated with Keith's words. He made it sound degrading, like Serena was an object—game to be hunted, a prize to be captured, of no consequence. And yet, wasn't that what he was doing in a sense? Going after her? His frown deepened. He *was* going after her, he acknowledged to himself, but not exactly as a conquest. Instinctively, he somehow knew it went deeper than that. He wanted to get to know her, wanted to see those lips smile at him, for him. He *had* to talk to her; he had no choice.

He gave a wry smile, feeling a flicker of excitement course through him as he picked a spot where he would see Serena when she came off the escalator. He felt intrigued by her, wanted to talk with her and see where it would lead from there. He waited patiently, knowing she might be some time in coming, as the flight crew would have to go through their postflight routine before leaving the aircraft.

Ah, there she is. Kyle picked out Serena easily as she came off the escalator. She looked around—apparently searching for someone—gave a sigh and took out her cell phone. As he made his way toward her, she drifted to one side of the passageway so she was not blocking anyone's path. He was close enough now to overhear her conversation.

"Where are you? Please tell me you're parking the car and not leaving now." She listened a moment and spoke again. "Oh, come on, you know it takes a while to get here. Couldn't you have tried to leave a little earlier? You always do this to me," she complained, seemingly in frustration. She listened some more and responded, "Yeah, yeah, I love you too."

She snapped the phone shut with a sigh and turned around. He masked his feeling of disappointment even as she gave a gasp of surprise on seeing him standing in front of her. He gave her a wry smile and said, "Pity."

He started to walk away. He was two steps away when he heard her blurt out, "It's my cousin."

Kyle stopped dead in his tracks, a fierce rush of exultation coursing through him. Those three words knocked out the huge disappointment and inexplicable feeling, which had come over him of something precious slipping away when he overhead her telling the person to whom she was speaking, "I love you too." He thought it might have been a boyfriend or her husband, but obviously, he was wrong.

He turned around, walked back to her, and, with a slight smile, said, "I'm Kyle Drummond. Would you like to join me for a cup of coffee while you wait for your ride?"

She looked back at him solemnly and replied a little breathlessly, "I'd love to."

Kyle and Serena made their way through the bustling throngs found at any international airport—arriving and departing passengers, family and friends dropping off or picking up travelers, some moving purposefully, others ambling about aimlessly, limo drivers with name placards looking for their passengers whom they didn't know and only hoped to find through their signs, security personnel and airport workers. The level of noise rose and fell: a continuous background mix of voices, intercom announcements, snatches of television programs, harried parents trying to keep their wayward children in line.

They made their way to the Atrium—the food court at Hartsfield-Jackson Airport—and were fortunate to secure an empty table. Kyle pulled out a chair for Serena. She eased into it with a sigh of relief, rolling her wheeled bag up close to her. Kyle rested his hands on the back of another chair and turned to Serena, a small smile still on his face.

"I'm going to get a coffee. Can I get you one as promised, or would you prefer to have something else?"

"I'd love a hot chocolate, thanks."

"F'sure. Would you like anything to go with that? Danish or cookie or anything?" She shook her head.

"Back in a sec, yeah."

He turned and strode away, not quite believing she had stopped him leaving and was now sitting at a table waiting for him to rejoin her. It didn't take him long to return with the two beverages.

"Here we are. Careful with that, it's hot."

"Yeah, I think that's why they call it hot chocolate," she quipped.

He chuckled in acknowledgment at her dig, taking the seat next to her and resting his overnight bag on another chair. Kyle took a sip of his coffee, not saying anything, allowing the moment to weave a connection between them. After a few sips, he caught her eyes and asked her directly,

"Why did you tell me it was your cousin?"

She didn't answer for a few moments and then looked at him and said, "Honestly, I don't know. I was as surprised as you were."

"Well, I'm glad you did. I wanted to talk with you since I saw you on the aircraft."

"I know," she said softly, almost under her breath. Kyle bent his head and smiled into his coffee cup.

She pulled out her phone, clutching it as if it were a lifeline, and said, "Excuse me one moment. I need to tell Adrian where I am so he's not wandering outside looking for me."

He gestured in compliance. She punched in a number and held the phone up to her ear. He was absorbed in watching the little details: her fingers tapping the keys, her head tilting on one side as she placed the phone to her ear, her hair swinging lightly away from the side of her head, her lips moving as she spoke, catching glimpses of white teeth as her mouth opened and closed. He swallowed convulsively. She snapped the phone shut and took another sip of hot chocolate, her hand carefully gripping the cup.

"So what's it like being a flight attendant?" he asked, trying for something neutral to put her at ease, seeing she looked a little nervous. It was the right tack; her face lit up with a smile.

"You're kidding, right?" She laughed. "Do you mean when passengers board with luggage that should definitely have been checked and stuff it in the bin so no one else's can fit? Or you pass up and down about three times and each time you ask so sweetly if they would pull their seats up and put their tray table *to the upright and locked position*," she intoned, "and when you pass back, they're still in the same positions? Or how about the toddlers who cry from takeoff to touchdown?"

Her face was animated as she laughingly described the trials and tribulations of being a flight attendant. Kyle smiled indulgently. He could see she wasn't really bothered by it and enjoyed what she did. He watched the words leaving her mouth and wondered what it would be like to kiss those lips. He bent his head to hide his expression and took another sip of coffee.

"How long have you been a flight attendant?"

"Oh, a little less than three years now. I'm glad I made the change." A faint shadow touched her face briefly and then was gone. "I love flying to all the different states. I can't wait to get one of those cool trips, like the Bahamas or maybe Puerto Rico!"

Her eyes sparkled with remembered pleasures and happy anticipation, and he smiled in return. She looked so beautiful and alive; he couldn't think of anywhere else he wanted to be at this moment.

"Notwithstanding the Bahamas and Puerto Rico, which places do you like the best?"

"Oh, there isn't just one. They're all so different, you know."

She paused for a moment as if gathering her thoughts and then continued.

"I love Florida, especially Miami in the winter. It's so warm, and their carnival is fabulous too. New York is great; I love Manhattan and going into Greenwich Village when we have a long layover. New Orleans is wonderful; you can't beat the jazz in that place. Of course, I don't have to tell you about Las Vegas; you were just there. Aren't the casinos and cabaret shows simply spectacular? I love those costumes, don't you? And, ooh, San Francisco, those trolley cars are fabulous! I love to ride up and down on them."

She laughed unselfconsciously. The conversation flowed so easily and naturally, Kyle felt as if they had known each other for years and not mere minutes. He was amazed at how easy it was to talk to her.

"Why did you become a flight attendant? Don't be offended, but isn't it like being a waitress—in an unusual setting, of course—but still a waitress?"

Kyle was curious to hear her reply. He admired flight attendants. They worked so tirelessly and often had to cope with rude, abusive, and unruly passengers—sometimes a combination of all three—and wondered why they did it, what motivated them. Serena looked irritated for a moment, and then she shrugged and answered his question.

"You sound just like my friend, Annette. 'Glorified

servants' she calls us. But it's not just that. Do you know how good it feels when you have someone flying for the first time, sometimes so scared, and you're able to reassure them that everything's all right? Especially a small child travelling alone? I remember my first flight; I was ten years old, and the attendant was so kind. She took me up front to visit the captain, and I saw the cockpit with all the lights and equipment ..."

Her voice tapered off as she became lost in time with happy memories. She blinked and smiled, coming back to the present.

"Of course, that doesn't happen now, with all the safety restrictions and regulations, but we try to make the flight as enjoyable as possible." She focused more fully on his face.

"Well, you know what I do. What's your line of work?" Serena asked.

"Oh, I'm just an officer of the law, trying to keep the peace."

Kyle was deliberately vague. He didn't think he could bear it if she looked sexually excited if he told her he was a deputy US marshal. He would *like* to see her sexually excited in connection with him, for sure, but not because of his job.

"Only trying to do my bit to make the world a safer place."

"Yeah, I'm sure you do."

She gazed at him as if she were trying to assess him, figure him out. He wondered what she was thinking.

Serena was doing exactly that. She was thinking he probably gave criminals one look and they toed the line. She couldn't believe she was chatting away with him as if she had known him a long time and not met him a few hours ago. Now that she wasn't talking, she studied him closely, in silence. Just as quietly, he looked back at her. There was something about him, but Serena couldn't quite put her finger on it. Then it struck her. He was so still, it was unnatural. He didn't fidget or twist in his seat, didn't move his legs much that she noticed, his hands only to sip his coffee. His eyes, however, moved quite a lot, flickering from side to side before coming back to rest on her face as she spoke.

She cast her mind back to the flight. His legs had been stretched out and his eyes closed, but she would've bet anything he wasn't asleep. He was just … still. In a flash of whimsy, she thought if he ever wanted a job as a guard at Buckingham Palace, he'd get it, no questions asked, no problem. But it was more than not moving and being still, she thought. She sensed an explosive energy held in check, a feral quality to him. The man radiated power and danger. She gave an involuntary shiver. She didn't think she wanted to be on the other end of any gun if he was the one looking down the barrel.

She raised her head from her perusal and looked into his eyes—gray eyes the color of slate. He was watching her calmly as if he knew what she was thinking. For the first time, she hoped Adrian was really late, not knowing he was thinking the same thing. She was having such a good time chatting with him; she wanted it to last a little longer. She couldn't remember when was the last time she had done something so spontaneous concerning the opposite sex.

As Serena continued to look at him, the air felt charged, electrified. Her glance dropped to his lips—he had such gorgeous, kissable lips—and she felt a sudden hunger to feel those lips pressed against her own. Without conscious thought, she ran her tongue over her upper lip and caught the bottom one between her teeth. She heard his sudden intake of breath and looked up again. His eyes locked unwaveringly on hers. She thought his eyes were gray, but they darkened now with the intensity of his expression until they blazed at her like twin coals of fire. The air between them shimmered with heat, a sense of expectancy. Serena felt she couldn't tear her gaze away if her life depended on it.

A woman passing behind the table miscalculated the

space for her wheeled suitcase and bumped into Kyle's chair, breaking the connection between them. Serena didn't realize she had been holding her breath until she felt it leave her body in a shuddering gasp. The woman apologized, smiling at Kyle warmly as she took in his good looks. Kyle waved her apology away but took the opportunity to shift his chair closer to Serena's. He looked like he could stay right where he was for a long time. For once, Serena was glad Adrian was late. She simply didn't want to leave as yet.

Kyle placed his hand lightly over hers, where it rested on the table, the hot chocolate having long been consumed. Again she felt that slight tingle, that warmth, when his hand touched hers, just as she had on the aircraft. She didn't remove her hand but waited for him to speak.

"I'd like to see you again, Serena," he said softly. "Maybe we could get together, have dinner and take in a movie, if that's all right with you, yeah?"

She didn't reply right away but watched him intently.

"Yes, I'd like that too," she said softly. With a slight shock, she realized that she had neglected to introduce herself when he had invited her to join him for a cup of coffee. She had been enjoying his company so much since then that it had totally slipped her mind. She cocked her head on one side, studied him with a slight frown marring her brow, and asked curiously, "How did you know my name?"

"I heard one of the flight attendants call you by name." He raised one eyebrow as if to say, *Does it matter? I would've asked you anyway.* She shrugged, decided it wasn't really important.

He took out his cell phone.

"If you let me have your number, I'll give you a call. That's if you're not too busy wrestling oversized bags from hapless passengers," he teased.

Serena laughed but felt a bit wary. She bit her lip, undecided, even though she agreed to go out with him moments ago.

"I'm not a serial killer, honestly. No bodies in the basement or in the backyard," Kyle said in a reassuring tone.

Serena made up her mind, squaring her shoulders and giving another shrug. She recited her number, watched as he programmed it into his phone. Almost on cue, she looked up, saw him swing his head around to follow her gaze. A young man was wending his way toward her, looking faintly apologetic. He reached the table and bent down, giving her a kiss on the cheek.

"Hey, cuz, I'm really, really sorry to be so late. At least you had some company." He appeared relieved even as he looked at Kyle questioningly.

"Yeah, you should be sorry," Serena rebuked lightly. "This is … my friend, Kyle. Kyle, my always-late cousin, Adrian. He's going to be late for his own funeral."

Adrian rolled his eyes like he had heard this countless times, reached across, and extended his hand to Kyle.

"Hey, man, nice to meet you."

"Likewise," Kyle responded, returning the handshake.

Adrian picked up Serena's bag, snapped the handle upright, and swung it around on its wheels.

"Ready?" he asked, not waiting for an answer, already starting to move away. Serena and Kyle both stood up together.

"Thanks for the hot chocolate," Serena said, feeling a little self-conscious.

"My pleasure," Kyle replied. "I'll walk with you; we're both going the same way."

They left the Atrium, following her cousin as he moved quickly past baggage claim and out of the terminal. Once outside, Kyle looked down at her and said, "I'll call you, okay." He brushed the back of his knuckles down her cheek, lifted her hand, and gave it a quick squeeze.

"Have a good night."

"You too," she responded, feeling slightly dazed. She

turned and hurried to catch up to her cousin as he disappeared into the parking lot.

Kyle watched her go, feeling as light as air; the past few days with its long stakeout and subsequent action—the capture of the fugitive, wrapping up the assignment—all that felt like nothing now.

She liked him. She was very much aware of him sexually. First on the plane and now he had talked with her, he was even more certain of that. He saw how she ran her eyes over his body when she thought he wasn't looking, how her eyes widened and her breath caught in her throat when he pinned her with his gaze. He still felt a bit shaken by that intense connection while they were sitting at the table. When she had run her tongue over her upper lip and then nibbled on the bottom one, his groin had tightened, and an involuntary hiss of breath had escaped him. He had wanted to replace her tongue with his own, nip at her lips himself. Thank goodness that woman had bumped his chair just then.

He couldn't wait to see her again. But just as he noticed her interest in him, he also picked up on her restraint and caution. He could tell that sitting down with a perfect stranger was not something she normally did, and she was torn in two about it. He would wait two days, he decided—short enough to still be on her mind and long enough for her to wonder why he hadn't called. Kyle smiled to himself again, feeling more energized at the end of the evening than he had at the beginning. Georgia had suddenly become an interesting place to be.

Chapter 3

Serena sat in near silence as Adrian sped onto I-285, her thoughts turned inward. He seemed not to notice, bobbing his head and singing along with Bob Marley, who lamented that "No Woman No Cry" and all he could remember when he "used to sit in a government yard in Trenchtown." Her cousin loved Bob Marley and other reggae artists. The music flowed over Serena as she thought about the evening.

Kyle Drummond, Serena mused. Now there was one fine specimen of pure, undiluted male. On the aircraft, he had looked uncomfortable with his long legs stretched out in the aisle but resigned, as there was no other choice. His dark curly hair looked carelessly untidy, probably from running his fingers through it. When she made eye contact with him on the flight, she felt such a strong physical attraction to him, she almost gasped aloud. He exuded an air of complete confidence, as if whatever he undertook, he knew he was going to be successful and failure was not an option. His eyes had seared her, holding her with his gaze almost effortlessly until she felt compelled to take the few steps to his side. When he offered his hand, she felt a sharp tingle as he enclosed her hand in his. It was unnerving to say the least, and given her wariness with members of the opposite sex, it made her pause to reflect on her reaction.

Three years ago, Serena was happy and overwhelmingly in love. Her fiancé, Danny Morton, was an up-and-coming accountant with a midtown Atlanta firm. They were seeing each other for nearly six months and only recently gotten engaged.

In a horrendous betrayal, Danny shattered her heart and destroyed her trust in relationships. Returning unexpectedly from a trip with her girlfriends, she discovered him in bed with a coworker of his. His face mirrored her shocked and horrified expression.

It was then that she changed her job, successfully applying and training to become a flight attendant. She enjoyed flying, the fact that her routine was ever-changing, flying to different states, the passengers always transients, seen once and never again. Although she might fly with the same crew from time to time, even they rotated regularly.

Serena never fully recovered from the devastating blow. It shattered her confidence in herself as a woman. She never again allowed either herself or any man to get close emotionally. Whenever a relationship appeared to have the potential to develop into something stronger, she cut it off ruthlessly at the knees.

But now, here came Kyle Drummond, who—seemingly without trying—made her heart beat a little faster, who flicked a spark somewhere within her, had her agreeing to see him again. Serena uttered a small groan, telling herself she was crazy to think of seeing him again; he would be dangerous to her frame of mind. *He* was dangerous. There was no denying his animal magnetism. It pulled at her like a strong current pulled an inexperienced swimmer out to sea, inexorably washing over her and leaving her practically defenseless.

Adrian reached her apartment by this time and pulled into one of the parking spots. She got out, opened the back door, and reached in for her bag. He promised to pick her up in the morning to take her to the mechanic to collect her car. The warning light indicating a possible problem with the oil had been coming on, and she left it with the mechanic to be checked out while she was on her flight.

Serena let herself into the apartment, still in a thoughtful frame of mind but also experiencing a warm feeling of excitement. Her roommate and best friend from college, Annette—who was practically like her sister—was lying on the couch, looking at a show on television. She moved in with Serena about a year ago, after her family returned to New York. She looked around as Serena came in, her words of greeting breaking off as she took in the look on Serena's face.

"What's up? You look like you're not sure whether to smile or frown, like a Christmas tree with sputtering lights."

Serena laughed, hesitating while she tried to think of what to say. Annette swung her legs around and sat up, looking more interested. Serena assumed her inner turmoil was blatantly displayed on her face.

"What happened to you?" she asked. "Come, sit, tell Auntie Annette." She patted the sofa next to her.

Serena sank down on the sofa and replied, speaking slowly as she thought through her reactions.

"I met this guy on the flight tonight, some sort of law enforcement officer. He never really said what he was," she suddenly realized. "Adrian was late picking me up, as usual!" She rolled her eyes. "And he invited me to have a cup of coffee with him while I waited. I think he was deliberately waiting for me in the concourse." She turned to look at Annette helplessly.

"Cool," Annette responded, "what was he like? Did you like him? What did you all talk about?" She fired the questions at Serena like bullets from a gun. "At least you know he's not a low-life weirdo if he's in law enforcement."

Serena ignored the last statement. "I … I did like him, Annette. He was really easy to talk to, even though he was a little quiet. I probably did most of the talking. His voice, Annette. Uhhh! His voice gave me the shivers. He has the sexiest drawl you could ever imagine."

"But?" Annette prompted. Annette knew her too well.

"I don't know how to describe it. When we were on the plane and he looked at me, I was just so very aware of him, and when I shook his hand, it was as if there was a current flowing from his hand to mine. It happened again when we were at the Atrium but not as strong."

"No kidding," Annette murmured, looking awed. "It's called chemistry, girl. Did he ask to see you again? Did he give you his number?" Annette was beside herself with excitement.

"He asked me for mine, said he'd like to take me out to dinner."

"Please, please, tell me you're going to say yes."

"I don't know," Serena murmured. "I get the feeling he could be quite … dangerous."

"He's a policeman, or whatever, for God's sake; he's supposed to be dangerous!" Annette retorted. "Listen to me, Serena," she said softly, taking her friend's hand. "There are some good men out there, not everyone is a bastard like Danny. You have to give yourself a chance, honey. You've got so much love in you to give. And it sounds like you and this officer already have a connection. Why don't you give it a try and see how it goes? What's his name, by the way?"

"Kyle," Serena answered, still undecided. "I really don't know, Annette. I'll have to think about it, I guess."

"Don't think too long," Annette warned. "Be like Nike. *Just Do It.*"

Serena laughed. "We'll see," she said, "and now, I'm going to bed. G'night."

"Have a good'n, honey, sweet dreams," Annette teased.

Serena waved a hand as she disappeared down the hallway to her room. She couldn't stop a shiver of excitement as she thought about Kyle Drummond. Did she want to take the next step and get to know him? She wasn't sure she could stop herself, but, God help her, she was sure it would be the most dangerous thing she would ever do in her life.

Chapter 4

True to his word, Kyle called Serena after a few days and invited her out to dinner. Urged on by Annette, Serena accepted. Unfortunately, the first available free time she had was the coming weekend, as she was once again in the air. At first, she had wanted to meet him at the restaurant, but Annette persuaded her she was being overly cautious, so she agreed to let Kyle pick her up at the apartment.

He arrived promptly and she invited him in. God, he was even better looking than she had remembered. How in the world was that possible? Were his shoulders really that broad the first time and his legs that long, his thighs so muscled? How come she hadn't noticed before? She could feel her breathing start to speed up, and she stammered a little as she introduced him to Annette.

Annette had deliberately stayed behind to meet him before going off to join friends. She teased Serena that she needed to vet him, make sure he was worthy of her best friend. Although Annette made her remarks lightheartedly, Serena realized—with fondness mixed with a tinge of exasperation—that Annette was also serious in her intent. Serena had retreated into her shell where members of the opposite sex were concerned since that fiasco with her ex-fiancé, Danny Morton. Although there were one or two relationships in the three years since then, nothing had intrigued Serena as much as meeting Kyle.

She knew it made Annette hopeful, and so she was more than routinely interested in meeting Serena's date, the mystery law enforcement officer, Kyle Drummond.

Annette took one look at Kyle and thought, *Hot mama!* He looked as good as Serena described, and she could understand the attraction Serena felt. He wore a black shirt with ivory buttons, tan Dockers which molded to his long legs, and black loafers with thin black socks on his feet—the ensemble gave him a look of casual elegance. He was sexy as hell, and he gave off an aura of power and confidence—a heady combination. Plus, when he looked at Serena, she could see the attraction was not all on Serena's side. He couldn't seem to take his eyes off Serena, glancing her way every few seconds. Annette was pleased.

"Hey, I'm Annette. Pleased to meet you," she greeted him, holding out her hand. To her disappointment, there was no electric current when his hand grasped hers and shook it. Apparently, that only worked between him and Serena.

"Same here," Kyle returned pleasantly. He appeared slightly amused, and she wondered if he knew she wanted to size him up, give him the once-over, and decide if he was good enough for her friend. Probably. His eyes looked intelligent and worldly, like they had seen a lot of things, too many things. They also looked like he was touched she cared so much for Serena she was willing to go to such lengths for her.

She looked at him steadily, her gaze telling him he had better not turn out to be a jerk to her friend. He looked back, his eyes silently reassuring her she had nothing to worry about, that Serena was safe with him. Message received and understood. Annette smiled.

"You two have a good time. I'm on my way out myself."

"You do the same, yeah," Kyle responded. The two friends embraced, and everyone headed for the door.

Kyle led Serena to his truck, a black Chevy Silverado with

tinted windows. He helped her up into the seat and made his way swiftly around to the driver's side.

"I thought we might try this club, it's called the Black and White Pussycat. Have you ever heard of it?"

Serena shook her head. Her voice seemed to have deserted her.

"I guess it's going to be new to both of us, yeah," Kyle answered easily.

He felt—happy, he realized. The last few days seemed to crawl by extra slowly, agonizingly. He had never wanted to see anyone, any *woman*, as much as he wanted to see Serena. He thought about her constantly since they parted at the airport after sharing coffee and hot chocolate. He had realized on the flight she was attracted to him but fighting it. He would have to be very gentle in his approach to her, put her at ease. He caught glimpses of an outgoing nature when they were chatting, but she had a natural reserve, which came out from time to time and wrapped around her like a shield.

The drive to the club took fifteen, maybe twenty minutes. Kyle found a parking space near the front of the building, and they made their way inside. Soft music played from hidden speakers, and waiters in white shirts with black aprons around their waists scurried to and fro, taking orders and carrying platters of food. There was a fair-sized space in the middle of the floor for persons who wanted to dance. A number of indoor plants were dotted around the room, giving the place a casual but slightly upscale look.

Kyle pulled out Serena's chair after the hostess led them to one of the tables in a far corner, near a statue of a young boy holding a jug. A fountain of water poured out of its spout onto a bed of rocks. The scene was artistically backlit with muted, colored lights. In addition to the tables, there were also a number of booths.

A waitress appeared and said in a chirpy voice, "Hi, I'm Terri, and I'll be your server tonight," and handed them two menus. After perusing them for a short while, they decided to have calamari as an appetizer. Serena opted for chicken marsala while Kyle decided to have oven-baked salmon. Both ordered Coca-Colas. They handed the menus back to the waitress. She bounced away and silence descended on the table.

Kyle looked across at Serena as she nervously fingered the cutlery, which Terri had placed before them. She had left her hair loose, and as he suspected, it looked glorious, thick and curly, falling softly around her face and down past her shoulders. She wore a green top with a slightly cowled neck. When she moved, it offered him tantalizing glimpses of the top of her breasts. Just enough to make him wish he could see more.

She wore jeans, black ones that followed every curve of her luscious figure. They outlined her hips, drew his eyes again and again. He enjoyed walking behind her as they were being seated, taking in the jiggle and sway of her hips. He thought she looked beautiful, and clearly, he wasn't the only one. A young man two tables over was openly checking her out while the hostess was taking them to their table but hastily looked away when Kyle pinned him with an icy glare.

Serena fidgeted in her seat, looking nervous. She had been fairly relaxed while concentrating on her meal choice, but now that she was no longer occupied, she seemed acutely aware of him sitting across from her at the table. He smiled as a relieved look came over her face and she rushed into speech.

"So are you going to tell me which branch of law enforcement you're in? Are you a cop? A sheriff? Coastguard? CIA? FBI? NCIS? CSI? RED DOG?" She ran through the alphabet soup of agencies, babbling a little in her nervousness. Kyle chuckled.

"What do you know of RED DOG?" he asked, amazed she had even heard of that particular group.

"Oh, my cousin has a friend who's one, and I had asked

him what it meant. I thought it was cute—*Run Every Drug Dealer Outta Georgia*," she quoted. "So, which one is it?"

Kyle gave her a grin. "None of the above."

She started again. "Undercover detective? GBI? DEA? ATF? ICE?" With each agency she named, he shook his head, still smiling.

"Why don't you try a little closer to home, yeah?"

Terri returned with the drinks and the platter of calamari and placed it in the middle of the table. The lighting was muted, but it wasn't so dark that you couldn't see what you were eating either. Kyle gestured for Serena to help herself. She took one absentmindedly, frowning in puzzlement, and then her face cleared, and she gave a little groan.

"Of course, a federal air marshal! You would think, being a flight attendant, that's the first one I would call! That's why you were on the flight, but I'm sure it was someone else." She looked puzzled.

Kyle held up his hand. "No, I'm not, but something like that."

"Okay, I give up. What are you?"

He hesitated slightly and said, "I'm a deputy US marshal," wondering what her reaction would be.

It was the complete opposite of what he was expecting. Her eyes opened wide, as if he had offered her a gold nugget, and she said, "Ooh, like Tommy Lee Jones in the movie! Do you transport prisoners, all of them shackled to the floor? Do you have to hunt down fugitives, like he did with Harrison Ford?"

Kyle grinned broadly at her enthusiasm. Any nervousness she had at the beginning of the evening had completely dissipated. She seemed enthralled with his profession, treating it more as an adventure like the ones she had apparently seen at the movies rather than the highly dangerous reality it often was.

He gave a laugh and replied, "Yeah, we do hunt fugitives,

but it's not always as exciting as Tommy Lee Jones made it look in the movies, you know. We do a lot of electronic surveillance and stakeouts and escorting federal prisoners to court and looking after judges. You know, boring stuff."

She gave him a disbelieving look, which said *yeah, boring, and pigs can fly too.* "I'm sure you do more than that. What else do US marshals do? Tell me," she demanded.

He looked at her eager face and felt he couldn't deny her.

"Okay, do you remember back in 2000, that young Cuban kid, Elian Gonzales? His mother died trying to get to the States with him, and his relatives in Miami didn't want to give him back to his father."

"Yeah, I remember. I was a teenager at the time."

"Well, when his father came to the States to take him back to Cuba, the US Marshals protected Elian and his father while they were waiting to go back to Cuba, yeah."

"Really?" She looked fascinated, her eyes wide. "Wow. I didn't know that. Tell me another one."

"There was that guy in '97, Timothy McVeigh; he bombed the federal building in Oklahoma City. The US marshals provided security for him and his coconspirator, Terry Nichols, when they came to trial."

"I remember my dad talking about it when it happened. He said it was terrible." Serena helped herself to some more calamari. "So why did you become a US marshal, Kyle?" she asked curiously.

"My dad was a deputy US marshal, yeah. He was part of an operation at Wounded Knee in South Dakota back in the seventies, before I was born. A Native American group took control of the town and held it for over two months before they surrendered. I grew up hearing my dad talk about it. I guess all I could see myself doing since I was a kid was becoming a US marshal. I'm really …" He hesitated. Deep down in his gut, he felt that it was important that she know—without her rose-colored spectacles—exactly what he did, how extremely dangerous his job really was. "I'm with the SOG."

She rolled her eyes. "More alphabet soup! And what, if I may ask, is the SOG?"

"It stands for special operations group. The group you send in when really bad things are going down, like, if a big-time drug dealer is going to court, we try to make sure everything goes without a hitch, that the judge and jurors are protected, that sort of thing. When the Wounded Knee operation started, it was the SOG who went in first. The police have SWAT, the marines have the Navy SEALs, and the US marshals have SOG. We work a lot with other federal agencies like the FBI."

For Kyle, this was a long speech, but he wanted her to know how serious he was. She picked up on the change in his body language and facial expression. Her own demeanor followed suit, the frivolity of the past few minutes disappearing.

"I see. That's like the cream of the crop, isn't it?" He inclined his head in acquiescence, helping himself to some more calamari while he waited for her response. She studied him in silence for a few moments before she replied.

"Well, you look like you can handle yourself in tough situations." She bent her head, bit her lip, and glanced away. She looked embarrassed at what she had revealed—that she had given his physique more than a passing glance.

Kyle decided not to push. He merely replied to her comment.

"I usually do, but on my last assignment, I got injured, so I'm taking it a little lighter for a while until I'm fully recovered, yeah. More routine stuff, you might say."

"How were you injured, Kyle? Was it very bad?" she asked in her soft voice.

Kyle felt pleased she had asked and told her what happened. "It was bad enough. We were covering a drug trial—one of the Colombian drug lords—and some of his people mounted a rescue operation. They failed and now he has a lot of company in jail. But two of them escaped. One of them tried to take out one of the key witnesses. It apparently was a joint operation—some for the rescue attempt, some to get rid of the witness. I shoved the witness to the ground, and the bullet got me in the arm instead."

He gave a nonchalant shrug as if it was just one of those things. The media had blown the incident out of proportion, gushing in their reports about what a hero he was, putting himself in the line of fire to save the witness. In his mind's eye, he saw the whole scene unfold before him once more—the movement of the barrel of the gun coming up, alerting him, his shout and desperate leap to get the witness out of harm's way, the stinging pain as the bullet ripped into his upper arm.

He still felt a white-hot rage at what had happened. If he had to do it over again, he would still try to save the witness, but he burned to find the felon and bring him to justice. In fact, he and the other deputies had already spread the word among their confidential informants, but none of the CIs had come back with any information. He figured it would take time. He longed to be back with the SOG—well, he *had*—up to one week ago. Life had gotten very interesting very unexpectedly.

Serena's eyes were growing bigger as he talked. She reached across and laid her hand on his arm. "I'm so sorry, Kyle. I'm sorry you got shot but I'm glad you're okay."

He placed his hand on top of hers and smiled at her. "You and me both, yeah."

Their entrees arrived, and the conversation paused while they gave their full attention to the meal. As they ate, Serena looked around and remarked, "This really is a nice place, Kyle. How did you find it?"

"Actually, I didn't." He chuckled. "I'm still learning my way around Atlanta. My buddy, Keith, recommended it."

"Your buddy?" Serena said in careful tones.

Kyle looked up, hearing something off in her reply but not

quite sure what it was that twanged his mental alarm. After a moment, he replied, "Yeah. Keith and I met here in Georgia when we were both training to be deputy marshals. I wanted to be in the SOG, so I went back to Louisiana for more training. Keith decided to stay here in Georgia."

"Oh, so that's your accent. You're from Louisiana. I was wondering what it was."

"*F'sure, boo,*" Kyle said in an exaggerated drawl, smiling as she laughed.

Their desserts arrived: for Serena, a thick slice of a rich three-layered chocolate cake with velvety chocolate icing while Kyle settled for a modest slice of cheesecake.

"Your cousin picked you up at the airport the other night. Is the rest of your family here in Atlanta too?" Kyle asked as he made short work of his dessert.

A shadow crossed Serena's face, and a look of sadness appeared.

"Actually, he and his brother, Nigel, are my only family here right now. I'm an only child, and my parents died in a car crash when I was in college. A drunk driver hit them head-on." Her face turned reflective. She looked up as Kyle laid his hand gently on her arm.

"I'm sorry. I didn't mean to upset you, bring back rough memories."

She smiled bravely at him. "It's okay. It gets a little easier to bear every year. I don't know what I would have done if it hadn't been for Annette and her family. They took me in and were there for me, long after the funeral was over. My uncle —my dad's brother—he and his family live in California, so they only came for the funeral and went back home. Annette's parents made her bring me for holidays—Easter, Thanksgiving, Christmas—you name it, I was there." She smiled at him again, not looking sad anymore.

Kyle returned her smile. "It seems you have a true friend

in Annette and her family. Not many people go out of their way like that for others, yeah."

"Yeah, I know," Serena agreed. "I'm very lucky to be a part of their family. They're like my second parents."

They finished their desserts, Kyle paid for their meal, and all too soon, it was time to leave. Kyle walked Serena to the truck, and they were on their way back to her apartment.

Kyle was surprised at how relaxed he was—but also pleased—and how much he enjoyed the evening. The food was great but the company was superb. His heart started to beat a little faster when he pulled into her apartment complex. He was looking forward to this part of the evening, had been since he met her almost a week ago. He wanted to kiss her so badly; he was sure she felt the vibes rolling off him all evening. Oh, he hadn't made any overt moves, but it was there, hanging in the air between them.

"I had a great time tonight, Serena. Thank you," Kyle said softly as they stopped outside her door.

"Me too," Serena stammered. Kyle curved one arm around her waist, turned her to face him, and lifted her chin with his knuckles. He looked into her eyes, letting her see all the heat and desire he felt. Her breathing accelerated. His head slowly lowered to hers, tilted at an angle as it came closer. Her lids drifted closed at the first touch of his lips as they softly rested on hers. They lifted for a second before returning, and his tongue explored her bottom lip. She gave a sigh of pure pleasure, and he took advantage of her parted lips to slide his tongue into her mouth. He teased her, flicking her tongue with his and dancing away when she would try to catch him.

Serena trembled, her arms around his neck, as he kissed her senseless. Lifting his head slightly, he pressed light kisses along the side of her neck and under her jaw before taking her mouth captive once more, sinking into its honey depths. He broke off the kiss, sliding his lips along her jaw and nibbling on the lobe of her ear. She was breathing as heavily as he was.

"I think it might be a good idea if I took my leave now, yeah," Kyle breathed into her neck. "We'll get together again soon, is that okay with you?"

"Yes," Serena whispered. Kyle turned her around to face her door and waited while she hunted in her bag for her key, his hands on her waist. He wanted to keep touching her for as long as possible. She opened the door, and he dropped a last kiss on her neck and reluctantly stepped back.

"Have a good'n, babe. Sweet dreams."

"Night, Kyle," Serena answered softly. He waited until she stepped inside and closed the door before he turned and walked away, a soft smile on his lips. Oh yeah, very interesting, very unexpectedly.

Chapter 5

Kyle stepped out the shower, ran a towel quickly over his skin and knotted it around his hips. He headed for the kitchen, opened his refrigerator, and took out the makings for a po-boy. Although Kyle was happy in Georgia—and even more so now he had met Serena—as far as he was concerned, nowhere else could make a po-boy as good as his native Louisiana. Kyle liked his po-boy dressed, and he quickly added mayonnaise, lettuce, and two tomato slices. Munching on the sandwich, he took a cold beer from the fridge and returned to the bedroom. Serena was working, and it was becoming the norm for them to talk each evening when she was away.

Kyle felt extremely frustrated. It was close to two weeks since he had last held Serena in his arms and kissed her, and it was driving him crazy. He thought they would have gotten back together the next evening, but she picked up another shift unexpectedly when one of the scheduled attendants became ill and she was asked to fill in. Then he went out of Atlanta to do some firearms training with the local police department in Brunswick.

By the time he got back, Serena was on one of her regular scheduled flights. It went on like this for the last week and a half, with their schedules overlapping each other, and he was ready to tear his hair out by the roots. The closest they got to any form of contact were these nightly phone calls, which had gotten pretty steamy the last few times. But even that was not enough for him. He ached to hold her in his arms, to taste her sweet lips, to smell the perfume of her skin. It was a slow burn steadily consuming him.

He pulled on a pair of lounging pants and sat down on his bed, picked up his phone from the nightstand, and dialed her number, already smiling in anticipation.

"Hey, Kyle." Her soft, beautiful voice flowed over him, making his gut clench.

"Hey, babe, had a good flight?" he asked.

"Yeah, it was *awrite,*" she said, mimicking his accent and laughing. "Not too full and we had a good tailwind, so the captain made good time. Wish there were more flights like these."

She laughed again, and he smiled upon hearing the sound. He loved to hear her laugh. He thought it was the sweetest sound on earth. "How're you doing?"

"I wish we could get together. I want to see you again, hold you, and kiss you, yeah," he told her bluntly.

Her sigh traveled across the line to him. "Oh, Kyle, I want that too. I'll be back tomorrow," she said in a hopeful tone.

It was his turn to sigh in frustration. "We're doing some night training for the next three nights. I can't believe this is happening, yeah!"

"I know, me too. I … hold on a minute, Kyle." He heard her yell to someone to get the door; there was some whispered conversation before she was back on the line. "Kyle? Listen, I've got to go. Are you going to be up late? I'll call you when I get back."

He ignored her question. "Get back? What's going on? Where're you going?"

"Oh, we're fixing to go out to dinner at the—"

"Who're we?" Kyle interrupted, feeling outraged. He was lying here, missing her, and she was out painting the town red. There was a small beat of silence, and then her voice came back on the line.

"The *crew,*" she said in frosty tones, "is going out to dinner. Do you have a problem with that, Kyle Drummond?"

Kyle backpedaled fast. "Uh, no, no problem. Just hope you have a good time and wish I was there."

Another short silence. "Oh. I see. For a moment there, I thought you were actually going to tell me … well, never mind. Anyway, I've got to go. Everyone is almost ready. If it's not too late, I'll call you when I get back, okay? Take it easy."

He barely had time to say bye before the connection was broken. He swore and flopped back on the bed. He didn't mean to come on all strong and heavy, but hell, he couldn't bear to think of some man sitting across from her and enjoying the pleasure of her company when he couldn't.

He doubted he would see her over the next three days, as there was some talk of incorporating the police in the night exercises, and if so, they would be staying in Gainesville. By then, Serena would, no doubt, be back in the air on another flight. He would know more when he went into the office in the morning. He sighed, got up, and went to get another beer out of the fridge.

A few days later, Kyle was back in Atlanta. The night training had gone well, but he felt short-tempered and irritable. He knew the reason was because he wanted to see Serena, but the situation was out of his control. Kyle liked being in control, and when he wasn't, it irked him. His phone vibrated at his waist, and he placed it to his ear without checking the ID, one hand on the wheel as he maneuvered the Silverado through downtown Atlanta.

"Drummond," he said in clipped tones.

"Uh-oh, who's been messing with you?" a soft voice teased in his ear. The clouds rolled away and the sun came out.

"Hey, baby," he said in a pleased voice. "You're in Tampa already?"

"No, I'm not. The flight was canceled, some problem with the plane, and we're not leaving till tomorrow. But I forgot I had let Adrian go with my car. By the time I remembered, I couldn't get a ride. Are you close by? Can you give me a ride home? If not, I can get a taxi or wait until Annette gets off." She sounded hesitant and unsure.

"You don't have to do that. I'll come get you. It'll be my pleasure, yeah," Kyle told her, pleased at the unexpected turn of events.

Within fifteen minutes, he had pulled up to the curb, and there she was, looking every bit as delicious as he remembered. She was helping a young mother pull her suitcases to the curb. The woman had a baby in her arms and a screaming toddler clinging to her legs and looked to be at the end of her tether. His blood rushed along his veins as his pulse sped up and he gripped the wheel tightly. His first impulse was to rush out of the vehicle and gather her tightly in his arms, kissing her senseless. He didn't think that would go over very well.

He leaned over, swung open the passenger door, and smiled warmly at her. She seemed equally as glad to see him if the wide smile she gave him in return was any indication. He couldn't help himself. He, Kyle Drummond—nicknamed Iceman because of his iron self-control—acted on impulse. He pulled her into his arms and kissed her hungrily. Lifting his lips away from her face, he nuzzled her neck and inhaled deeply, his eyes closed in pleasure. Her soft skin had a light citrus smell, a vague hint of oranges, causing him to think of Caribbean beaches and sunshine. Raising his head, he looked down into her face, his breathing heavy.

"I didn't think it was going to be so long before I actually saw you again."

"Me either," she said breathlessly.

He became distracted when she made a grab for a brightly colored purple bag sliding off her lap.

"What's that?" he asked with a smile.

"Oh, a little something I picked up for Annette. I spotted it in one of the shops when I was walking through the concourse. I just *had* to get it." She opened the bag while she was talking and took out a black T-shirt. "Annette is going to love this, look!" She held up the shirt.

He took one look and chuckled in appreciation. In bold white letters were three initials—CSI—and below that, the legend, Can't Stand Idiots.

"Nice one," he said, smiling at her enthusiasm. She looked quite pleased with herself.

"Yeah, isn't it?" she agreed happily.

Acting on another impulse, he said, "Why don't you come over by my place this evening? I'll cook you dinner, yeah." He cocked his head to one side as he waited for her answer.

"Dinner, huh? At your place …" Her voice trailed away, and she looked a little unsure and uncertain, moving out of his arms.

"What? You don't think I can cook?" He pretended to look offended.

"Oh, I'm sure you can cook. You seem to be very accomplished; you can do anything you want. It's not dinner I'm worried about, Kyle." She looked directly at him and gave it to him straight. "It's dessert."

He knew instantly what she meant, and just like that, in the space of a heartbeat, the atmosphere became charged with even more sexual tension.

"Oh-kay," he said slowly, "what about dessert?"

She looked uncomfortable. "I don't mind having dinner at your place, Kyle. It's just … I'm not ready for *dessert,* and I don't want to give you the wrong idea by coming over."

Kyle was quiet as he thought how best to answer, taking in her defensive body posture—her arms were folded across her chest, and she was slightly bent over.

"Serena," he said slowly, picking his words with care, instinctively knowing this was an important point in their relationship, "I'd like you to come by because I enjoy your company. I'm not saying I won't enjoy *having* dessert, you know that, but how the evening turns out is entirely up to you. I'm not rushing you, babe. You set the pace. Whatever makes you feel most comfortable is fine with me, okay?"

Serena bit her lip, not saying anything, still looking troubled. Unable to resist, Kyle reached out and folded her into his arms as he cradled her head against his chest and gently stroked her back.

"Dinner and a movie, that's all. Promise."

He knew the moment she decided to accept his invitation. Her body relaxed and she leaned into him a bit more. With her arms wrapped around his waist, she lifted her head and gave him a warm smile.

"Okay, I'll be happy to have dinner at your place. What time do you want me to come over? Do you need any help?"

"Nah, got everything covered. I gotta make a few groceries but I—"

"Make groceries!" she interrupted in a startled tone. "What do you mean?"

He gave a chuckle. "I just have to pick up a few things at the store, that's all. Half-seven good for you?"

"Sounds fine. I'll see you then. You can give me the directions when you drop me off, then you can go and *make* your groceries." She laughed in delight at the unusual term.

Dinner was a success. They started off with a tossed salad and followed with the popular Louisiana dish of jambalaya Kyle had prepared. For dessert, they had a pecan praline pie, as Kyle knew she loved sweet.

"As I can't have the dessert I *really* want, thought I might as well enjoy this one with you," he teased her. She punched him in the arm but seemed too interested in cutting a slice of pie to really think about doing any damage to him—not that she could, he was so perfectly muscled. She cut him a slice as well and they drifted over to the sofa.

"That was delicious." Serena sighed with pleasure. "If desserts didn't go straight to my hips, I'd have another slice. Dinner was fabulous too, Kyle. You really can cook!"

"Thanks, glad you enjoyed it. Here, you've got some crumbs on your mouth. Why don't I take them off for you," he whispered as he leaned in close and touched his lips to hers. His tongue licked the offending crumbs from the corner of her lips and proceeded to trace her upper lip before coming around to the bottom. She turned more fully into him, eagerly reaching up and running her hand through his hair, caressing his scalp.

Kyle deepened the kiss, exploring her mouth fully, his tongue dancing with hers, advancing and retreating. He trailed tiny kisses across her jaw, circling her ear before blowing gently into it. She shivered, her hand tightening on the nape of his neck. He continued his sensuous exploration, his lips moving to her throat.

His hand slipped under her blouse, softly caressing her satin smooth stomach before moving upward and coming to rest on her breast. He squeezed gently, flicking his thumb over her bra-covered nipple. He reached behind her and unhooked her bra, slid his hands back around and cupped her breasts. He felt aflame with desire and started to ease her back on the sofa.

She stiffened and started to pull away. He paused and looked down at her face. She looked ready for fight or flight; neither option was appealing to him. He let out a long slow breath, removed his hands from under her clothes, and pulled her back upright. Taking her left hand in his, he leaned back against the sofa.

"Sorry, Serena," he reassured her, his eyes closed, head tilted up toward the ceiling. "I guess I got carried away, babe.

You're too damn luscious for your own good, yeah." He opened his eyes and gave her a wry smile.

"I'm sorry," she said, biting her lip and looking worried and upset. "Maybe I should go."

"No, don't go. It's okay. Why don't we look at a movie? You remember, I did promise you dinner and a movie," he said, hoping to get her out of the somewhat tense state she was in now. She still looked slightly wary and poised for flight.

"What do you have?" she asked.

"Have you seen *Taken* with Liam Neeson? It's supposed to be really good, lots of action."

"No, I haven't."

"Well, let's check it out. *Taken* it is."

He got up, rummaged among his stack of DVDs, and popped the correct one into the DVD player. While the premovie credits were rolling, he went into the kitchen and poured a glass of wine for Serena and one for himself. He was a little angry with himself. After Serena expressed her doubts about coming over for dinner at his place, there he was, practically jumping her bones and giving her every reason to feel her concerns were not misplaced.

But damn, she was so fine, and he wanted so badly to take her to bed, it was eating him up. He remembered the first time he kissed her. She had tasted like a ripe Georgia peach, sweet and succulent and juicy. He wanted to eat her up.

Kyle blew out a tortured breath, trying to gain some semblance of control before returning to the living room. She looked up when he returned, gave him a small worried smile when he handed her the glass of wine. He settled back on the sofa, drew her to his side, and placed his arm around her shoulders. He took a sip from his own glass as the movie began.

"Wow, that was one hot movie!" Serena exclaimed as the credits rolled and the audio track faded. "I have not enjoyed a movie like that since I don't know when! Talk about nonstop action."

Serena couldn't stop bubbling with enthusiasm over the movie. As it had progressed and she got absorbed in the details of the film, her nervousness evaporated, and the only tension she exhibited came from the vivid action on the screen. Kyle was pleased he was successful in his plans.

"I know, I know," he agreed. "I was surprised myself; it was really good, yeah."

Serena wandered over to the dining table and cut another slice of the pie they had for dessert. He didn't remind her she said it went straight to her hips. After all, he liked the hips in question; he thought they were curvy and sexy as hell. They had a lively discussion of all the whos and whys and wherefores and continued to dissect the plot and characters of the film as she munched down on the pie. It was almost half an hour later when Serena gave a huge yawn, looking most surprised at herself before she gave a laugh.

"I really need to go, Kyle. Dinner was great, dinner and the movie," she corrected with a smile.

"I aim to please," Kyle said, turning off the television, which he had switched to a news channel before turning and giving her an exaggerated bow. "I'm glad you had a good time; it was fun for me too. Hold on a minute, let me get my keys."

"Your keys? You're going out?" she asked, looking surprised.

"Only to follow you home," he replied. He picked up the wine glasses and the plate Serena used for her slice of pie and carried them through to the kitchen.

"You don't have to do that, Kyle." Serena's voice followed him as he placed the dishes in the sink. He turned around and saw her leaning against the wall, smiling at him.

"I know I don't have to, I *want* to," he said as he walked

over to her. When she opened her mouth, he forestalled her comment by placing a finger on her lips.

"Just humor me, okay? I intend to see you reach home safely. Now, are you ready?"

Serena raised her hands in good-natured acceptance. "Okay, just let me get my things."

They walked out to her Chevy Cobalt, and Kyle opened the door for her to get in before sliding behind the wheel of his own vehicle. The streets were clear, and they reached Serena's apartment in a relatively short time. He walked her to the door and waited while she opened it. She turned around with a cheeky smile and said, "Okay, Kyle, here I am, safe and sound. You can sleep easy now."

He chuckled, his hand coming up to push the hair away from her face. "Yeah, I will sleep but I don't know about *easy.* This is why."

His mouth, hot and damp and eager, came down on hers, and he kissed her passionately, nibbling on her bottom lip before easing his tongue into the sweet, warm depths of her mouth. When he finally raised his head and studied her face, he smiled in satisfaction. She looked thoroughly kissed. But being Serena, she had to have the last word.

"Night, Kyle. I enjoyed dinner, the movie, and now, both desserts."

With a cheeky grin, she slid inside and closed the door.

Kyle laughed. He liked her spunk, couldn't help thinking about how good they would be in bed together, what fun they would have. He expelled a harsh breath. He hoped he wouldn't have to wait too long to find out.

Chapter 6

Kyle awoke with a feeling of well-being. The dinner the night before was a great success, even though he almost ruined it in his eagerness to make love to Serena. Thank goodness the movie was excellent and had grabbed her attention.

He went through his morning exercise routine quickly and efficiently, as always. He poured himself a cup of coffee, which he had timed to finish brewing after his shower, grabbed a muffin, and left his apartment.

He was two blocks away from the federal building when he picked up the distress call on the police scanner.

"Shots fired! Shots fired! We got a shooter! We need backup now! Now!"

"Hell!" Kyle swore loudly.

"Officers are on the north side of the Roosevelt Gateway Apartments on Roosevelt Avenue," announced the calm voice of the dispatcher.

He felt the adrenaline flood his body as he swung the Silverado around and headed for the address given over the scanner. It was automatic whenever an officer was under fire—all law enforcement agencies responded. More reports indicated a routine response by four police officers to a complaint by a tenant in an apartment complex, who thought his neighbor was dealing meth, was met with gunfire. The police officers were pinned down in the apartment of the tenant, who called in the complaint. The officers' path to safety was blocked by the suspects, who were firing at them repeatedly, two with handguns and one with a rifle. The officers' handguns—Glock 22s—were no match for the SKS assault rifle, commonly known as the poor man's hunting rifle, one of the suspects was using; and the officers were running out of ammo. The officers' reports continued over the scanner.

"We're in apartment 8B. They're shooting through the open front door, but they're not coming out into the corridor. We're gonna need rifle power."

Kyle reported in to his supervisor. "Someone's shooting rounds in an apartment complex on Roosevelt. I'm rolling that way now."

He fought his way through rush-hour traffic, but being so close, in a matter of minutes, he was on the scene. So far, only a few officers responded, but he knew the numbers would increase rapidly. He noticed some of his fellow deputy marshals—his buddy Keith, as well as Paul Spencer and Tim Munroe. They made their way over to the officer in charge and were briefed on the situation.

"We'll need to get some tear gas to smoke them out," Kyle suggested to the officer.

"The SWAT team should be here any minute now with their bag of tricks," the officer replied in grim satisfaction.

"Good," Kyle replied. "Have you got anyone covering the back?"

"Not yet," the officer replied. "We're concentrating on trying to get our guys out unharmed."

"Okay, we'll go around back and cover that side," Kyle said. He and the other three deputy marshals, as well as two police officers, took off at a fast pace to the end of the apartment building and headed around the back. Kyle hoped none of the suspects had made their way downstairs and out of the building. Since he arrived, he had only heard four shots fired; all had come from a rifle, none from a handgun.

As he came around the side of the building, a curse ripped from his throat. There was a small parking lot behind the apartments; and beyond that, he could see a path leading into a wooded area, which opened out to a shopping complex. Two men were hurrying across the parking lot and were almost to the path. He caught a glint of sun on a gun barrel. He also recognized the man and swore again.

"Federal agents! Drop your weapons!" he yelled.

At the same time, one of the officers yelled, "Police! Drop your weapons and put your hands up!"

The men spun around and fired. Kyle and the other officers took cover behind some of the cars in the lot and returned fire. In the silence following the exchange, he heard a groan to his right. His heart dropped in his chest. Someone had been hit!

"Who's hit? Thommo? Spencer? Munroe? You guys? Answer me, goddammit!"

An unsteady voice he didn't recognize said, "It's Hammond, looks like he got it in the leg. He's bleeding heavy."

"Call for an ambulance and get him out of here." More gunfire erupted again.

"Give it up, Parker. It's over," Kyle yelled. He heard mocking laughter followed by a jeer.

"You wish, Drummond. I ain't gonna let you get me."

A barrage of shots followed his voice, and Kyle and the other officers were forced to hunker down. The second the shots ceased, he sneaked a look around the car and saw Parker and his accomplice slipping into the wooded area. He leapt to his feet and raced after them. He would not let Parker escape him again. He could hear the others behind him. Parker's accomplice stopped and turned around.

"Take cover!" Kyle yelled as he slipped to one knee behind a tree. He took aim and fired, watching with satisfaction as the man screamed, dropped his weapon, and went down clutching his arm. Parker kept going. Kyle approached quickly but cautiously, picking up the man's weapon. He handed it over to Spencer and left him to take custody of the assailant. He and the other two deputies charged behind Parker.

Too late. Parker made it to the shopping complex, which was already teeming with people. It had been too dangerous, with innocent people around, to risk a shot at Parker as he headed for the complex. Now the man had literally disappeared. He looked around frantically but could not spot Parker anywhere.

Kyle swore savagely and ripped his radio from his belt. "We need some officers in the shopping complex behind the apartments. One of the suspects is here; we need to flush him out. And send some EMTs to the back of the apartments. An officer is down and also one of the suspects." He snapped the radio back on his belt, continuing to scan the area as he walked.

"You know this guy, Drum?" Thommo asked at his side.

"He's the bastard who shot me," Kyle replied grimly. Keith whistled. No other words were needed. The three of them continued to search.

Three police cars pulled into the shopping complex, and officers spilled out. Kyle described Parker and what he was wearing to the police officers; but not having seen the suspect, however, it was a hopeless cause. He didn't think Parker would be a fool enough to walk around with his gun in the air.

After searching for about fifteen minutes, he realized it was futile. Parker was long gone. He ground his teeth and turned to Keith and Munroe.

"Let's get back and see how Hammond's doing." He was worried about the officer. Leaving the police officers to continue searching, they made their way back to the apartment complex.

The action was all but over. The SWAT team had managed to subdue the remaining suspect by firing a tear gas canister into the apartment. The assailant surrendered, pushing his rifle through the door and emerged, hands in the air, his eyes red and streaming.

Kyle decided to go to the hospital. He felt personally responsible for Hammond getting shot and wanted to make sure the officer was going to be okay. He was also angry he couldn't give the man the satisfaction of knowing his assailant was in custody.

Serena stifled a yawn as she stumbled out of bed and headed for the living room. She turned on the television to a news channel and went into the kitchen to pour a cup of coffee, hoping it would jolt her awake. She smiled as she remembered the dinner last night at Kyle's place. It was a surprisingly good meal—she had enjoyed the jambalaya and the pecan praline pie—but she had gotten a little upset when Kyle had tried to force the issue of exactly what kind of dessert he wanted. However, he backed off when he saw how upset she was becoming, and the evening ended pleasantly, after all.

Taking her cup of coffee and toasted cheese sandwich with her, she plopped down on the sofa and looked at the news as she enjoyed her breakfast. The news anchor was reporting on a school board meeting the night before when there was an interruption for some breaking news.

The scene flashed to an apartment complex, which seemed to be overrun with law enforcement vehicles. Serena could see someone being wheeled into an ambulance; there was a SWAT vehicle to one side and about eight police cars and other unmarked vehicles scattered about. A number of persons in flak vests—some marked "Police," others "US marshals"—were milling about the area. Her eyebrows rose when she saw that, and she wondered if Kyle was there. The reporter on scene appeared in the foreground with the confusing scene behind him.

"Yes, Mark," he replied to some question asked by the news anchor, which Serena had not heard. "Two men have been taken into custody, but the one who appears to be the ringleader escaped into the shopping mall, which runs directly behind this apartment complex. One of the suspects was shot as he attempted to escape, but an officer was also wounded. That officer is … mond and he is currently being taken to Grady Hospital …"

The coffee sloshed dangerously in her cup as Serena jumped in shock. At the precise moment the reporter spoke the name of the injured officer, the ambulance siren came on as the vehicle started to leave the area, and she did not hear the name clearly, but it had sounded too much like "Drummond." Her heart started to pound in her chest. Snatching up the remote, she raised the volume on the television.

"Please don't let it be Kyle. Please don't let it be Kyle." The silent entreaty swirled around in her head as she waited for the reporter to repeat the name of the injured officer.

"… took the third suspect into custody after throwing tear gas canisters into the apartment. The apartment was the scene of an alleged meth operation. Again, one suspect eluded capture, two suspects are in custody, and one law enforcement officer has been wounded. We'll keep you updated on this story as it develops. Reporting to you live from the Roosevelt Gateway Apartments, I'm Jake Johnson, Channel 5 News. Back to you, Mark."

Serena gave a low moan. She still didn't know if Kyle was there or had been injured. Jumping up, she rushed into the bedroom and grabbed her phone off the charger. She speed-dialed his number with trembling hands.

"C'mon, Kyle, pick up, please, pick up." She sank down on the bed, the phone pressed to her ear. The phone rang and rang, but there was no answer. He didn't pick up. Serena closed the phone without leaving a voice message, her heart thundering in her chest. She drew a shuddering breath. Did she have enough time to go to the hospital?

She glanced at the clock; it read ten thirty. If she left now, she could get to Grady and still have enough time to get to the airport. The canceled Tampa flight the day before had been put back to three o'clock this afternoon.

Her decision made, Serena leapt off the bed and flew into the bathroom. She prayed Kyle was all right. She couldn't bear to think he might have been injured again.

Kyle stood as still as a statue, his arms folded across his chest. His face was expressionless; anyone looking at him would think it was carved in stone. Out of the corner of his eye, he saw Keith shift his weight from one leg to the other and give a small grimace.

A number of police officers had ended up at Grady Hospital, waiting to hear the prognosis on Hammond's injury. Hammond was in surgery. There were at least ten law enforcement officers crowded into the small waiting room, including the four deputy marshals. Most of the officers were pacing up and down, talking in low tones with each other. Only Kyle was totally motionless, remaining in the same position since arriving about twenty minutes ago.

Kyle was enraged that Parker had escaped him yet again. To have been shot by a career criminal like Parker and then, unexpectedly, have him almost in his grasp but unable to take him down—that stuck in his craw. The more he thought about it, the angrier he became. But there was nothing he could have done. He had held his fire as he pursued Parker toward the shopping complex for fear of injuring someone.

He turned to Keith. "Thommo, can you get word out to your CIs? See if they get any info on Parker? I am *not* going to let this guy slip away again." Kyle's mouth was a grim line.

"Sure thing, Drum. You talk to any of those guys yet?" Keith jerked his head in the direction of the cops milling around the waiting room.

Kyle nodded. "Yeah, I did, but I don't know if they'll 'remember.'" Kyle smiled mirthlessly. If the cops had a chance to make an arrest of someone who had shot one of their own, they would most likely notify the marshals after they had done so, not before. Kyle didn't mind; he wanted Parker safely tucked in the arms of the law, and he wasn't particular which arm it was that did the tucking.

He saw Keith look beyond him at something that drew his attention. Keith made a small sound under his breath—*hello*—and flicked his brows at him.

"Hey, Drum, ain't that your boo?" he asked quietly.

Kyle turned around and looked in the direction Keith indicated. His eyebrows rose and his eyes widened in surprise. Without answering Keith, he walked toward the woman, who had drawn Keith's attention. He could feel Keith's interested gaze following him.

Kyle strode rapidly toward Serena, surprised to see her. He saw the worry and fear on her face and swore silently. He recalled the television news van and the reporter at the scene. *Damn, she must have seen the news.* When she saw him apparently unharmed, the relief on her face caused him to swallow involuntarily, a funny feeling blooming in his chest. He braced himself as she hurled herself into his embrace, his arms going around her and holding her steady.

"Hey, hey, it's okay, it's okay, I'm awrite," he soothed her, one hand coming up to cradle her head. She raised her head, remnants of fear still visible in her gorgeous eyes.

"Oh, Kyle, I was so scared. I didn't hear the name properly 'cause the ambulance started up, and the reporter didn't call it again, but it sounded like he said 'Drummond,' and I thought it was you, and you had been shot, and I called you, but you didn't answer your phone and I—"

She was babbling and Kyle—still pumped with adrenaline from the morning's activities—did the only thing he could think of to reassure her. He kissed her.

Kyle moved his lips hungrily across Serena's mouth, taking his fill. A warm feeling spread through him, easing the rage that held him in its grip since Parker escaped him yet again. Serena clung to him and kissed him back just as strongly. Kyle forgot he was in full view of anyone passing by until he heard the raucous comments behind him.

"Woo-hoo! You go, Drummond!"

"Is *that* the Iceman?! Well, 'scuse me!"

"Iceman? More like Volcano Man. Nothing cold about that action!"

There was a burst of appreciative male laughter. Kyle slowly raised his head and looked at Serena, his eyes black as jet with the desire he felt. Her face was flushed, and she looked well and truly kissed. He didn't think she heard the comments, but he didn't want her to feel embarrassed. Keeping one arm across her shoulder, he turned her back the way she had come and started to walk.

"C'mon, let's go."

She looked startled and said, "Weren't you waiting to find out what happened to the officer who got shot? Who is he, Kyle? What's his name?"

"He's a police officer, not a deputy marshal. His name is Ty Hammond. He got shot in the leg but he's going to be okay."

He continued to talk as he steered her down the corridor, away from the raucous comments of the LEOs in the waiting room.

"They're patching him up right now. I'll come back in a minute. Right now, I'm more concerned with you. Are you going to be okay?"

He looked down at her, pulling her to one side as the corridor opened up into a small foyer with a nurse's station, and rested his hands on her shoulders.

"Now I know you're okay, I'll be fine, Kyle," she reassured him, giving him a warm smile.

"Come with me now," he said, looking deep into her eyes, letting her see the fire and need which burned in him. When he kissed her just now, he had wanted so much more. He wanted to kiss every inch of her delectable skin, wanted to stroke it and feel its satiny warmth pressed up close to his, wanted to bury himself in her body. He ached with a fierce need to make love to her.

"Now?" she said, her eyes huge and startled. "Kyle, I can't. I'm fixing to go on a flight now. Remember the one that was canceled yesterday?"

She looked bewildered by his sudden intensity. Two nurses passed by, both absorbed in a chart which one of them held. They were having an intense discussion, their heads close together and their expressions serious.

Kyle tipped his head back and blew out a long, frustrated breath. He looked at the ceiling as he struggled for control and then back at Serena. He hoped the smile on his face looked natural.

"That's right, I forgot. I'll call you tonight; let you know how Hammond is doing. See you when you get back?"

"Yeah. I'm so glad you're okay, Kyle. I was really worried." She hugged him again. "Did they catch the guy who shot the officer? The news said that one person escaped. Is that who—"

"It's that bastard, Parker," Kyle interrupted savagely, raking his hand through his hair in a violent gesture. Serena looked startled at his sudden explosion.

"Who's Parker? You know him?" she asked.

"He's the same bastard who shot me back in March. I almost had him this time, but he got away in that shopping complex. He's not going to be so lucky next time," he said grimly.

Serena drew in a shocked breath.

"Kyle, don't! Please don't go after him. You could be hurt, he could kill you!"

"Serena, that's my job, I go after bad guys."

"No, it's not. Your job is to protect. You only want to go after this guy because he shot you. Please, Kyle, don't do it."

She looked up at him with worried eyes, looking so upset at the thought of him being injured; it burned him that he couldn't give her what she wanted.

"I can't promise you that, Serena. I wish I could but I can't." He reached out a hand for her, but she stepped back, her lips tightening.

"Okay, fine, do what you want, Mr. Macho. I've got to go if I want to be on time for my flight. I only wanted to make sure you were okay."

Abruptly, she spun on her heel and walked off quickly, not looking back. Kyle cursed softly.

"Serena." He took a step forward but she never broke stride.

Kyle watched her go, his hands on his hips, filled with myriad feelings—anger that Parker had escaped, frustration that he couldn't promise Serena what she wanted, and most of all, an aching need to make Serena his. If things didn't change between them soon, he was going to explode. He had almost forgotten what a hot bath felt like; he took so many cold showers these days. Exhaling harshly, he turned around and headed back to the waiting area, bracing himself for the round of raunchy comments that were inevitable.

Chapter 7

Serena pushed her cereal around her bowl before gathering a spoonful and placing it in her mouth. She chewed and swallowed but all her actions were automatic. If someone asked her what she was eating or whether it was any good, for the life of her she would not have been able to answer. It could have been sawdust, and she would not have known or cared; so deeply preoccupied was she by her thoughts.

It was almost two weeks since she thought Kyle had been shot and rushed to the hospital, shaking with fear. The relief when she found he was unharmed was overwhelming. But that relief had quickly turned to anger when she inadvertently found out he was incensed that the suspect—the same man who had shot him—had escaped and that he intended to actively pursue him. When she left for her flight, she functioned on automatic all the way to Tampa, the anger fueling her blood. But when she had cooled down, fear for his safety had returned.

Her breath hitched when she thought of his well-muscled body riddled with bullets, and she almost choked on the mouthful of cereal.

It was now a little over a month since they first met on the flight from Vegas, but they had only managed to get together twice. Well, four times really, if you counted their first talk at the Atrium and their last emotional meeting at the hospital. They talked on the phone quite often though, and each conversation was getting hotter and hotter until she longed to touch him, be wrapped up in his strong embrace, and enjoy his bone-melting kisses.

She knew Kyle felt the same way from their conversations, knew he was getting more and more sexually frustrated. Strangely enough, she didn't think he was getting any on the side. She didn't know how she knew, but somehow, instinctively, *she knew.* Maybe because he seemed so *hungry* when he was with her? How he seemed ready to tip over the edge? His reaction when she reminded him she was flying to Tampa seemed to make that a certainty. If a man was getting some on the side while he waited for what he obviously decided was the main course, surely he wouldn't be as tense and strung up as Kyle seemed to be, as if he was balancing on a high wire strung between two skyscrapers, trying to get to the other side, and one false move would send him plunging down to oblivion.

Serena didn't understand what was happening to her, how she could feel so strongly about someone she had only seen so few times but talked to almost every night. She wanted to, oh God, she so wanted to make love to him. She wanted to feel him joined to her in the most elemental way. This feeling had intensified over this last month. Her body burned as she sat there at her breakfast table thinking of him.

Outside the window, two squirrels chased each other up the bark of a pine tree, one of the teenagers from the apartment two doors down revved his car and pulled out of the parking area with a squeal of rubber, a door slammed in the apartment below—all normal, ordinary activities. Serena neither heard nor saw; all her attention was focused inward on her thoughts. The light breeze blowing in through the open kitchen window and ruffling the curtains did nothing to cool her. She felt hot all over, inside and out.

In the few brief relationships she had after Danny, there hadn't been any sex. Once she felt the relationship heading in that direction, she cut it off. Firmly and finally. Sex with Danny had been physically satisfying. She wasn't promiscuous by any means, but she always felt that there was something more to be had. It hadn't really bothered her because she had loved Danny. But here was the kicker. Sex with Kyle was *not* going to be just a physical thing—well, it was, but it was going to be so much more.

Instinctively, she knew sex with Kyle was going to consume her, mind and body and soul. She was not going to be the same, ever. Was she ready for that? Did she *want* that? Or was she going to allow the pain of Danny's betrayal continue to dominate her life and color her relationships? She needed to take a serious leap of faith here, to believe that what she and Kyle could have was worth going after, in spite of the dangers of his job and the doubts that she still had.

Serena swayed on the horns of her dilemma, uncertain of what to do. Kyle had called her a few times since she last saw him at the hospital, but she hadn't answered. At first, she was too angry, and then she wanted to sort out her feelings before seeing him again. She had deliberately avoided him by picking up a few extra shifts, and she still wasn't sure if that move had been smart or stupid. She had finally left a text message, asking him to give her some space, that she would call him soon. That was three days ago and she hadn't heard from him since.

So here she now was, still trying to come to grips with her feelings. Her mind tried to deal with the problem pragmatically, dispassionately, but her body apparently had a mind of its own as well. Or was she truly listening to what her inner self was trying to tell her? That she was fighting a lost cause, that it was not only mind and body but also her *heart* that was involved? That she was already consumed because she loved him? That he sneaked in past her defenses before she knew it; and she had fallen for him, wholly, solely, and completely?

Serena sighed. The truth was out and it was staring her in the face. She loved Kyle and that was what was scaring her.

She didn't know how or when it had happened, but it had. From the very first time they met, there had been that instant connection, something on a deeper, primal level that went beyond "Wow, he's so hot!"

The thought of him being injured forced the truth to the front of her mind, and she could no longer deny it. She loved him, and when you loved people, you became vulnerable. That was what she was fighting so hard. But as hard as she tried, her defenses weren't good enough. She loved him, and she had better learn to deal with it; there was no turning back. The fear and panic she felt on her way to the hospital and the gut-wrenching relief when she saw him—safe and whole and unharmed—was testimony to that. And now she knew why. She loved him; it was that simple.

All of a sudden, she grinned. She had her answer to the question plaguing her since she met him at the airport a month ago—should I sleep with Kyle or shouldn't I? Why fight it any longer? She wanted to. Kyle wanted to. There was nothing to stop them any longer. Well, one more thing, which was entirely in Kyle's hands. Feeling much more cheerful and energetic, she polished off the cereal, got up, and placed her bowl in the sink.

Annette came in and started to prepare her breakfast. "What's going on?" she asked as she shook one of those nutrition-conscious cereals into her bowl—Raisin Bran with Granola or Shredded Wheat or One Million and One Grains with Fruit, Serena thought flippantly. Annette took her breakfast very seriously. She placed the box back on top of the refrigerator, and Serena saw it was Kellogg's Special K; that wasn't too bad. She liked Special K herself.

"Oh, nothing, just been feeling a little out of sorts this week," she prevaricated, watching Annette drizzle honey on top of her cereal as she waited for the coffee to finish dripping. "Are you fixing to go to the mall today to look for your parents' wedding anniversary gift? Shopping way in advance, aren't you? What did you have in mind?"

The coffeemaker clicked off, and Serena poured a cupful, the steam rising from the cup in lazy aromatic drifts. She sniffed appreciatively. French Vanilla Roast, her favorite. She hated it when Annette was on one of her quirks and would try different flavors before settling on one. It seemed like this was the week for French Vanilla. She hoped it was also the month.

"I thought I told you," Annette said in surprise. "I was really getting frustrated because I couldn't think what to get them; it's getting harder every year. I was browsing at Perimeter Mall, and I went into Things Remembered or whatever is the name of the place."

She paused to crunch and swallow a mouthful of cereal and continued. "I decided to get them an engraved photo album with a compilation of photos from as many wedding anniversary parties and occasions as I can lay my hands on. It will mean a bit of work, but I've still got some time; their anniversary is two months away. I thought they'd like that better than some generic thing from a shop, you know." She shrugged deprecatingly.

"I think it's a fabulous idea," Serena exclaimed.

"You do?" Annette said, looking pleased.

"Yeah, it's really great. It will send them down memory lane but have a central theme—wedding anniversaries. That's really, really good. I'll help you with it, if you like, just let me know what you want to do," Serena gushed.

"Thanks, you're the best, girl," Annette said gratefully. She finished her cereal and poured herself a cup of coffee and popped two slices of wheat bread into the toaster. "What do you have planned for today? Are you seeing Kyle? I haven't seen him around in a while."

She looked at Serena sharply. Serena ignored the look. She knew what it meant—*I hope you haven't broken up with him.*

"Well, I thought we would be in the mall, so I don't know. I'm at rather a loose end now."

"Why don't you try that new hairstyle we were talking about? You remember, last week you were moaning you wished your hair was straight 'cause you were getting so frustrated with your tangled curls. Not with chemicals cause I know you don't like that, but you could try using a flatiron. I'm sure Jeralyn could fit you in if you call her early enough, like now," she hinted meaningfully.

Serena mulled it over. It was true. Of late, her curls were driving her crazy. They seemed to get more and more tangled every time she washed her hair. Neither the detangling shampoo nor the double-toothed comb seemed to help. Having it straight, huh? The last time she had her hair straight was in college, and it was one big experiment she vowed never to do again. The chemicals burned her scalp and she disliked the smell. But using a flatiron didn't involve chemicals. She made up her mind.

"All right, think I'll go for it." She picked up her cell phone and scrolled through for Jeralyn's number.

"Okay, see if she can fit me in too, or one of her girls. I might as well get mine done too," Annette replied. She spread strawberry preserves on her toast and took a big bite, licking the edge of her lips at a bit of preserve that had escaped her mouth. "Time we looked even prettier than we normally are."

She winked at Serena, who laughed. Serena had just finished making the arrangements with Jeralyn when the doorbell rang. Annette disappeared into her bedroom, and Serena made her way to the front door. Before she could reach it, there was another insistent peal.

"All right, already! Hold your hor ...ses ..." The last word died away in her throat as she yanked the door open and looked at Kyle standing on the step. He was wearing a dark blue T-shirt that hugged his chest and showed off his toned arms. Blue jeans fitted his hips and legs as if they were sewn on to his frame. Serena swallowed past a sudden obstruction in her throat. He looked good enough to eat.

"Kyle. What are you doing here?"

He raised his brow. "I think we need to talk. Can I come in?"

She bit her lip. "I told you I was going to call you. Oh, all right, come in, Mr. Macho," she muttered ungraciously, feeling off balance. He didn't look like he was going to take no for an answer.

"Thank you," he said drily. "So you still mad at me?" he asked abruptly. She guessed he thought that because she called him Mr. Macho, which was the last thing she had said to him at the hospital when she *was* mad.

"No, I'm not, but I just don't want you to get hurt again, that's all," Serena said, rubbing her arms as she held them in front of her across her body.

"Serena, it's the nature of my job. I'm a special ops man; there's always danger involved. Why is that so hard to understand?" He raked his fingers through his hair.

"Yes, but you're not special ops now, at least that's what you told me. You're doing regular duties while you're here. But you *want* to go after this guy." She glared at him.

"You think I should just let him get away? Don't make any effort to find him if I get the chance? I can't do that, Serena." He looked frustrated that she wasn't getting it.

She looked at him, all the fear she had felt when she had seen the news report rushing back to her. "Do you know how afraid I was when I didn't know if it was you who had been injured?"

Kyle sighed. "I know, baby. But I'm very good at what I do. I *like* my job; I don't take unnecessary risks. But I'm not the only one here with a dangerous job, you know." He looked at her pointedly.

Serena jerked back in surprise, her eyes going wide. "Me?" she exclaimed in surprise.

Kyle nodded grimly. "Yes, you. Every time you go on a flight, I wonder if this is the one time some fool is going to try something—explosives in shoes or luggage, even an out-of-control drunken passenger, or, God forbid, something like 9/11. Did you ever stop to think how *I* feel, hmm?" He folded his arms and looked at her.

Serena was taken aback by his statement. She had never viewed her job as dangerous—annoying sometimes, irritating at other times, but always loved. She loved to fly; it was a grand way to see the country. Yes, everyone in the airline industry—as well as the entire world—was aware of 9/11, but wasn't that why federal marshals were now on flights?

But it put a different perspective on everything. She couldn't very well be angry with him because he was perpetually in danger. As he so clearly pointed out, she was too.

"I never thought of it like that. It's not just flying, is it?" she said wonderingly.

Kyle reached for her, stroked his thumb over the back of her hand. "No, it's not. Look, I'm not making light of your fears. I just want you to know that I do take every precaution when I work. Why do you think they want me to train recruits? Because I'm one of the best they've got. I was injured, yes, but it was because I was saving the life of someone else. If I hadn't done what I did, the man would've been dead."

He said this without any trace of modesty or arrogance; it was just a matter-of-fact statement. Serena didn't say anything. It really didn't matter what he said; she knew she would be terrified when he was actively on a case, more especially now when she admitted to herself that she loved him.

He placed his hand on her shoulder and looked into her eyes, his intent gaze holding her as effortlessly as a snake charmer playing a flute holds a snake captive.

"Look, let's call a truce, okay? I'll promise to be really careful if you promise not to worry too much." He twirled his finger around one of her curls and pulled gently. She felt it snap back when he let go.

Serena sighed. "Okay, Kyle. I promise I'll *try* not to get too upset or worried when you're on a case or mission or whatever you call it. It's just this particular guy you're chasing; I just have a bad feeling about him." She shivered.

"Don't worry about him. I'll handle him." He tilted her face up. "I'll try not to think of what could happen when you're on a flight, okay? We have a deal?"

"Deal." She smiled at him and he smiled back. His big calloused hands cupped her face. His eyes slowly darkened from gray to onyx just before he lowered his head and his hot mouth closed on hers hungrily. His tongue swept in, plundered her mouth, laid it bare with a hunger that mirrored her own. He hauled her up against him, his pelvis grinding into her belly. His hands stroked down her back, one hand moving lower to cup her bottom and press her more fully into him.

Serena could feel him, the hard ridge of his arousal pressing into her, and she wanted him so badly she was shaking. She moaned in his arms, dimly conscious of Annette somewhere in the apartment. Regretfully, she eased slightly away from him. Hot damn, the man could kiss. He could lead a saint to sin.

He lifted his head, looked at her with eyes that were still bright and hot before he pressed his lips to her forehead. His hands tightened briefly on her shoulders before he raised one hand and caressed her cheek; the other hand slid around her waist.

"Want to go for a drive? I've got to go down to Griffin, and I hoped you might want to come with me."

Serena gave a regretful sigh. "I'd love to have done that, but Annette and I have prior commitments today. Actually, I was going to call you today to ask you if you wanted to have a drink later."

"Sure, I can do that, sounds good." The disappointed look on his face was replaced with a smile.

"Can you pick me up around eight o'clock?"

"F'sure, baby. I'll see you then." Kyle gave her one last kiss and left.

Serena closed the door and then leaned back against it. She was glad that he showed up and they cleared the air, but she still had something else to talk about this evening, and that was a whole different matter altogether.

Chapter 8

Kyle walked briskly up the steps to Serena's apartment, eager as always to see her, an involuntary smile turning up the corners of his mouth. As Keith would say, he really had it bad for this woman. He was glad that he had come around earlier and they had worked things out, to some degree. It had made him uneasy when she had sent him the text saying she needed some space. He was afraid that the next text would be telling him she was ending the relationship. He had forced the confrontation between them, and now they had a truce. But he wasn't a fool. He knew she was still scared for him because of the dangers of his job, and he had done his best to convince her that he wasn't being reckless in his pursuit of Parker. Now he could only wait and see. Once again, he pressed on the doorbell but gently this time.

Annette opened the door.

"Hey, Kyle, come on in. How's it going?" she greeted him, swinging the door wider to allow him to enter. He stepped over the threshold, but before he could answer, Annette continued.

"Serena will be out in a minute; she's running a little behind. Sit down and take a load off. I'll let her know you're here." Annette was already heading down the hall toward the bedrooms.

"Thanks," Kyle replied, sinking down on the sofa.

He looked around with interest. He never really spent time at Serena's apartment. This morning, all his attention had been focused on easing her fears and getting her to continue their relationship.

He noted they had the usual furniture—television, CD/DVD player, sofa and loveseat, a few houseplants, small occasional table. But now he apparently had time on his hands while he waited, so he gave the living room more than a cursory appraisal.

There was a runner at the front door and two smaller area rugs scattered around the room. The sofa and loveseat were dark blue and were full of light, fluffy throw cushions in contrasting pastel shades—cream, light blue, and light green. The sofa and loveseat sat at a ninety-degree angle to each other, turned so they faced the focal point of the room—the forty-two-inch flat-screen television. It was not mounted on the wall but sat at eye level on a stand, below which were a CD/DVD player and the cable box for whichever service they had a subscription. Off to one side was a DVD stand three quarters full. He ambled over to have a closer look.

In addition to the expected chick flicks like *The Memory Keeper's Daughter* and *How Stella Got Her Groove Back,* there were also comedies, suspense thrillers, and collections like the *Harry Potter* and *Die Hard* series.

Wandering over to the overflowing bookshelf, he saw the reading material was as varied as the DVD selections. His eye was caught by a slim book: *Here Are Your Heroes, Caribbean* by Standhope Williams. He drew it out and quickly flipped through it.

It appeared to be about outstanding Caribbean people, who had been awarded the Order of the Caribbean Community, the Caribbean region's highest national honor. Interesting. Kyle was fascinated, getting this glimpse into the multi-faceted layers that made up Serena. Before he had a chance to peruse the CDs, however, he heard the bedroom door close.

He looked up when he heard her come into the room, relieved she was finally ready. It was not like Serena to be tardy for their date; she was usually a very punctual person.

Her hair was different. It was smoother and sleeker and lay close to her head, sweeping over at an angle from one side of her face. The ends were curled softly under, resting some way past her shoulders. He hadn't realized her hair was so long as it was always curly—scratch that—it was *usually* curly.

"Hmm, going for a new look, I see."

"Yeah, what do you think?"

Kyle was no fool. "It's different. I prefer your curls, but this looks good too. You're still beautiful, either one, yeah." He smiled softly.

Serena blushed even as she gave him a glowing smile. "Very good answer. Okay, I'm ready, let's go."

She picked up her purse and led the way out the front door. Kyle followed.

He sat quietly, watching her, trying to decide her mood. Edgy, he thought, edgy and distracted. She was never still for more than five seconds, fidgeting first one way and then the other, playing with her hair, crossing her ankles, picking up her drink, putting it back down without actually taking a sip, looking around without, he was sure, focusing on anything. What bothered him the most was that she was not looking at *him*. Every time her gaze rested on him, she bit her lip and quickly turned her head, almost as if she were afraid of him, afraid to look at him.

She didn't talk either. They were at the club for about half an hour now, and for someone who was ordinarily very chatty and always liked to tell him about her day or what her friends did—or something funny and hilarious she might have experienced with a passenger on a flight—this silence was unnerving him, to say the least.

He started to feel somewhat uneasy. He was normally

very self-assured, so this feeling did not sit well with him. He thought back to all that had happened recently. She had been very upset when she thought he was injured during the call for assistance and rushed to the hospital. Her relief at seeing him unharmed was palpable, but there was nothing for snatching the rose-colored spectacles from your eyes like cold hard reality. Coupled with that reality and after their earlier conversation—now that she realized how extremely high risk and dangerous his job was, especially as he fully intended to pursue Parker—did she want to call it quits and didn't know how to broach the subject? He didn't think he could handle it.

Even though they weren't together as often as he would've liked, the two occasions he spent with her he remembered with contentment and pleasure. Each time he thought he had her figured out, she would always say or do something that would cause him to pull up short in surprise or wonder—something as simple as buying that T-shirt for Annette just because she thought Annette would like it.

Kyle didn't understand his fascination, his yearning, his *hunger* for Serena. Of all the women he had met, what made her so special? Why did she stay on his mind? Why did the thought of never seeing her again cause his gut to clench and actually cause him physical pain?

He loved being with her; he always felt more alive, more in touch with himself, not so much cynical and world-weary. He loved touching her, kissing her—oh man, did he love kissing her. She always gave all of herself whenever they kissed, no holding back.

At first, when he tried to push the relationship—take it to the next level because he was on fire to get her into bed, to lose himself inside her—he sensed a reserve, a sort of panic, saw it in her eyes. It was as if she was saying "Slow down, buster, or I'm out of here." He backed off immediately, giving her space, letting her move at her own pace, even though he wished that pace was faster.

It seemed to be the right approach because she was much more relaxed on the phone. There was no lack of salt in their conversations either. Many times after he hung up the phone, it was a cold shower for him if he was to have any chance of sleeping.

She was a very sensual person but didn't seem to realize it herself. When she had come over for dinner, she had touched him constantly—on his hand, playing with his hair, caressing his arm, resting her chin on his shoulder if he was sitting down, giving him quick hugs when he didn't expect it.

Once, when he had said something that needed a response and she didn't answer, he looked over at her, and she had this sleepy, sexy smile on her face, one which sent an immediate message straight to his groin. It was like a triangle—her look, his brain, his groin—all at once. And the hell of it was he didn't think she realized what she was doing! Because loosely translated, that look said, "I can't wait to jump your bones."

He knew she wanted to sleep with him—perhaps more than she knew it herself—maybe not as much as *he* wanted to sleep with *her*, but he knew it was there. He debated with himself whether he should push things again, step up the tempo, but was afraid he would scare her away if it wasn't what she really wanted. But damn, this waiting was killing him, not to say what it was doing to his libido. And now, tonight, this total air of distraction and uncertainty had *him* on edge. He wondered again if she was beginning to have doubts about her decision earlier on.

All at once, he just had to touch her, to feel she still wanted to be with him and wasn't planning on giving him the boot.

"Serena", he said softly to get her attention. Her head snapped around and she looked at him silently. "Let's dance", he said, praying she would say yes. A pleased smile—a natural smile, one he knew—appeared on her face.

"Sure", she said, already jumping to her feet eagerly and stretching out her hand to him. Taken aback by her ready acceptance when he had all but convinced himself this was going to be their last date—that she was getting ready to end things—he recovered quickly nonetheless and stood up, taking her hand and leading her to the dance floor.

Luck was with him; a nice slow tune was playing. Double luck, it was one of her favorite groups, The Temptations. He folded her into his arms with a silent sigh, feeling like he was home, where he was supposed to be. With something close to relief, he felt her arms come around his waist. If she was planning to leave him, she wouldn't wrap herself so closely around him, would she? She was petite but had a nicely shaped body with good muscle tone. He couldn't wait to see her naked, to feel those legs wrapped around his waist. It was something he had imagined since he met her and at the most inopportune times—like when he was in the midst of a meeting—but he couldn't stop thinking about her.

He thought she was beautiful, not pretty like a beauty queen in a pageant, but a beauty that came from within, shining through and giving her such a special glow he was always amazed everyone couldn't see what he did. Her skin was a lovely shade of caramel and was so soft and smooth he could stroke it all day long and never get tired of its silky feel.

She usually wore her thick hair in a natural style, her curls reaching down to her shoulders. However, she was sporting a new getup tonight, something straight and sleek that hugged her head. She hardly wore makeup—not that she needed to, her skin was so flawless and beautiful—just something around the eyes and maybe some lipstick. She pointed out, with a twinkle in her eyes, that she didn't know why she bothered, as he would just kiss it off. Her eyes were large and dark brown, a lovely chocolate color. Oh yeah, she heated his blood, all right.

They moved slowly on the floor, arms wrapped around

each other. She had moved her arms from around his waist and placed them around his neck. What was it she once mentioned to him about couples who danced really close to each other, so closely linked they were hardly moving? He remembered laughing heartily. It was—as was so often the case with her—something completely unexpected. Ah, yes, *rent-a-tile.* While they hadn't remained in the same spot, they weren't waltzing around the dance floor either. He didn't want it any other way anyhow. He just wanted to feel her close in his arms.

In silence, they listened to The Temptations crooning "Just My Imagination (Running Away With Me)." He wondered if *his* imagination was running away with him, thinking Serena was getting ready to dump him. He didn't really think so, but for right now, he decided he wasn't going to borrow trouble. He was going to enjoy dancing with her and feeling her trim little body in his arms.

The Temptations gave way to John Legend singing about "Ordinary People." Ah, well, it felt like even the very music was mocking him. If he was going to be tormented, he might as well broach the subject. He was always someone who met problems head on. If there was something wrong, he wanted to know sooner rather than later. Bracing himself, he asked softly, "You're a little quiet tonight and you seem distracted. What's wrong, Serena?"

She didn't answer for a moment, and he heard her soft voice say hesitantly, "Well, there's something I want to ask you, but I'm concerned you might, uhm, be a little angry or maybe feel insulted."

She looked up at him with worried eyes, biting her bottom lip. He didn't reply right away but looked at her with a puzzled expression.

"What do you mean, babe? Why do you think I'd be angry or feel insulted at anything you would have to tell me? Does this have anything to do with what we talked about this morning? I don't understand," he admitted with a bewildered look on his face.

She gave a small sigh. "Can we dance some more first? I like this music, and I like dancing with you, Kyle," she replied with a dreamy look on her face.

"Sure, as long as you like. I like dancing with you too," he said softly with a smile on his face and while tightening his arms around her. From that little exchange, it didn't appear he was about to be sent packing. But he was now full of curiosity. Angry? Insulted? What on earth could be in the woman's mind that would elicit these two reactions?

He tried to amuse himself by thinking of different scenarios, but nothing came close to anything that would encompass both reactions. Once again, she took him by surprise, and he couldn't wait to find out on what strange little side trip her mind had gone this time.

They spent another half an hour or more on the dance floor, enjoying the music and being in each other's arms. Kyle was beginning to have to exercise some control over his body south of the border. When the music changed to a faster beat, they broke apart and turned to leave the dance floor.

Serena took his hand and said, "Do you mind if we leave now? Let's go so we can talk. We'll have to shout too much to be able to hear each other in here; it's too noisy."

"Awrite by me," Kyle responded.

They picked their way through the crowd gyrating on the dance floor and headed for the exit, Kyle leading the way, his arm wrapped around Serena's waist and shielding her as much as he could from being shoved against the other patrons. Once outside, the air felt cool, and there was a slight breeze blowing. As always, Kyle paused and surveyed his surroundings carefully.

His gaze passed over a battered Ford Fusion parked out on the street. It sparked his interest for some reason, but before he could give it a closer look, it started up and pulled out, blending into the line of traffic moving by. Kyle kept his gaze on the car as it moved up the street. As it drew further away, he shrugged away the odd moment.

Fingers interlocked, he and Serena strolled unhurriedly to the parking lot and made their way to his truck. He unlocked the passenger door and helped her up onto the seat before moving around the front of the vehicle and getting in behind the wheel.

"Let's go down by Centennial Park. It's nice to sit there and relax."

"You know me, baby. I aim to please." Kyle smiled at her and swung out of the club's parking lot and onto the street. As he headed for downtown Atlanta, he wondered what secrets the night would unfold.

Across the street, Dave Parker slouched down in the passenger seat of a battered Ford Fusion. He felt rage flow through him as he watched the deputy US marshal leave the club accompanied by a woman.

"That's him," he growled, "that's the bastard who screwed up my game up north and got Leroy in the arm couple weeks back."

His cousin, Tyrone, sitting in the driver's seat, looked over at the two people, who had just come through the door of the club. The man placed a hand on the woman's arm, holding her back when she would've walked forward, his gaze sweeping the area quickly and efficiently. His unhurried perusal stopped when he spotted the Ford. Tyrone shivered as he watched the man watch them. Even from this distance, he could sense the aura of danger and leashed power the deputy presented.

Without having to be told, he put the car in gear and pulled quickly out into the street. He could sense the deputy following the car's progress as it moved up the street. He shivered again.

"Damn, Dave, that man is dangerous. You think he followed you down here?"

"Nah, Leroy only called me two weeks ago, and Drummond looked surprised when he saw me at Leroy's place on Roosevelt. Word out is that he's been here a couple months. That fool, Leroy. If he had waited like I told him to, instead of setting up shop in his own apartment, we could've been handling some good product. Now he's got a banged-up arm and about to join Lenny in jail." Parker cursed angrily.

"Lucky it wasn't you," Tyrone said. "If I was you, man, I'd head back north. I'm telling you, that guy is bad news."

Tyrone shook his head as if shaking off the uneasy feeling he had gotten when the deputy had first glanced and then stared fixedly at his car. For all he knew, he had probably memorized his tag number. Damn Dave and his wish for vengeance. He would have to be careful over the next few days, stay clean, and give the cops no reason to pull him in. He glanced at his cousin, who had straightened in his seat once they had left the club behind and wished Dave had stayed the hell away from him. This kind of trouble he didn't need. Damn Dave.

Parker ignored Tyrone and continued to scowl as he thought about getting even with Drummond. Twice now, the deputy had messed up his plans for getting a quick buck, and he was enraged. What made him angrier was that he knew Tyrone was right.

The word on the street was that Drummond was a special ops man, like a Navy SEAL, and everyone knew those guys were damned dangerous. You didn't mess with them. He could count himself lucky he had escaped twice from Drummond, but he didn't want to be lucky. He wanted revenge.

He could either be smart and get the hell out of Georgia before his luck ran out and Drummond caught him or he could take a chance and try to take Drummond out. Even to his own mind, the second option sounded like a damned stupid idea. He knew Drummond was looking for him, and sooner or later, some snitch was going to give him up. So which was it going to be? Smart and safe back in New York or revenge and risk down in Georgia?

Parker smiled evilly.

Chapter 9

Serena looked out the window as the truck rolled down the relatively quiet streets. Her heart was going like a trip-hammer in her chest, and she was surprised Kyle couldn't hear it. It sounded extremely loud to her. She was not all surprised he picked up on her distraction earlier in the evening. After all, given that he had specialized training, it stood to reason he was acutely observant of his surroundings and the people within those surroundings.

She surmised he was probably trying to figure out exactly what she wanted to talk about, what her cryptic statement meant, but there was no way he could possibly guess, not in a thousand years. She wondered if she wasn't being a fool, but every time she thought of how his kisses melted her bones—along with her newfound discovery of her love for him—she figured the time had come to take it to the next level before she self-combusted.

God knows she wanted to, even though she was a little scared to take that step. Hence the upcoming conversation. Would he think her a complete flake? Would he consider it an insult to his masculinity? Men could be such complete asses. There was no telling how he would react, whether with anger or feel insulted. Of course, he could also listen quite calmly and react with his usual equanimity, but who could tell the mind of men? Then, too, she had stronger reasons, personal reasons.

Well, the die was cast now; she could only play it through. She could only hope the feelings he had for her were strong enough to overcome whatever would be his initial reaction to her request. After all, he had come looking for her this morning to talk about her fears for him. She knew he wanted to make love to her very, very badly. Hell, if it had been left to him, they would have ended up in bed when she had gone by his place for dinner. He was a very primal animal, and she was left in no doubt whatsoever of the extent of his reaction to her, of the effect she had on him. She wondered almost idly if he realized the effect he had on *her*.

With a start, she realized they reached their destination and had stopped while she was still lost in her thoughts. She turned toward Kyle, knowing she would find him watching her. He was, very intently, almost as if he was willing himself to lift the very thoughts from her brains. He raised his eyebrows slightly and said, "Those must be really deep thoughts. We've been here almost ten minutes, yeah."

Astonished, Serena said, "So long, why didn't you say something?"

"Just giving you the time you seemed to need, babe. There's no rush, is there?" he asked, almost tentatively.

Knowing Kyle to be one of the most positive, assured persons she had ever known, it was strange to hear him being so uncertain of himself, and Serena gave him a closer look. It seemed to her he had a slight air of worry, as if he was afraid of what she might have to say. Strangely, it made her feel protective of him somehow and much more confident.

"Do you want to stay here in the truck or sit outside on one of the benches?" Kyle asked quietly.

"Oh, let's sit outside. It's such a beautiful night, and I like to see the water fountain displays."

"Awrite, outside it is," he agreed lightly.

When they were seated comfortably, slightly facing each other—Serena with her jeans-clad legs draped over his thigh—she turned to him, took a deep breath, squared her shoulders, and plunged into speech.

"Okay, Kyle, here's the thing. We've been seeing each other for a little while now, and I know you'd like like to … to … to have things move to the next level, to make love …" Here her voice faded away almost inaudibly before Kyle interrupted.

"Yes, I would but only if you want that too. I don't want you to feel we have to because it's what I want. I'm not rushing you, babe" he added somewhat anxiously before Serena placed a finger against his lips.

"Shh. Let me talk before I lose my nerve. You see, I want that too. I want to make love with you so that's what we have to talk about. Your sexual history."

She saw his eyes flare wide and a look of masculine triumph, which he quickly masked, appear in them when she talked about wanting to make love with him, but now he looked puzzled as he frowned and queried, "My sexual history? What do you mean? Do you want to know how many women I've been involved with?"

"No! What I mean is, well, you're a very sensual man. You must know you're very sexy and attractive to women—and wipe that smug look off your face!" His lips started to twitch. "And I'm sure you've had your fair share of … of sexual encounters over the years, so what I'm asking is, what sort of precautions have you been taking?"

"Well, I most times use a condom, but most of the women have been on some form of birth control." He answered frankly but still seemed slightly puzzled. "Is that what you meant?"

Oh, for Pete's sake, would she have to spell it out? For someone so intelligent, he was being incredibly obtuse. Taking a deep breath, she said, "What I really meant was, there are a lot of STDs out there. Do you get tested regularly for AIDS and that sort of stuff?" There, she'd said it. It was out. Let the chips fall where they may.

There was a short, pregnant silence. Serena didn't dare lift her eyes from where their hands were entwined in her lap.

"Ahhh, I see," he murmured at last. "Serena, babe, look at me, yeah."

She peered up slowly, not knowing what she would meet. To her relief, he didn't appear angry and was, in fact, looking grave and thoughtful.

"I have to say, even though it was the last thing I expected, that's a damn good question to ask in these times. And I'm ashamed to admit I haven't gotten tested as often as I should for someone with, uh, a healthy sex appetite," he said, quite tongue-in-cheek. "I haven't really been in a relationship in a while, so I guess I let it slide. I do get tested but like I said, not recently. That's no excuse, I know, and just not good enough. I'll set up an appointment with my doctor right away, okay, babe?" he promised softly as he raised her hand and kissed it.

"Yeah, somehow I knew you'd lose no time getting that done. So you're not mad?" she asked, wanting to be sure. He could be mad all he wanted, but he was going to get tested if he wanted them to have sex.

"Nah, I'm not mad, though I have to admit, I couldn't, for the life of me, imagine what you would have to talk about that would have me either angry or feeling insulted. Why did you think that, by the way, the angry part?"

"Well, I know a lot of men like to feel they're *in charge,*" she said, holding up her hands and making exaggerated quotation marks with her fingers, "when it comes to sex, and I didn't know if you might feel angry I'm asking you to do something you might not want to do. Likewise, that you might feel insulted because you've already done so—taken tests, I mean—and you might feel I think you're not responsible. But it's *very* important to me. No test, no sex," she finished with a shrug.

He sat in thoughtful silence for a long minute, his lips pursed and brow furrowed.

"You're absolutely right," he agreed. "It's something I should have been more vigilant about, and I'm sorry. I never want for you to have to worry about that, okay?"

"I won't. Glad you're taking it so calmly."

He shrugged. "When you're right, you're right. What about you, are you going to get tested too, hmm?" he queried lightly.

"Of course, that's only fair," she replied. She bit her lip and looked away quickly. Not quickly enough, however, for that sharp-eyed lynx. He took her chin in his hand, turning her face toward him.

"Serena?" he questioned. She saw him frown as he puzzled out why she was suddenly looking so self-conscious, and then his face cleared as the penny dropped.

"Hold up, you've already had yourself tested, haven't you?"

"Yeah," she whispered.

"And birth control? Did you get set up for that too?"

"Of course," she replied, looking at him like it was so obvious and why would he even need to ask such a silly question.

He looked at her for a long moment before hugging her tightly and giving a rueful chuckle.

"Damn," he said softly, "if I was on the ball, we would've been having a hell of a night, yeah."

"Well, you snooze, you lose" she said impudently, sticking out her tongue at him now that she once again had the upper hand.

"Ah, you"—he laughed, pulling her more fully onto his lap—"I'll get you for that."

He cupped his large hand on her nape, holding her head steady as he lowered his head and kissed her quickly and gently. She didn't care for public displays of affection any more than he did, but it seemed he was getting quite comfortable doing that—first at the hospital and now here. His kisses were so heavenly, Serena didn't mind at all. As the kiss ended, he stroked her cheek up and down with the backs of his fingers. She sighed with pleasure. He was such a great kisser. She could kiss him all night long.

He started to chuckle again.

"What's so funny?" Serena asked, smiling as well, relieved he was taking it so well. He might have gone all macho on her, like her friend Donna's boyfriend, and look how well *that* had turned out.

He turned toward her and looked serious for a moment as he answered. "I thought you were planning to tell me you didn't want to see me any more 'cause of what happened last month, even though we talked about it this morning. I know my job's dangerous, and I won't blame you if that's what you decide to do, especially since you know I'm not going to give up on bringing in Parker. I take the best care I can when I'm out there, but accidents do happen." He paused and a smile returned to his face. "But I didn't think you were getting all bent out of shape 'cause you wanted me to take a simple test and wear a condom."

Serena stiffened, slid her legs from across his thighs, and pushed away from him. His eyebrows rose at her sudden action and climbed even higher when she folded her arms across her chest. She felt incensed. How dare he belittle her concerns and make fun of her?

"Well, I'm glad this is all so amusing to you. And you're right, it *is* one simple test. *One simple test* you men seem to feel you don't need to do and get all pissed about it. My friend Donna found that out the hard way. Her oh-so-macho boyfriend refused to get tested, felt insulted she would even think to suggest he might have AIDS. And she loved him so much, she didn't insist. Well, guess what? She *died.* Died because he lied to her. He had HIV—it hadn't turned into full-blown AIDS yet—but he knew it. And I had to watch her suffer—my best friend since kindergarten—watch as she wasted away and died. Because she was scared he'd leave her if she insisted on the test. That just about tore me up. So don't you dare sit there and laugh at me and tell me you think *I'm getting all bent out of shape* and it's just a little thing."

Her hands dropped from across her chest as she spoke but were tightly clenched into fists at her side. Her lips were pressed tightly together when she finished speaking.

Kyle looked at her flashing eyes and heaving breasts and knew he was in trouble. Deep trouble. Normally very sweet-tempered, she was capable of great passion once she felt strongly about something. He had tasted a hint of that passion in her kisses and her embrace, and he wanted more.

After their conversation tonight, he was looking forward to receiving the full force of her passion. That hope was evaporating rapidly. Or rather, the *manner* in which he hoped to receive all her passion was evaporating because she was certainly letting him have it now in full flow. If he didn't defuse this situation quickly, he would be lucky if she even spoke with him again, much less went to bed with him.

He stretched out one hand toward her and said softly, "I'm not belittling your concerns, Serena. Truly, I'm not. I'm sorry you lost a good friend like that. I *am* going to get tested, I promise. You won't ever have to worry about that with me."

He took one of her hands in his, easing open the clenched fist and slowly rubbing his thumb over the back of her hand. He waited. He didn't have to be psychic to know she was thinking of her friend. Tense moments passed, and it was close to two minutes before she gave a small shudder and looked at him. His heart squeezed as he noted the sadness on her face, the trembling lower lip.

"I'm sorry," she said quietly. "I didn't mean to blow up at

you like that. But it's very important to me, not only because of that, but … well, never mind." She shook her head.

"C'mere, baby," he said softly, lifting her and resettling her on his lap. He tucked her head into his shoulder and stroked her back. "It's my fault. It was in poor taste to make a joke about something like that. I'm sorry."

She didn't answer but leaned into him, one arm wrapped around his neck. They sat in silence, watching the activity before them. The fountain displays were beautiful, with their intricate combinations of light, water, and music. There was a smattering of people enjoying the evening—mothers watching their small children running in and out of the displays created by the fountain, trying to dodge the water sprays as they shot up and fell back to the ground; teenagers wrapped up in each other; young couples with eyes only for each other; here and there, a lone person taking in the tranquil beauty of the evening. It was a beautiful night, not too hot with a cool breeze blowing over their skin.

"What are you plans for next weekend?" Kyle asked, almost ten minutes after Serena's outburst.

"I'm off. I have two flights later this week—tomorrow to New York and on Wednesday to Tampa—and then nothing till next week. Why, what are you thinking?"

"Well, to make up for my poor taste and to help celebrate the soon-to-be new status in our relationship"—he dropped a quick kiss on her lips—"I thought we could do it in style. How'd you like to go somewhere quiet and relaxing for the weekend, far from all the crowds?"

He looked into her lovely brown eyes, feeling the weekend couldn't come fast enough for him, knowing what would happen between them would be on his mind 24-7—even more so than it had before—because finally, it was about to become reality.

"Cool, where are we going?" Serena asked. The sad look was gone from her face, and she looked interested.

Kyle was glad he brought up the subject, as it put a spark of life back in her face, took away that haunted look of grief that he had brought about with his careless words.

"Well, I haven't really decided yet. I just thought about it, remember? Why don't I let it be a surprise?" he answered. "And seeing as how you're going to be flying early tomorrow, we'd better go so you can get your beauty rest, yeah."

"Yeah, beauty rest, right," she scoffed. "All right, let's go."

Lifting her off his lap most reluctantly, Kyle stood up, reaching down and curving her to his side. They were soon on their way and a, short while later, reached her apartment in Lithonia.

When Annette's family had relocated to New York, Annette had decided to stay in Georgia, as she had quite a good job with Verizon Wireless and didn't want to relocate with its attending worry of securing a position as lucrative as the one she currently held. Serena and Annette were both pleased with their living arrangement, but lately, Kyle wished fervently Annette had gone with her family to New York.

After a lengthy and pleasurable good night—with Serena promising to call him when she arrived in New York—Kyle took his leave, feeling much more upbeat at the end of the evening than he had at the beginning.

He thought over the events of the evening: his conversation with Serena, her surprising but oh-so-welcome announcement that they needed to move the relationship along, her unexpected outburst when he was fool enough to make an asinine comment. He was happy they resolved the situation and it had not spiraled out of control. He was also happy with the major decision to step up the relationship, a decision with which he concurred 100 percent. Thinking about it now had him so hot; his jeans were getting way too tight and uncomfortable.

To take his mind off his discomfort, he thought about where they could go for the weekend. He figured she was in the air so often with her job that, unless they were going international, she would probably prefer a road trip. So where to go within a reasonable time and distance that was conducive to a hot, sexy weekend?

Mulling it over, he decided he still had some time to finalize that plan. The more important order of business was making an appointment with his doctor. He knew, or at least was reasonably certain, he didn't have any STDs, but Serena was right. It was important and prudent to be tested. Better to be safe than sorry. And he would never put her in jeopardy or have her feeling less than comfortable with any aspect of their relationship. He was annoyed with himself that he had not thought to get tested, especially since he had been hell-bent and determined he and Serena were going to end up in bed together—sooner rather than later.

Chapter 10

"Hey, Drum, hold the elevator, will you?" a voice yelled.

Kyle turned around to see Keith jogging across the aisle in the parking garage, hurrying to catch up to him.

"What's up?" Kyle asked as he continued to stride along toward the elevator in the parking garage.

"Where's the fire? Why are you in such a hurry?"

"Just wanted to check what's happening. I've got some stuff I need to handle—"

"Ah-hah! Personal stuff, eh?" Keith interrupted with delight. Kyle sighed. Keith never missed a chance to tease him.

"What're we talking about here? Grocery shopping, dentist appointment, or would it have anything to do with that hot little flight attendant who's been occupying your time these last couple of months, the same one you almost burned to a crisp there at the hospital?"

Keith's teasing reminded Kyle of the hot kiss he had shared with Serena.

"Give it a rest, Thommo," Kyle answered absently, his mind still on the personal errand he needed to run. The elevator door opened and they stepped inside. Kyle pushed the button for their floor. "What choice would you make if *you* had a woman and she thought you had been hurt?"

Keith laughed. "Point taken. Listen, did you hear they

need some guys to assist with some training down in Valdosta? And I think the Mounties have someone they need taken off their hands too."

"Well, aren't you just full of news today?" Kyle said mockingly. "Which one are you thinking of doing 'cause I know you, bro, you've got your eye on something, yeah."

"Yeah, I do. Unless something else comes up, I thought I might head out to Valdosta, whip those guys into shape. Who knows, someone may be interested in recruitment. What about you, feeling interested?"

"Haven't really thought about it. Valdosta sounds interesting enough. Who's the target group? The local law enforcement? When do they want to start? Would be nice to take a run up to Canada too."

"This week, I think. You've probably got some mail on your computer. Check and see. I think Spencer and Monroe are eyeing that Canada trip; they've never been up there."

The elevator dinged and opened and they stepped out. Kyle walked down the corridor, stopped at his cubicle, and turned on his computer. While he waited for it to boot up, he went into the little kitchenette and poured a cup of coffee. Steaming cup in hand, he returned and clicked on his e-mail.

He went through his inbox, noting the response on some information concerning a probation violator he had relayed to New Jersey. From his e-mail, he learnt the Valdosta Police Department wanted to conduct some specialized training in building entry and search, search and seizure, and evasive driving. It was scheduled for the following week for five days.

Kyle reasoned that at least he would only be gone for one week rather than a more extensive assignment that could take him to another state. He smiled to himself, thinking of the coming weekend, and chuckled under his breath when he remembered the night just past. He had been kissing Serena good night, very passionately indeed, when she suddenly asked, as if it only now occurred to her, "Why are we waiting until weekend? I thought you would've, you know, wanted to do it as soon as you were set. Nowadays, it doesn't take long to get back test results, you know. The same day."

Breathing a little hard, Kyle looked at her, the fire burning in his eyes, and replied softly, "One night with you is not going to be enough, babe. Not long enough to do all I want to with you and love you as you should be loved. Not hardly long enough."

She looked back at him, wide-eyed, and her mouth rounded in an O; but as his words penetrated her brain, he could see the fire appearing in the depths of her eyes; and that sexy look that turned him to mush appeared on her face. Kyle groaned and kissed her fiercely, hungrily, like a starving man getting his first meal in days.

So caught up in his pleasant daydream of the night before, Kyle didn't realize Keith had come to his cubicle and asked him a question. Getting no response, Keith was now silently looking at him with a slight grin on his face.

"Must've been one heck of a night, man."

"Lay off, Milk, unless you want me to wipe that smirk off your face for you," Kyle growled.

"Ooh, fighting words! Okay, okay, truce." He laughed as Kyle advanced threateningly on him. "Listen, I meant to ask you if you want to get in some time at the gym later. Thought I'd do some upper-body work. You can spot me if you're not too *tired* to work out, after your hectic night and all." Keith laughed.

"Sure, why not. I'll show you how it's done. Let me handle my business first, and I'll catch up with you later, yeah. Six o'clock good for you?"

"Six is good. See you later then."

Kyle continued checking his e-mail, deleted some junk mail, and sent updates to two queries from deputy marshals in Florida. As he continued scrolling down his inbox, he noticed Serena's name in the subject line. His heart gave a sudden jump and speeded up slightly. He had given her his e-mail address a few nights ago when she had asked him, but she had not yet sent him any mail. It seemed that was about to change.

He clicked open the mail, read what she had typed, and smiled. It was short and to the point.

Just wanted to tell you I'm thinking about you and looking forward to the weekend.

He smiled and typed his response.

So am I, baby, so am I.

He hit send, finished checking the rest of his mail, and turned off his computer. He stepped into the chief's office to let him know he was going to be out for a few hours taking care of some personal business. He was an SOG operative, but that didn't mean he was a law unto himself. He still had to follow the chain of command like everyone else. The chief acknowledged his request, checked with him on his schedule for the day, and waved him away.

Kyle headed for his truck and the first phase—an appointment with his doctor—of what he hoped would turn out to be one of the best weekends of his life. Serena's e-mail left him with a warm feeling, and he smiled as his thoughts drifted to her. He hadn't heard from her and wondered idly which leg of her trip she was currently on. She had three stops on this rotation before returning to Georgia.

The clank of metal weights being hoisted on bars, the whine of pulleys, the familiar smell of sweat, and the sound of male voices grunting and groaning with exertion greeted Kyle as he swung open the door of the gym. He was looking forward to a strenuous workout with Keith. He needed to work off his sexual tension, and if he couldn't do it how he would've preferred, what better way to burn it off than with some good old-fashioned physical exertion.

He spotted Keith sitting on one of the padded workout benches and made his way over to him. A few of the guys called out to him as he circled the floor, and he acknowledged them with upraised hand but did not pause to chat.

"Hey, see you got here, good. Give you a minute to warm up. Changed my mind, thought we might work on abs today instead. We haven't done those suckers in a while. Taking it to the max today, Drum," Keith greeted him with a challenging grin.

"Bring it on. I can handle whatever you've got," Kyle responded. After doing some stretching to loosen up his muscles, he and Keith made their way over to the chin-up bars.

"What're you starting with?" he asked Keith, letting him take the initiative, knowing he always liked to push their sessions to the maximum.

"Hanging knee raises," Keith responded with an evil leer. "And no shortcuts with the straps either," he warned, talking of the straps which could be used to take the stress off your grip.

Kyle cocked an eyebrow at him questioningly. "You ever see me use those, bro? Why do you think I'm going to start now?"

"Oh, I don't know, something to do with how *tired* you seemed earlier," the ever-jovial Keith joked.

Kyle snorted in derision. "Let's get this show on the road. Four by twenty-five?" he looked at Keith for confirmation.

"Yeah, let's do this," Keith agreed.

They started their grueling workout. Hanging from the chin-up bars with their hands shoulder width apart, they started to work on their lower abdominal muscles. Bending their knees so their thighs were now parallel to the floor, they swung their knees as high as they could into their chests—using only their ab muscles, not their bodies—and rotating their hips upward. Holding for a brief moment, they lowered their knees until their thighs were again parallel with the floor.

They did four sets of twenty-five repetitions, allowing twenty seconds of rest between each set.

Keith always made it a personal challenge whenever he and Kyle worked out. At first, right after his injury, Kyle was unable to exercise on the chin-up bar, and Keith had bested him. He had been shot in the upper arm—luckily for him, only a flesh wound, neither penetrating nor nicking the bone—but he still needed rest and rehabilitation. But his superb physical condition ensured he healed rapidly, and his arm and shoulder were now much better able to handle the stress of the exercise. Keith was no longer able to take advantage of Kyle's temporarily weakened condition.

Next, they moved on to work on their obliques and upper abs with twisting crunches on the decline bench. They alternated sides, again doing four sets of twenty-five repetitions and resting twenty seconds between each set.

The twisting crunches were followed by machine crunches, which worked the upper body as did the cable crunches, which followed. After that, it was reverse crunches on the incline board for their lower abs. Same sets, same reps, same rest before moving on to the final exercise—split leg crunches to work their upper abs and obliques.

Lying on floor mats with their feet shoulder width apart and straight up in the air so their soles were parallel to the ceiling, they reached up with both hands to touch their toes, holding for brief seconds and alternating each side. Kyle usually managed to actually reach his toes, whereas the bulkier Keith could only manage his ankles, to his everlasting irritation.

"Someday, Drum, someday," he grunted out. Kyle gasped out a laugh.

They rested for thirty seconds, each taking a drink of water before starting the circuit once again. They did three circuits before calling a halt.

"Whew!" Keith exclaimed. "Feel that burn!"

"Yeah, that was a good one," Kyle agreed, breathing a little hard himself as he took a swig of water. "Took it to the max indeed, Thommo."

He rotated his shoulder experimentally and flexed his biceps as he probed with his mind for any feeling of strain or pain. It felt good to have his muscles back up to optimum fitness.

Keith grinned, still catching his breath. "Don't I know it. Let's hit the showers, man. I got a hot date tonight."

"Yeah, when do you not ever have a hot date?" Kyle asked wryly.

Keith chuckled in acknowledgment. "When you're the man, you're the man. What can I say? How's it going with that flight attendant of yours?"

Kyle looked over at him with eyebrows raised questioningly in warning.

"Hey, man," Keith said quickly with palms upraised, "you know I'm not up in your business. We've had each other's backs for a good while now; you're my brother." He paused and hesitated. "I've never known you to be so intense about any woman before, and I was wondering what's up with that."

Kyle didn't answer; his steps slowed as his thoughts turned inward. He knew Keith wasn't being malicious or nosy, just concerned about him. The trouble was he didn't really know the answer to that question either.

"I'm not sure," he said slowly.

"You think she might be the one?" Keith looked at him curiously.

"I don't know," Kyle replied, running his fingers through his sweat-drenched hair. "She's different, you know. I don't feel bored when I'm with her. I love her spirit. Even if I've had a hell of a day, when I'm done talking with her, I always feel better. She always does something I never expect that surprises the hell out of me."

"Are you in love with her?" Keith asked incredulously and with what seemed like a tinge of disbelief.

Kyle shrugged. "Don't think so," he responded nonchalantly, not missing Keith's exaggerated gesture of wiping the very real sweat from his brow even as he asked himself, *Am I in love with Serena? Hell, we haven't even slept together yet!*

He knew that one thing had nothing to do with the other, but he didn't like how Keith had just thrown up the L word so quickly. But still, he remembered how she always managed to bring a smile to his face whenever he thought of her—which was more and more often of late. How he was always pleased to hear her voice whenever they spoke on the phone, how he never felt the need to be on his guard or cautious around her. He recalled how panicked and uneasy he was last weekend, when he thought Serena wanted to call a halt to their relationship. The reality of her distraction was the complete opposite of his anxiety of course, but he couldn't forget how scared he was the relationship might be over. He sighed.

"Let's get that shower." He quickened his pace toward the locker rooms.

"Sure thing, man," Keith responded easily. Kyle was not fooled. He knew Keith would still have more to say on the subject of his girlfriend.

Sure enough, Keith asked, "Could I at least know her name?" He grinned, irrepressible as ever.

Kyle couldn't help but grin back. "Serena," he said, his face and voice soft, not realizing how much he was revealing at that moment. "Her name is Serena."

Chapter 11

Finally, Friday! Serena couldn't believe how much she was looking forward to this day, the start of her weekend getaway with Kyle. True to his word, he kept the location a surprise, only promising she would enjoy where they would be going. She knew she would—she was always happy when she was with him, wherever they were—but if truth be told, she could care less where they were going.

All she could think about was the coming night and the rest of the weekend, alternating between nervous anticipation and shivery delight. Every time she thought of Kyle—remembering the spread of his broad shoulders, his well-muscled body and firm thighs, how snugly his bulging biceps filled out his polo shirt, imagining herself getting familiar with all that hot hunk of masculinity—a deep warmth would settle low in her stomach, and she would have to take slow deep breaths before she started hyperventilating.

He wasn't half bad to look at either—his skin a delicious shade of mocha, his lips firm and sensuous eyes that always seemed to be smoldering whenever he looked at her. It was what she called his bone-melting look, and it always gave her the shivers.

The two flights she worked this week and the return trips were riots. She was sure her fellow attendants must have thought she was becoming ill, the way she would suddenly stop and blow out a long slow breath.

Her overnight bag was already packed, and she waited impatiently for Kyle to pick her up. He had told her not to bother with any night attire, and he was serious about it. They were leaving late afternoon and would be driving for about an hour, hc said. Just when she was looking at her watch for what seemed to be the hundredth time, "What's Going On" sang out on her cell phone.

"Two minutes, babe," Kyle said when she answered. "Want to come down so I don't have to park?"

"Sure, see you in a sec." She wondered if after this weekend she would be changing Kyle's ring tone to "Sexual Healing."

The black pickup pulled to a stop in front of her, and Kyle reached across to push open the passenger door for her, giving her a sensuous smile laden with the promise of wonderful things to come. He was so damn fine, and suddenly she had to touch him so badly, feel connected to him. She slid across the seat, ran her fingers through his curly hair, and pressed her lips to his. His eyes widened in surprise and he looked pleased. He returned the kiss with interest.

"Well, hey to you too! Missed me a little?" he teased.

"No, missed you a lot," Serena breathed as she looked at him hungrily.

Kyle let out a long slow breath. "Uh, babe, we've got some driving ahead of us. I'd like to do that in a reasonably comfortable frame of mind and physical condition. So help me out here, okay? Sit back and behave yourself."

Serena sighed and sat back in her seat. Kyle leaned across and turned her face toward him.

"I'm not saying I don't like it. Just, hold that feeling until tonight, why don't you," he whispered in a sultry voice. He kissed her on her cheek and stroked it quickly with his tongue. Serena shivered, anticipation a fiery curl in her belly.

They headed out onto I-20 West, exiting onto I-285 South

and onto I-85 South. Serena tried to think where they were going, pumping Kyle for information, but he only smiled and shook his head. When he turned yet again, she decided she might as well fully enjoy the drive and the company. After going down a few local highways, Kyle turned the pickup in at the entrance to Regency Gardens.

Serena drew in an excited gasp. "Regency Gardens! Oh, Kyle, I've heard of this place! It's supposed to be really fabulous! Ooh, thank you!"

"Glad you like it. I aim to please." Kyle smiled. He seemed pleased to see her so happy and excited. "Let's check in. I booked one of the cottages."

"A cottage?" she asked, surprised. "Not one of the rooms or suites?"

He looked down at her and smiled. "I'll tell you why tomorrow."

"Okay," she replied, a little mystified.

After they had checked in and gone to their cottage—a cute little one-bedroom affair nestled among the pine trees—Kyle had thoughtfully left her to freshen up and change for dinner while he scouted out the surroundings. By the time he returned, she had already finished dressing, opting for a cool sleeveless cotton shift in a flowered print. Kyle's eyes heated when he saw her, and it stirred an answering hunger in her own. He showered and dressed quickly, and they decided to visit one of the many restaurants on the site, The Victoria, for dinner.

Serena was sure the dinner was tasty, but if anyone had asked her, she would not have been able to say what she had eaten. All she could think about was Kyle; they were finally going to make love. Every minute that passed seemed to be longer than the last, and she was practically squirming in her seat, thinking about the room back at the cottage.

"What do you want for dessert, babe?" Kyle asked with a smile.

"Chocolate," she whispered.

"Of course." He smiled at her favorite preference for sweet. "Do you remember what they had on the menu? Chocolate cake, ice cream?"

"It's not on this menu," she said softly, looking up at him, the desire clearly stamped on her face. As he realized which chocolate she was referring to, his eyes darkened with desire and turned to liquid coal, the heat that suddenly blazed out of them scorching her with their intensity.

"Let's get out of here," he growled, his voice deep and low and husky.

Silently, she pushed back her chair and stood up once Kyle took care of the bill. Kyle folded her hand in his, and they made their way quickly back to the cottage. The second they were inside, Kyle swung her around into his arms, crushed her to his chest, and slanted his lips across hers in a hot hungry kiss. Serena felt all the sexual tension he had been holding in for the past few months explode. She gave a little whimper as he overwhelmed her with the force of his passion, winding her arms around his neck and holding on tightly.

Kyle plunged his tongue into Serena's mouth, dancing around hers while exploring every nook and cranny. She tasted of the wine she had drunk at dinner and her own special essence that was uniquely Serena. Hearing the little sound she gave, he thought to pull back so he wouldn't scare her, but knowing that this time, this night, he would not have to stop their lovemaking was acting like a drug on him. It swept him away and brought out all the pent-up sexual hungers he had been banking these past few months.

He slid his arms across her warm shoulders, one hand cupping her nape, holding her neck steady while he ravaged her mouth, the other hand moving down her back to cup her bottom, bringing her up against his erection, which was straining mightily against his pants. He felt like he was on fire, that he would explode any minute, knew he couldn't wait, couldn't take it slow this first time. He needed to bury himself in her, needed to do it now before he completely lost his mind.

"Serena, babe, I can't wait any more. I've got to have you now." He barely got the words out through gritted teeth.

"Huh, huh, ohhh," she moaned, holding him just as tightly.

Somehow, they reached the bed without him realizing how they got there, and they tumbled down on the covers. Kyle pushed the hem of Serena's dress up her thighs and quickly whipped her panties down her legs. She writhed on the bed, tossing her head from side to side.

"Yeah, baby, I know. It's going to be so good."

"Kyle, Kyle," she moaned as her hands reached out for him frantically.

"I've got what you need, baby. I've got it right here."

He stood up and tugged at his zipper, yanking his jeans and briefs down in one movement, freeing his erection. It burst forth, jutting proudly from his loins. He stepped out of the puddle of clothing at his feet and kicked them aside. Hands shaking, he got one of the packets from the nightstand and put on the condom. He parted her legs and knelt between them, positioned himself, and, with one strong thrust, impaled himself to the hilt. She arched up with a small cry as she clamped her legs around his waist and squeezed him tightly, inside and out. Kyle shuddered and moaned, knowing he didn't have too much control left. It didn't feel like Serena had any either. She appeared to be on fire as much as he was.

He started to move, withdrawing and thrusting, sliding into her hot depths. They were so hungry for each other, had denied themselves for so long that in no time at all, he felt her muscles start to contract. He knew he wasn't going to be too far behind her when she exploded and started to thrust faster and faster.

She gave one last squeeze and held him fast in her grasp. He squeezed her buttocks as the gurgling cry burst out of her throat, ratcheting up in volume as the orgasm hit her. Then he was plunging faster and faster until, with a groan, he emptied himself into her.

Shuddering, he collapsed onto his elbows before rolling onto his back, pulling her with him and cradling her into his side as he fought to control his breathing. Her breathing was just as erratic, and he could feel her trembling in his arms, her passion spent.

It was all Kyle could do to raise his hand and move aside the damp strands of hair clinging to her face. He was amazed to see his hand trembling as he slowly tucked the hair behind her ear. God, that was mind-blowing! His breath huffed in and out of his chest as he lay next to Serena, his fingers moving in a soft caress over the back of her neck.

When he felt like he had some semblance of control over his legs, he eased away from her and went into the bathroom. He carefully removed the condom and cleaned himself with a washcloth before returning to the bed and doing the same to Serena. Gathering her into his arms with a sigh of rich contentment, he pulled the sheet halfway up their bodies as they lay on the bed.

Kyle looked down at the beautiful woman in his arms—at the look of intense satisfaction and bliss on her face—still in shock over what had taken place moments ago. He had never been so blown away, never felt such a savage pleasure as what he had just experienced. He knew he had been rough, but Serena had met him stroke for stroke, giving him as good as she got and increasing his own pleasure in the process.

His woman. And she was his woman, by God; she would know it too before the weekend was over. He was going to lay his stamp on her every way he could. Amazingly, he found himself getting hard again as he thought about what they had shared. He wondered what was going through her mind right now.

Serena felt like she had just exploded into a million tiny pieces. She knew Kyle was a man very much in tune with his physical and sensual self, and she had felt like a warrior princess as he took her so savagely and completely. She reveled in his fierce lovemaking, glad the first time between them was as raw and hot as it was. She felt like they were fused together, not knowing where one started and the other ended. She hugged him fiercely and felt his answering hug and more in return.

Serena felt his erection poking her through her dress, which was bunched up around her waist as she lay on her side, cuddled up to Kyle. Her eyes flew up to his. He was watching her intently, smolderingly, raw passion in his gaze. His features were hardened by sexual arousal.

His cheekbones appeared more prominent, his skin flushed, eyes bright and glittering. Even though they had just come together so explosively, he didn't look at all sated. That little romp barely seemed to have scratched the surface of his desire for her.

"Ready for round two?" he whispered. He planted a searing kiss on her lips as she tilted her head up to him.

"I like a man who can rise to the occasion, and so magnificently too," she purred.

His smile was pure male, pure satisfaction. "Let's get out of these clothes. I want to see you, every inch of you."

"I want to see you too," she breathed, pulling the hem of his shirt up and running her fingers softly across his chest and down his finely chiseled abs.

He sucked in his breath sharply. "Oh, baby, what you do to me," he groaned. He stood up, quickly yanked the shirt over his head, and tossed it carelessly aside. He turned back to her and started to reach for her clothing but stopped. She was sure it was the look on her face. She felt a combination of wonder, hunger, and a fierce possessive pride.

"Like what you see?" he murmured, hands on his hips, his desire for her obvious to both of them.

"Ooh yeah," she moaned. "Why don't you come over here and let me show you how much." She stretched her hands up to him in mute invitation.

"I'm all yours. However you want me, baby."

Kyle sank back down on the bed next to her and slid the zipper down her back and pulled the dress down her legs. It quickly joined his shirt and other clothing somewhere on the floor. He unsnapped her strapless bra and her breasts sprang free. His breathing—now beginning to return to a more normal rhythm—started to get ragged again as he gazed down at her.

"I like what I see too. You're so freaking beautiful," he whispered. He dipped his head into the curve of her neck and shoulder, kissed her silky skin, his mouth fanning the growing flames of her desire. She shivered in delight as his lips trailed down her neck onto her collar bone, his right hand at the same time stroked slowly and enticingly down her left side, over her hip and down her thigh.

"This time we take it slow, Serena. Now that we've taken the edge off, I'm going to love you long and slow."

He whispered his promise onto her skin as he stretched out on the bed next to her. His hand cupped her breast, and he rubbed his thumb over the nipple. It pebbled immediately into a tight little nub. His head dipped, and he slid his tongue in a circle around the nipple. Serena breathed in gasps and moans—*the air, what happened to the air?*—as he took her breast into his mouth, suckling like a baby. He turned his attention to the other breast, giving it the same treatment as her passion mounted and desire burned like a wild flame in her.

Her fingers wound into his hair, pulling and caressing

mindlessly. He placed soft, feathery kisses onto her stomach; her muscles clenched with every touch. His hands stroked over her skin; he seemed to love its texture. He spread her legs and kissed her inner thighs. She arched her back and collapsed back onto the bed. He worked his way down her legs with small kisses, light as a butterfly, touching down and moving quickly, giving her the sensation she was being tickled by a feather; they were so soft. She had her eyes closed. She felt ecstatic. How could it get any better than this?

"Open your eyes, babe. Look at me," he whispered.

She complied, protesting softly, "I don't want to look. I just want to feel and it feels so good." Her eyes drifted shut again.

"You want to feel, huh? All right. How does *this* feel?"

And he exploded over her, kissing and licking, stroking and kneading every inch of her skin with his hands and lips.

Serena did not believe such pleasure could exist. His tongue and lips trailed liquid fire wherever they touched on her skin. His nimble fingers followed the molten trail; sometimes they blazed a path of their own.

Serena went into sensory overload, feeling the fire building within her again, hotter and hotter as he stoked it with his sure touch. She groaned and twisted on the bed, wanting, needing his final possession; but the slow, sweet torture continued.

"Kyle, please, please," she begged, almost out of her mind.

"Tell me what you want, babe," Kyle crooned. "Tell me and it's yours."

"I want you!" she practically screamed at him. "Now, now, now!"

"You've got me, babe. I'm all yours."

He slid on another condom, spread her thighs further apart, lifting her legs so she was completely vulnerable to him and entered her. She was so wet and ready for him; he fit like a hand in a glove. They both moaned in rapturous pleasure.

"Ahh, baby, you're so tight. It feels so good," he groaned. He paused as if he were savoring the sensation. He started stroking, slowly withdrawing and plunging back in, letting her enfold him in her silky sheath. Serena wrapped her legs tightly around his waist, her arms around his back as she sank into the rhythm, lifting her hips and clenching him with her internal muscles before sinking back down.

"Oh, it's so good, it's so good," she moaned. She could feel the spiral start to wind up from low down in her stomach, getting her ready for another trip to the stars.

Seemingly out of nowhere, a random thought popped into her head. She remembered one of those television talk shows her friends loved to watch, always some ridiculous dirty laundry people were forever airing for the world to see—"I slept with my sister's boyfriend" or "my father is after my girlfriend" or some other ludicrous subject. This one had been about lovers, who didn't give their partners satisfaction in bed, only concentrating on themselves. The girl in question said when everything was going well in bed, her boyfriend would change his action and leave her feeling frustrated.

I'll kill him if he does anything to mess up this rhythm. I'll kill him, I'll kill him, I'll kill him, Serena thought fiercely.

Without realizing it, the chant became the rhythm, taking her higher and higher as she strained to reach the top, to take that leap off into the stratosphere. It was coming; she could feel it in every pore, closer and closer and closer.

Kyle stroked faster and harder. She couldn't begin to imagine what he was seeing on her face, only knew she was getting closer to her climax, that heavenly feeling she had just experienced with him and greedily wanted again. Her inner muscles clenched and released around his shaft. And then her legs tightened even more around his waist, her back arched until she was almost bowed, lifting her buttocks off the bed as she went over the edge, the scream ripping from her throat.

"Yes, yes, yeeesssss!"

Serena felt as if her whole body was exploding from the inside out; it was the most intense feeling as she erupted. The pleasure was beyond belief, and it went on and on and on. Slowly, she drifted back to earth, back to the world, holding on to Kyle as he pounded into her, followed her into the realms of pleasure with his own release.

"Oh, Serena baby," Kyle moaned as he collapsed on top of her. After a breathless moment—or two or three, she lost count—he raised himself up on his elbows as if he felt he was too heavy to stay where he was. Serena gave a whimper of protest and clung to him, her legs still locked about his waist.

"Awrite, baby," he soothed as he turned onto his side with her in his arms. "It's awrite."

Serena purred, her hand at the back of his head, running her fingers through his hair. Every few seconds, the aftershocks would hit her, and her inner muscles would clench around him as she continued to milk him. It was an incredibly erotic sensation for her and, apparently, for Kyle too as he seemed quite content to lay there and enjoy.

Serena knew Kyle was an incredibly sensuous man, knew that sex with him would have been fantastic, but this was beyond what she dreamed and, if she didn't miss her guess, what Kyle suspected too. They drifted off to sleep in each other's arms, exhausted but totally replete with contentment.

Chapter 12

Serena awoke to find herself lying spoon fashion, Kyle nestled behind her, his arm resting on her hip, her buttocks tucked up against his groin. She felt pleasantly sore and smiled as she thought of the reason for her mild discomfort. They had come together twice more during the night—the last time before dawn—and each time, it had been as intense and rapturous as the previous one.

"You awake, babe?" Kyle asked in a drowsy voice, his arms tightening around her waist as he kissed her neck. She shivered.

"Just about," she replied softly, turning around. "Lying here being lazy."

He chuckled. "Well, no time for that today. C'mon, up and about, woman. We've got a schedule to keep."

"Why, what's on the agenda?" she asked with interest.

"Well, I thought you might enjoy a massage this morning," he said with a wicked leer, "and I'll check out the fitness center while you're being pampered. After that, we'll have lunch and visit the gardens this afternoon. I know you like your plants, so I figured you'd enjoy the setup out here. Are you awrite with that? I only want you to enjoy yourself this weekend."

"Sounds really great, Kyle. A massage! Wonderful. Why didn't you get one too?" she asked curiously.

He gave her a look which plainly said, "I'm a man. I pump iron."

She threw her hands into the air. "All right, all right. What time is my massage scheduled?"

He plucked his watch off the bedside table and looked at the time. "In the next hour. If we hurry, we still have time for a light breakfast, that's if you want it."

"Yeah, let's do that. Okay, let me take a shower, and we'll get this show on the road."

Serena went into the bathroom, humming a tune under her breath. She stepped into the shower, smiling a little as she thought back over the incredible night they had shared. *Kyle is some man and he's all mine*, she thought with fierce satisfaction. She felt herself becoming hot all over as she thought of the coming night and being back in his arms for some more mind-blowing sex. It was more than anything she had expected, and she couldn't wait for them to get back in bed.

Get a grip, she admonished herself as she turned off the shower, *or it's going to be a very long day*. After brushing her teeth, she wrapped the towel around herself and stepped out of the bathroom to give Kyle his turn while she got dressed.

They left the room a short while later and headed back to The Victoria but decided to try another restaurant later for lunch. Tucking into the slices of fruit she put on her plate, she suddenly remembered something she wanted to ask him earlier.

"Oh, you were going to tell me today why you booked a cottage, remember?" she said, looking across at him as he sipped his coffee with quiet enjoyment.

He looked across at her, starting to smile in that sexy way that always went straight to her gut and lower down. Her breathing automatically started to get choppy. He leaned forward, lowering his voice as he said softly, "I know you're a very sensual woman; you've got a great capacity for loving and compassion. I figured you'd come hard, with everything you've got. That usually involves some amount of volume. But you're also incredibly reserved, in some ways. I didn't want you to feel embarrassed or that you had to hold back because we were in a room close to other people."

Serena looked at Kyle, her eyes getting bigger and bigger as he spoke, feeling mortified. He scooted closer and took her hand.

"Don't," he said. "Don't ever feel embarrassed about that. I love how you're so giving and free and don't hold back. It's an incredible turn-on, and I don't want you to change that because you feel constrained by circumstances, okay?"

Serena nodded silently and went back to her breakfast. She mulled it over in her mind, as was her wont, thinking things through. When she looked over at him with a smile of acceptance and acknowledgment of what he said, he was smiling in response.

"Figured all that out by yourself, huh? Come hard, huh?"

"Oh, yeah, baby," he breathed. "Thought I was riding a wave." He paused and then said with a wicked smile, "I might need ear plugs next time too."

She blushed, even though she knew it was a little hard to tell with her complexion, and she felt a little self-conscious.

"C'mon, let's go. I've got a massage waiting."

"Running away, Serena?" he teased indulgently.

"That, I am, and not ashamed to say it," she replied jauntily.

He chuckled. "Enjoy yourself, babe. I'll meet you back at the cottage when you're done, awrite?"

They left the dining area and turned in different directions to go their respective ways.

The rest of the weekend flew by much too fast for Serena. Following her incredible hour of pampering with her massage, they had lunch at the Wellington Café and strolled around the different garden layouts. Kyle smiled indulgently as she oohed and aahed over the magnificent flowering blooms and the vegetable gardens.

The next day they spent partly at the beach and simply hanging out, relaxing in the tranquil spots around the resort. The two nights were incredible. Serena didn't think she would ever get enough of Kyle, never tire of drawing him into her body, feeling him possess her so thoroughly that it was almost too much to bear at times. She wondered how she would get through the following days and weeks when they were not together. At least, she hoped they had days and weeks together.

All too soon, it was Sunday afternoon and time to take leave of their idyllic weekend retreat. They headed out for the hour's drive back to Atlanta. She felt she was leaving a little bit of heaven behind, and judging by the way Kyle kept touching her and pulling her close to his side, she figured he felt the same way too. She flipped up the tray section between the seats of the pickup and snuggled up close to Kyle, wanting, *needing* to stay connected to him for as long as possible before they had to part.

Kyle drove one-handed, his right hand resting on Serena's shoulders, often playing with her hair as they headed back to Atlanta. She had reverted back to her natural hair, and even though he said she looked good in the other hair style, he seemed to prefer her wild, untamed curls.

The middle seat was not all that great, and he suggested she might be more comfortable if she could lean back and relax her neck on the headrest, but she shook her head and stayed where she was. She liked him touching her; his warm hands on her skin brought to mind their incredible weekend and the pleasure they had given each other. She wondered if he, too, were thinking of how fantastic they had been together and when they would get together again.

As Kyle drove swiftly toward Atlanta, his mind was filled

not only with the weekend but also with the past week. He was extremely glad Serena had brought up the subject and suggested—no, *demanded*, he thought wryly—that he be tested for STDs. And that she had the foresight to be on birth control. He wished he could've felt himself sliding into her with no barriers, flesh on flesh, but knew instinctively Serena would not feel comfortable with that step until they were more of a couple, seeing each other exclusively. And especially after what she revealed about her friend's death from AIDS. He could wait. Hell, after the weekend they just spent, he could wait for a lot of things. Besides, right now, he didn't feel interested in any other woman, only Serena.

He thought that once he made love to her a few times, the sexual hunger and tension he was carrying around for the last few months would have eased, but it never abated. If anything, it seemed to get stronger the more he made love to her.

And that was another thing. His previous affairs with women primarily focused on sex, but when it came to Serena, he always thought of *making love.* He was a little uneasy about the distinction but was so wrapped up in the intense connection they had that he pushed the disturbing thought away to the back of his mind. Time enough to worry later. For now, he wanted to dwell on the pleasurable memories and sensations of the weekend.

He wondered when they could get together again. That reminded him he had yet to tell her he would be gone for about a week or more. He always enjoyed the training assignments, but he wished now he didn't have to go to Valdosta.

She was a little quieter than usual since they left the resort, but he thought, like him, she was dwelling on the incredible experience they shared. Still …

"Everything okay, babe. You awrite?" he asked softly.

"More than okay, more than all right," she replied, looking up at him with a warm smile tinged with hints of the passion that had enveloped them. Her soft brown eyes looked like melted chocolate. He could drown in those eyes and die happy. He smiled back and gave her shoulder a squeeze.

"I'm going to be out of town next week, unfortunately. We're doing some training down in Valdosta with the local police department. I'm going to be passing this way again really early in the morning."

"Oh," she replied, "when will you be back?"

"Hopefully, by weekend. It depends on how large the training group is and how quickly we get through the sessions."

"I've got some flights this week, but I'll miss you," she said with a sigh.

"Miss you too, babe. I am not done enjoying that luscious body of yours, not by half. You know that, don't you?" he said fiercely.

"Is that all you're going to miss, only my body? I'm more than just a … a …," she spluttered indignantly, the right word she wanted eluding her.

Kyle used one of the more well-known street words for female genitalia.

"Was that the word you're looking for?" he asked mildly. "If so, I've never thought that. I'm going to miss *you,* the whole package. You make me laugh, make me feel so good. Not many people do that," he said seriously.

Serena looked slightly chastened. "Sorry, didn't mean to snap your head off, it's just …" Her voice trailed away.

"I know, I want you too," he said simply. He felt her quick gaze before she swung her head away.

Serena looked at him sharply. He did know exactly what caused her bad-tempered outburst. She wanted him, so badly it was like a flame consuming her. She hoped she wouldn't become one of those needy clinging women, who, because they had earth-shattering sex with a man, felt they owned him. Because she knew if she did that, it would drive this man away faster.

He was not your average citizen with a nine-to-five job, a membership at the gym, and kicking back with his buddies at Super Bowl parties. He lived dangerously, hunting fugitives and handling explosives and God knows what else the US Marshals did. She had died a thousand deaths when she thought he was shot again recently. The relief when she found him whole and unharmed had been absolute. She shuddered when she thought of him involved in high-speed chases and shootouts with wanted criminals—especially Parker, the one man he was determined to find and arrest—who felt they had nothing to lose. In fact, wasn't that why he was here in Georgia now? He had been injured, bad enough he had been shot, but thank God it was not as terrible as it so easily could have been. An inch or two higher, a slightly different angle, and he could have lost the use of his arm and shoulder entirely, not just for a few months.

She resolved fiercely to give him his space. Even though she was terrified for his safety, she would be her own independent self, the person who first caught his interest. She realized she was already ahead of the game, her assets being that he liked spending time with her and, after this weekend, *really* spending time with her. She made him laugh, he said. Okay, she'd go from there.

"I'd ask you to come spend the night with me, but like I said, I have to be off early in the morning and, uhm, I need a clear head and some rest. You wore me out, woman," he said with a sexy grin.

She laughed and responded, "What do you think you did to me?"

"Oh, I think you handled yourself extremely well. Every time I was ready to sleep, there you were, stirring up trouble again."

"I was not too!" she instantly denied hotly before she saw the grin on his face and realized he was teasing her.

"Oh, I'll get you for that!" With her right hand, she walked her fingers down his right thigh, going around his knee and coming back up his inner thigh, advancing and retreating as she got closer to the bulge between his legs.

He started to squirm on the seat.

"Have mercy, Serena. I'm driving," he groaned. "Don't let me have an accident."

"On the road or in your pants?" she asked mischievously. He burst out laughing and placed a quick kiss on her grinning, upturned face.

The miles sped away beneath them, and all too soon, they were back in Atlanta, and he was dropping her off at her apartment. Serena noticed that Annette's car was parked in its slot and knew she would be waiting eagerly to hear all the details of her weekend. Too bad because there were some things Annette was never going to hear—how Kyle played her body like it was a Stradivarius and he was a master violinist bringing forth the sweetest music imaginable.

"Don't look like that, babe, or I swear, you will be coming home with me," Kyle whispered hoarsely.

Serena blinked in confusion. She hadn't realized her thoughts had been telegraphed on her face, and he was reading all the passionate memories she was reliving. She gave a rueful smile and opened the door.

"Sorry, didn't mean to do that. Go get some rest, okay, so you're fresh for tomorrow. What time are you leaving?"

"Around four in the morning," Kyle replied, caressing her face. "We want to get to Valdosta by eight o'clock, get started around nine."

"Be careful."

"Always."

"Hurry back."

"I will."

"Call me when you can, okay? Thanks for a really fabulous weekend, Kyle. It was perfect, really, really perfect," she whispered softly.

"My pleasure," he responded, leaning in to kiss her more intensely. "I—"

"I know, I know, you aim to please," she interrupted.

"That I do," he said and leaned in to demonstrate, to her complete satisfaction and approval.

Chapter 13

Serena closed the door with a soft click and leaned back against it, a sweet smile of remembrance on her face, her fingers clutching the strap of her overnight bag. She glowed.

"Well, now, don't you look like the cat that swallowed the cream *and* the canary!" Annette teased as she pulled herself upright from where she was sprawled on the sofa, looking at *Extreme Makeover* on television.

"No need to ask you how your weekend was. But I think I will anyway." She laughed. "I'm dying to know, how *was* your weekend?"

Serena's smile grew wider as she beamed from ear to ear. She straightened, dropping her bag to one side, in front of the bookcase.

"Oh, Annette, it was simply … wonderful, fabulous, spectacular!"

Annette's eyebrows rose as the superlatives rolled off Serena's tongue and a grin lit her face.

"I feel like Maria and Eliza," Serena continued.

"Who?" Annette asked in some confusion.

"You know, Maria, from *West Side Story*." The TCM channel was one of their favorites. Serena threw out her arms and started to sing, "I feel pretty, oh so pretty, I feel pretty and witty and bright!"

"Oh, *that* Maria!" Annette acknowledged with a chuckle.

"And Eliza?" she queried with interest, racking her brains as she tried to remember a movie with an *Eliza* in it.

"Eliza Doolittle, My Fair Lady," Serena replied as she waltzed around the room and trilled again. "I could've danced all night, I could've danced all night, I could've spread my wings and done a thousand things, I've never done before."

Annette burst into laughter at Serena's antics. "Girl, you are so funny. Dancing you call it, huh?" she teased.

Serena laughed and plopped down on the sofa, her eyes bright and sparkling.

"Oh, Annette, it was such a perfect weekend. Kyle is so … so …" Her eyes and face grew dreamy as she thought back to the incredible weekend and the wonderful moments of lovemaking with Kyle. "He's a fantastic lover, Annette, I've never felt so …"

Again words failed her as she tried to convey how fantastic her weekend with Kyle had been. However, while her face and words obviously proclaimed the wonderful experience she had enjoyed, her body was exhibiting a slight hint of tension. She could see Annette studying her with a frown on her face.

"If it was so fabulous, why do I detect an edge of panic about you?" she asked curiously.

Serena looked at her drily, the happiness easing from her face.

"You're so like Kyle, can never hide anything from you." She sighed. "He's going to be away this week. I'm going to miss him."

She shrugged, turning away and looking down. The explanation was feasible, but she knew that wouldn't fool Annette. She was too sharp. Sure enough, it didn't.

"Serena," Annette said gently, holding her friend's hand in hers, "you love him, don't you?"

Serena nodded slowly, face still averted.

"And it's scaring the hell out of you," Annette continued.

Serena turned back, looking at Annette with a pained expression as the words tumbled out her mouth.

"Oh, Annette, I love him so much I don't know what to do. What I felt for Danny is a joke compared to how I feel about Kyle. But I'm so scared, Annette. Suppose he's only having a good time, and it's not as important to him—*I'm* not as important to him as he is to me? It would tear me up if he's just playing me." She trembled with the force of her emotions.

Annette gathered her best friend into her arms and hugged her tightly.

"Oh, girl, you've really got it bad, haven't you? But honey, there aren't any guarantees in life. Sometimes you have to trust your instincts and plunge right in."

Serena gave a wry grimace. "Like Star Trek, huh? *To boldly go where no man has gone before* or, in this case, no woman."

Annette nodded. "Exactly. I can't tell you what's going to happen between you and Kyle. But I can tell you this. From the little I've seen of Kyle and seeing the two of you together, I won't say it's all one-sided on your part. The man is crazy about you, girl."

"You really think so?" Serena asked, looking marginally less stressed.

"I really think so," Annette replied solemnly.

"Thanks, Annette," Serena replied, giving her a hug. "You're the best." She sat back, feeling relaxed and happy once more.

"Okay, girl, so tell me now, what was the weekend *really* like? What's Kyle like? Did he lay it on you but good?" Annette looked ready and eager to hear all the juicy details, but Serena merely laughed and sidestepped neatly.

"All that and more, but as you said, that's between Kyle and me."

"Serena!" Annette wailed. Serena laughed again, her

equilibrium restored, knowing she wasn't going to give Annette anything but the most general noncommittal description.

"All right," Annette sighed in defeat, "if you're not going to tell me about Kyle in bed, at least tell me where you went. Where did he take you?"

Like Serena, she had tried to guess where Kyle would take Serena for their romantic, naughty weekend getaway.

Serena's eyes lit up again. "Oh, Annette, it was so beautiful. We went to Regency Gardens."

"Regency Gardens?" Annette repeated doubtfully. "I've never heard of that. Where is it? What is it?"

"It's like a retreat, I suppose, a relaxation spot. There are all these beautiful flowers—I guess that's where the "gardens" part of the name comes in—really lovely blooms. They have cottages and rooms, a spa, a fitness center; there's even a beach, but we didn't go down there much. And tons of restaurants with some really fabulous food. Kyle even got me a massage. It felt so good." She smiled remembering. "Oh, there's golf too, I think," she added thoughtfully. "I'd like to go back some time."

"Sounds like you had a blast, Kyle notwithstanding," Annette said. "Where did you say it was?"

"Down south. I know we took I-85 and after that, a couple of other highways and stuff. I'd probably have to Google it to get proper directions, but it wasn't so far out. An hour and some. I'm surprised Kyle even heard of this place, especially as he's not from Georgia."

"He's not?" Annette asked in surprise. "Where's he from?"

"Oh, he's from Louisiana. All his family is back there—mother, father, brother, sister, cousins, aunts, you know, the works."

Annette looked at her with raised brows. "Really know your man, don't you?"

Serena felt the flush warm her face.

"Well, we do talk a lot on the phone, you know. It's been really challenging trying to get together, not to mention frustrating. I'm either flying or he's off doing some training course or looking after prisoners or something. We've been very good customers of Verizon. You should be pleased." She laughed again.

Annette said, "Tell me about his family. You said he has brothers and sisters?"

"One brother, one sister," Serena corrected. "He's the eldest; next it's his brother, Junior. He's named after their father, Steven. Their sister, Akilah, is the youngest; I think she was a surprise baby for his parents."

She chuckled as she recalled Kyle telling her how he remembered his mother being initially dazed when she discovered she was pregnant with his sister.

"She's eight years younger than he is, but they seem really close. I get this feeling when he talks about her there isn't anything he wouldn't do for his baby sister. His brother is a firefighter. Did you know his dad was a deputy US marshal too?"

Annette shook her head. Judging by the rapt look on her face and her unusual nonparticipation in the conversation, she was enjoying this first-hand look Serena was providing into the life of the very reserved Kyle Drummond.

"Yeah, Kyle says he grew up hearing stories of his dad's different assignments. Apparently, he was one of the deputy marshals on some big case years ago, at some place called Wounded Knee in South Dakota. He said it's all he ever wanted to be since he was a kid."

Serena yawned suddenly, taken by surprise. "Gosh, my bed is calling to me." She got up off the sofa, picked up her overnight bag, and headed for her bedroom.

"Night, Annette. I'm feeling a little tired. I'm sure you can understand why. After all, I had a really hectic weekend."

She chortled as her voice floated down the hallway back to Annette.

Annette smiled as she flopped back down on the sofa, pleased that Serena was happy and her love life finally seemed to be heading in a positive direction. She liked Kyle. She thought he was exactly what Serena needed—someone to spoil her and pamper her and make her feel loved and special. And he did spoil Serena. How many men would wait so long to have sex with a woman? These days, even with AIDS and all, sex was still pretty much a free and easy commodity, easily obtained. Kyle's staying in the relationship so long without sex was a mark in his favor, a huge plus in Annette's book. But if he hurt her friend, Annette scowled fiercely, if he only dared, she would make him pay.

The images on the screen flashed by unnoticed as Annette's thoughts were taken up with Serena and Kyle's relationship. Yep, she thought, he'd better not be playing her friend or else there would be hell to pay.

Chapter 14

It was going to be a scorcher today, Kyle thought, but which day isn't in Georgia during the summer? No wonder they call it *Hotlanta*. He was out on the firing range, getting ready for some firearms skills training with other deputy US marshals. He was a crack shot, good with both handguns and rifles. Most of the other deputies who were taking part in the training session were already there and putting on their equipment.

Kyle walked briskly across to the group busy preparing themselves and their equipment.

"Hey, fellas. How's it going?" he greeted them as he reached the table and put down his bag.

"Hey, Drummond," Deputy Alan Martin responded. "Joining us or teaching us today?" he inquired curiously.

Everyone was aware that Kyle was a full-time member of the special operations group, injured on an assignment and working his way back to full fitness. He had conducted a number of firearms skills training with them and practiced with both his Glock handguns on the indoor range—the Glock 35 he used on assignments and the Glock 27, which was his backup weapon—but not participated in the actual firing of the weapons in simulated conditions as his arm and shoulder had not been fully recovered.

"Just one of the guys today," Kyle responded easily. "Felt much better during my last workout, so I thought I'd give it a tryout with the AR-15, see how it goes. No problems with the Glock."

He put on his duty belt, holding his handcuffs, baton, gun holster, and magazine clip. He was dressed as he would be if he was out on assignment. He put on his protective gear, vest, safety glasses, and hearing protection.

Earlier in the day, they had done some indoor training, stripping down and reassembling both the Glock .40-caliber handguns and the AR rifles. Kyle could strip and reassemble a Glock in his sleep. He sat down at the table and placed the bullets in his magazine, continuing to exchange pleasantries with Deputy Martin and a couple of others.

Once everyone was ready, they all moved to the firing position for the first shoot—paper targets about twenty feet away. For the next three hours, they practiced numerous scenarios using both the Glock handguns and the AR rifles. They practiced shooting from standing positions, down on one knee, and lying prone on their stomachs.

Kyle felt pleased with his progress. At first, when his arm and shoulder began healing, he was unable to use the rifle, as the recoil was too painful. But Kyle's body, his muscles, were in superb condition; and his rate of recovery from injury was extremely rapid. Already he was back to maximum efficiency with the Glock, and the recoil from the rifle was more than passingly bearable.

Another week or two and he would be back, he thought with satisfaction. Uncharacteristically, he did not fully follow the thread of this thought to its conclusion. He didn't want to think what this would mean with regards to his relationship with Serena and him returning to the SOG full time.

Once the group completed the training session, they picked up all the shell casings—*policing their brass* as it was known, a tactic usually followed by snipers to leave no clues for law enforcement—sat down, and discussed the training session. Kyle and the two other senior deputies in charge of the training session gave pointers and advice on various questions posed by the participating deputies.

Kyle felt a deep sense of contentment after the training came to a close. He always enjoyed firearms training, took it very seriously. When you were out there in a tense situation, very often it came down to superior skill and ability, and he always made sure he was ready with the necessary skills he needed to stay alive. Not only that, but a team was also only as strong as its weakest link. If one person was not operating at maximum efficiency, the whole team and, subsequently, their mission, were put at risk. You needed to know you could depend on each other totally because your life might be in someone else's hands.

"Think I'll grab a cold one at Hunter's," Martin said as they packed up their gear. "I need to get that smell out of my nose."

"Yeah, that sounds like a good idea," Kyle agreed. "Let's do it."

Kyle quietly eased his way through the door of Hunter's Bar and Grill, followed by Martin, and headed for the long counter. He was always amused by the name each time he came in for a drink, considered it fitting. The US Marshals *were* hunters, hunters of fugitives and lawbreakers. As usual, the place was crowded with office personnel. It was a popular hangout for the US marshals after hours, to down one or two after a hard day's work and catch up socially before heading home.

He ordered a Bud Light—not given to much heavy drinking—slid onto a stool, and exchanged a few words with the deputy next to him, a guy named Lewis. He and three other deputies had completed a successful fugitive apprehension and were celebrating. They were working on the case for two weeks.

A husband was suspected of arranging the killing of

his wife for a hefty life insurance policy and was initially questioned by the local police department. However, he fled the jurisdiction mere hours before a warrant was issued for his arrest, and a fugitive task force led by the marshals sprang into action. Thankfully, they recaptured the fugitive without violence.

Kyle congratulated the three men and one woman, knowing the heady feeling that came after you brought a lawbreaker to justice and especially without bloodshed or loss of life.

Hearing his name called, he turned in the other direction and spotted Keith at a table with Spencer and Monroe. They waved him and Martin over. He remembered Keith mentioning Spencer and Monroe were the ones who had made the Canada trip. Picking up his beer, he and Martin wove between two tables and made their way over to them.

"Pull up a chair, Drummond, Martin," Spencer invited. "Take a load off."

"Don't mind if I do," Kyle replied, easing his long length into the empty chair on Spencer's right. "What've you guys been up to?"

"Spence and I took some prisoners up to Augusta and also did some courthouse duty. You know, the usual," Monroe replied with a shrug of his shoulders.

"Haven't seen you around the office today," Keith remarked, looking a question at Kyle.

"Nah, we were up at the range, getting in some firearms practice. Session really went well, especially with the rifles. What'd you think, Martin?" he asked, turning to Martin.

"Yeah, it was a good session for me too and good discussion afterward. I picked up some good pointers," Martin agreed.

Irrepressible as ever, Keith asked, "How's the arm coming along?"

"Turned out much better than I hoped," Kyle mused thoughtfully. "The recoil's not too bad now with the AR-15, but it's still a little jarring. The Glock is fine."

The men continued to discuss guns and weapons training, arguing good-naturedly on the merits and disadvantages of the Glock versus the SIG Sauer, which was the weapon of choice for the US Coast Guard.

Kyle listened in, contributing to the conversation every now and then with a telling comment but content for the most part to let the discussion be carried by the others. As was becoming more common, his thoughts turned to Serena, and he decided to give her a call. He couldn't remember when her next flight was and hoped they could get together later.

He called her number, feeling an immediate uplift in his spirits as well as amusement as he thought what Keith and the other deputies would say if Serena ever called him. She had programmed the popular Marvin Gaye tune, "Sexual Healing," on his phone as her ringtone. He turned away slightly from the table for some privacy.

"Hi, babe, what's up?" Kyle asked lightly, the smile evident in his voice.

"Oh, hi, Kyle."

He picked up on the distress in her voice immediately. "What's wrong? Are you okay?"

"I'm all right," she assured him quickly. "Well, at least physically, I'm okay, just a little stressed." She sounded both irritated and on the verge of tears.

"Okay, calm down, take a breath, tell me what's wrong," he coaxed gently, feeling a little anxious. He could hear her take some deep breaths over the phone.

"I'm on my way to work and my car just up and died! I don't know what's wrong with it. I'm about to call the HERO people. I hope they get here in time to fix it so I can get to work."

"They may take some time to get there. I'll come and get you. Where are you exactly?"

"You don't have to do that. I'm sure it's nothing major, Kyle."

He gritted his teeth. She was so stubborn but so was he.

"I will come and get you," he bit out. "Now where are you?" he asked again.

"Okay, fine! I'm on 285, a little way past the 675 exit."

"All right, I'll be there in a few minutes. Is your car off the road?"

"Yeah, I managed to get it onto the shoulder before it gave up the ghost, the piece of junk!" She sighed. "Thanks, Kyle. Sorry I lost it for a minute."

"Anytime, babe. Just sit tight and I'll see you in a few, yeah."

He ended the call, stood up, and paused, debating something in his mind.

"Sorry, guys, I gotta run. Something came up," he said, draining his beer. "Keith, gimme a minute?" He stepped away from the table.

"What's up?" Keith asked.

"Serena broke down on 285. I'm going to pick her up and take her to the airport. She's on her way to work. Thought you might like to meet her," he explained to Keith, raising his eyebrows in query.

"Sure. I could take a look at her car while you drop her off. It may be something minor."

"That'll be good. Thanks, man."

Keith shrugged as if it was not worth mentioning. They went out the door and headed for the Silverado.

"Well, I'm glad I'm finally going to get the chance to actually meet Serena. You've been keeping her under such close wraps, I thought I'd be old and gray before I ever spoke with her." Keith laughed as he swung up onto the passenger seat.

"Want to meet the woman who's managed to make you *appear* human. Do you know the other day I overheard two of the women in admin talking. One of them said you gave her a smile when you had went in to check on something. She said she was about to pass out from the shock."

Kyle frowned. "C'mon, I'm not really that terrible, am I?" he asked doubtfully.

"Not saying you are," Keith replied, "but you've never been given to light conversation. Hell, the most talking you do is when you're conducting a training course. All I'm saying is, since you met Serena, you've become more approachable. And this is a good thing," he added hastily as Kyle's frown deepened. "Not soft, mind you, just not as tough as ever. *Now* you're human."

Keith was grinning. Kyle was still frowning as he absorbed Keith's words.

"Are you saying I've lost my edge?"

"Nope. Ops-wise, you're still the same tough son of a bitch. People-wise, you're a better human being, and to me, it seems that all this has been since you met Serena."

Kyle digested this information in silence. Was Keith right? Had he mellowed a little bit since he met Serena? Lately, he found himself smiling a lot more, and every time it was because he was thinking about Serena. Hell, he probably was doing just that when he apparently *smiled* at this woman.

He scowled. Great, just great. Now it would be all over; he was losing his edge, never mind what Keith said. He scowled some more.

They drove past the Bouldercrest exit and approached the exit to merge onto the I-675. A little way beyond that, Kyle could see Serena's red Chevy Cobalt on the side of the road and Serena standing by the passenger door. He could see how stressed she was by the way her arms were folded across her chest and how she fidgeted from side to side.

She relaxed visibly when she caught sight of the black truck easing off the road and rolling to a stop behind her car. He stepped out of the truck and made his way quickly to Serena's side, giving her a warm smile of reassurance.

"Hey, babe. It's going to be awrite. This is my buddy,

Keith." He turned around to introduce Keith, who came forward with a smile, hand outstretched.

"Hi there, Serena. Pleased to meet you."

Serena shook his hand quickly. "Pleased to meet you," she responded quietly.

Kyle slanted a quick gaze at her, feeling something a little off in her greeting, but putting it down to her stress over the car and being late for work.

"Keith's going to take a look at your car, see if it's something he can fix while I get you to work."

"Okay. Thank you. The keys are in the car," she said politely, unsmilingly, half turning in Keith's general direction but not quite meeting his gaze.

Kyle felt his brows pull together in a small frown. There was something wrong here.

"Can we go now, please, Kyle? I have to get to crew scheduling, and I can't afford to be late," she said quietly, turning to him.

"You go. I'll call you as soon as I check it out," Keith said.

"Thanks, man."

Kyle walked Serena to the Silverado and waited as she settled into the passenger seat before he closed the door and walked around to the driver's side. Watching for a break in the traffic, he pulled out and waved a hand in acknowledgment to Keith as they passed before accelerating away.

"You okay?" he asked quietly. Serena had not said a word since they got in the vehicle.

"I'm worried about the car. I hope it's not anything major. I really can't afford any big expense right now." She sighed.

It sounded plausible, a reasonable response, but Kyle had a gut feeling it was something deeper, and somehow, it had to do with Keith. He decided not to push the subject, as she was stressed right now about the car, but if she didn't bring it up later, he would. He didn't like unexplained mysteries.

Serena willed herself to stay calm and not panic. She had felt a shock go through her when Kyle's friend, Keith, stepped out of the truck with him. She figured Kyle had friends, but it was always in the abstract, nebulous. Now, abruptly, she was face-to-face with the fact, and the sudden and unexpected contact threw her off. Her mind and emotions immediately clamped down and went into defensive mode, able to respond to Keith by rote only, in an automatic fashion.

She could sense Kyle looking at her and wished he wasn't always so observant and astute. She knew he wasn't really fooled by her response but probably decided not to press the issue, as she was upset over her car troubles. She was thankful for that, figuring any reprieve was better than none. At least she would have a couple days grace while she flew.

She had to face her fears, she realized, but it was such a painful subject. She was afraid to go there. Ever since she decided to let the relationship with Kyle evolve, she knew this moment would come. What she hadn't realized was how unprepared and unwilling she would be to examine it closely.

What she also hadn't prepared for was the fact that she had fallen in love with him. Because somehow, somewhere, before she could get her defenses up, she had fallen hopelessly and overwhelmingly in love with him. It excited her. It terrified her. It made her shiver with delight. It plunged her into the depths of despair. She was an emotional wreck.

Kyle pulled into the curb and Serena prepared to get out.

"If you give me a call, I'll pick you up when you get in, as you won't have your car. I'll have it fixed for you by the time you get back, yeah."

"Oh, you don't have to pick me up. I can get a ride with one of the girls, or Annette can come get me," Serena responded quickly, almost babbling.

Kyle studied her in silence. She felt like a bug pinned on a slide. He knew. He knew she was running, trying to avoid him.

Ordinarily, she would've made some quip about his mechanical prowess when he promised to have her car fixed.

"It's not a problem. I'll come get you," he answered quietly.

Serena deflated. "Okay," she said, resigned. "Thanks for coming out to get me today."

"Anytime, babe. I'm at your service. Have a safe flight, yeah."

He tilted her chin up and kissed her a little more thoroughly than he usually did in a public place. She sensed he wanted to reassure her, wanted her to know it was all right, that whatever had her worried and out of sorts, she could depend on him for support. They broke apart and Serena looked into his eyes.

"Thanks, I needed that," she said softly. "Drive safe."

She slid from the truck quickly, opened the back door, took out her bag, and waved good-bye before heading into the terminal. She gave a little sigh of resignation. She might as well face it; the bulldog would be waiting to question her when she got back.

Chapter 15

Serena was getting off the escalator now and heading toward baggage claim. He felt his face curve into an involuntary smile until he saw the man walking next to her and engrossed in their conversation—a captain or first officer, judging by his uniform—put his hand on her shoulder. His lips tightened, and he pushed himself upright, away from the wall against which he had been casually braced. She twisted around as if looking for him, effectively dislodging the hand on her shoulder. When she turned back, he was right there in front of her.

"Oh, hey, Kyle. I didn't see you for a minute."

She seemed pleased to see him but also looked a little wary. He wasn't sure if this was because of the pilot she was walking with or because of the manner in which they last parted. He was damn certain she was aware he picked up on her unusual restraint when she met Keith.

She glanced toward the captain. "See you later, Somerset. Good flight," she said casually and turned back to Kyle.

His face grim, he took Serena's bag, placed *his* arm across her shoulder, and headed for the exit. He neither spoke to nor acknowledged Somerset's presence. Serena eased slightly away from him but stayed by his side. He recognized from the way her shoulders stiffened that she was irritated with him. Well, tough. He was irritated himself too. He didn't like to see any man touching her.

They made their way to his truck in silence. He opened the passenger door and she climbed in. He placed her carry-on bag on the backseat and then slid under the steering wheel and onto the seat. Before he could start the engine, she turned to him, arms folded, face mutinous, and said in an annoyed tone, "Well, you might as well get it off your chest. You looked really pissed just now."

She waited, her lips pressed tightly together. He obliged her.

"So who's that you were snuggling up to? Your out-of-town man? Y'all looked real tight."

"No, he is not my out-of-town man!" she retorted. "He happens to be the captain of the flight I just worked. He also happens to be engaged."

"F'true? Well, he didn't look like he remembered that. I know what I saw, and he looked like he was fixing to get to know you a *whole* lot better than just one of the crew."

"Just because he's interested in me doesn't mean I return the feeling."

He pounced. "Oh, so you agree he's interested in you?"

She gritted her teeth and glared at him. He glared back. Some Iceman he was. Tense moments passed as they faced each other. The atmosphere in the cab was volatile and electric; it only needed one spark to make it explode. He didn't back down; neither did she. Outside the truck, people passed by, pulling wheeled bags, either heading to their cars or into the terminal. Snatches of conversation floated in the air.

Kyle wasn't sure how much time had passed; he thought possibly two minutes, though it seemed much longer. He felt both aggravated and angry, but as he looked at her, her lips quivered, and he could see the hurt she was trying hard to conceal. It sent a jolt through him, and instantly he felt the tight band squeezing his chest ease a little bit. He exhaled slowly, feeling the irritation and tension drain out of him.

"I'm sorry, baby. I tend to lose it around you." He reached out and pulled her to him, his eyes locked on her lovely face. "Forgive me?"

She didn't relax, still held her arms folded across her chest. She didn't look at him but kept her gaze fixed somewhere in the region of his neck. He could kick himself for having caused her pain.

"I know you're not from Georgia, but don't you have friends at work, Kyle? People you share jokes with and y'all hang out together occasionally? Is it so hard to believe I have friends like that too? I need you to lighten up, Kyle. Don't smother me."

She blew out a frustrated breath and finally looked at him. He could see that she was angry, yes, but hurt as well.

"I know, I'm sorry," he whispered, caressing her face. He couldn't tell her he was afraid of losing her, that she would end things between them because she was scared for him in his job and the fact that he intended to get Parker. Every time he saw her with a guy, *any* guy, he was afraid she was moving on. He refused to examine too closely what that meant.

"Forgive me?" he asked again.

Serena's face softened slightly but she still looked mutinous. She sighed, unfolded her arms, and cupped his cheek.

"I'll think about it," she replied tartly, seconds before his lips came down on hers in a gentle kiss. He lifted his head and stared at her broodingly. She was making him do a lot of things he didn't normally do, like public displays of affection. And the hell of it was he didn't care.

Her hand had moved from his cheek to the back of his head, which she caressed, sending tingles of pleasure radiating through his entire being. She looked into his eyes and continued softly, just a hint of frustration in her tone. "I'm only interested in you. I'm not stepping out on you, honest. A little trust, please, huh?"

He nodded, dipped his head, and sampled her luscious lips again before he reluctantly pulled away and started the engine.

They were soon making their way down I-285, Kyle driving one-handed as he usually did when they were together, the fingers of their hands intertwined in the middle of the two seats.

"Will you come home with me?" Kyle asked softly, giving her a heavy-lidded look.

"Kyle, I need to shower," Serena protested weakly.

"You can shower at my place. I do have running water, you know," he said, trying to keep it light as he neatly deflected that argument. He wanted to make it up to her for acting like such a jealous fool just now. He also knew that she was upset when she left a few days ago, and he wanted to hold her and comfort her. But who was he kidding. He wanted to love her too. He always wanted to love her. She was like a fever in his blood.

What puzzled him was her reaction to Keith. Keith could offer no insight either when they had spoken later as they worked on replacing the water hose on Serena's car.

"I missed you, Serena."

"I missed you too, Kyle," Serena replied softly, squeezing his fingers.

"So will you come home with me now?"

She nodded. He smiled in response and raised their intertwined fingers to his lips, placing a kiss on them before lowering them.

Serena turned off the shower and stepped out on to the bath mat, quickly toweling herself dry. She put on clean underwear from her overnight bag, wrapped the towel around herself, and stepped out of the bathroom, intending to ask Kyle for one of his T-shirts, as she wanted something light and loose, which his large T-shirt was sure to be.

He was standing right outside the bathroom door and swallowed her involuntary exclamation of surprise as his mouth closed over hers, his arms going around her hungrily. He kissed her like she'd been gone for a month. She kissed him right back. God, she loved him so much it was like a physical pain at times.

Her hand slid into his hair at the back of his head, the other hand wrapping around his neck as he bent slightly and lifted her into his arms. She leaned forward and kissed him on the side of his neck, running her tongue down the long graceful column. He gave a slight shudder, and she could feel his throat moving under her lips as he swallowed.

He turned swiftly with her in his arms and made his way into the dimly lit bedroom, lowering her gently onto the bed. He shed his clothes before following her down, lying on his side and cradling her face between his palms. Serena wound her arms once again around his neck. Somewhere between stepping out of the bathroom and lying down on the bed, the towel disappeared, but she would have been hard-pressed to say when this happened.

Kyle gazed at Serena, his feelings at the moment showing starkly on his face.

"I missed you. I'm so glad you're back," he whispered, punctuating his words with kisses all over her face.

"I was only gone three days, Kyle," she said, surprised to see him so emotional.

"I know, but it really seemed longer this time," he replied.

His hand slid down her side and up her back, caressing her. He rose up on one elbow, pressed her gently onto her back while his lips made their way down to her stomach. Along the way, he stopped to take her breasts into his mouth.

Serena moaned with pleasure, enjoying the way Kyle made

love to her, the intensity he brought to each kiss, each caress. He seemed totally focused on giving her complete pleasure, not allowing her to reciprocate. His tongue circled her belly button, dipped into the indentation. Serena moaned and arched, her stomach muscles clenched, and the fire began to build between her legs.

Kyle hooked his fingers under the scrap of lace Serena was flaunting as underwear and slid it down her legs, flicking it aside impatiently. He wanted to see her, all of her, without interruption. He could feel his desire for her heating his loins.

Her head was thrown back, eyes closed. Her arms moved restlessly, running over the top of his head when he returned to her stomach. Her muscles clenched every time he kissed her middle. God, he loved how she was so responsive.

Her thighs were beginning to tauten with tension. He elbowed them further apart and slid his finger into her, started to stroke her, his thumb teasing the tight little bud at the center of her treasure. Her muscles clenched and released, her breath came in a shuddering gasp. She was already wet, ready and welcoming. His finger continued to slide in and out of her in a tormenting fashion, and then he added another finger.

Serena moaned, straining against his hand as he continued the unrelenting pleasure. He removed his fingers and she gave a whimper of protest.

"I've got something better, baby," he whispered. He lay between her legs, grasped her hips, and pulled her toward his mouth as he replaced his fingers with his tongue, flicking it over the tiny nub begging for attention before sliding into her sweet passage and tasting her essence.

She bucked under the pressure of his mouth, and he held her firmly, his agile tongue swirling in and out as he explored her fully, licking and sucking.

Serena moaned in ecstasy, "Ooh, yeah, be like Sprite!"

Kyle froze, thinking, *What the hell?*

He raised his head and whispered questioningly, "Uhh, Sprite, baby?"

Serena still had her eyes closed, twitching on the bed, her fingers running through his hair.

"Yeah, you know, *Obey Your Thirst*," she quoted the popular slogan for the Sprite advertisement.

Kyle couldn't help it; he started to shake with laughter and collapsed against Serena's thigh.

"What?" Serena asked, bemused.

"Obey your thirst," Kyle sputtered with laughter, absently caressing her arms as he rose up on one elbow and looked at her.

Serena squirmed in embarrassment. "Yes, well, uhm …"

"Shh, baby." He chuckled, placing a finger against her lips. "I'm not laughing at you. You're so funny, you always take me by surprise, yeah."

Serena smiled at him, and he smiled back, the laughter fading from his face.

"I think I'll take your advice," he whispered, his eyes like twin orbs of onyx as they heated with sensual desire. "I'll start right up here." His fingers flicked lightly over her nipple.

Serena shuddered, her eyes glazed over.

"And work up an appetite. How does that grab you?"

"It sounds fine as hell. Why are you still talking?"

He gave one last chuckle, his breath blowing over her nipple just before his tongue and teeth started to work in tandem as they nipped and licked the tiny bud. Serena sighed in pleasure as Kyle picked up where he had left off.

He kissed and caressed her nipples before sliding that talented mouth down her stomach, moving past her belly button and back to her core. He slid his tongue inside her sheath, his fingers moving her folds aside.

Serena's breaths started to come in short gasps, like there

wasn't enough air. She gasped and sobbed; her fingers clutched his hair as she choked out broken pleas.

"Oh, God, Kyle … yes, yes, yes … like that … don't stop, don't stop … oh, oh, oh!"

Her body started to twitch, contracting and releasing, faster and faster until she arched, giving way to the incredible, pulsing movements as she climaxed.

Kyle slid up her limp, unresisting body like salmon flowing upstream, and her hands reached out for him eagerly.

"Breathe, baby, we've got all night. I'm not going anywhere," he whispered in her ear as she continued to gasp short, uneven breaths. He ran his tongue around her ear and inside, nipped the lobe, and immediately soothed the area with his tongue.

Rolling a condom onto his erection, Kyle knelt in front of Serena, lifting her legs onto his shoulders. He could feel himself trembling with need, a fierce urgency to feel her tighten around him. He sheathed himself inside her with a groan of sheer pleasure, the sensation as she contracted around him almost making him lose himself. Making love with Serena was indeed ambrosia.

Kyle held himself still for as long as he could before slowly withdrawing then plunging back in, sliding out again and returning eagerly, over and over. Serena's whole body was trembling, and she made little mewling sounds.

Kyle increased the pace, plunging faster and faster as her sweetness beckoned him on, feeling that he was holding on by the edge of his fingertips. Serena was chanting his name like a litany every time he sank into her, alternating with the deity.

"Oh my God, Kyle! Oh my God, Kyle! Oh my God, Kyle!"

It drove him to a frenzy, spurred him on as he clutched at her shins, felt her lift her hips with every thrust. He felt her start to go over the edge as she reached for the stars again; outwardly her hips stilled, her inner muscles clenched and squeezed, and every muscle in her body convulsed as she gave way to the powerful sensations.

Kyle couldn't hold on any longer. With a harsh cry, he let his body empty itself as he hurtled forward and followed her into the beyond. His breath shuddered in his chest. He released her legs, and they slid bonelessly down the sides of his body to thump onto the bed. Again, he fell forward onto Serena's body.

Two sets of harsh breathing were the only sounds to be heard until they had both regained enough breath to attempt some semblance of speech. Kyle got a cloth from the bathroom and cleaned them both. He eased onto the bed and pulled Serena toward him.

"I need to come here more often when I return from my flights," Serena wheezed, wrapping her arms around him and kissing him gently.

"I'd love it if you do," Kyle said in all seriousness.

"Yeah, sure you would," Serena replied lightly.

He could feel her heart thumping, but whether in response to his comment or their recent physical activity, he didn't know. He didn't press her on the subject; he had a more important topic he wanted to address. He turned onto his back, adjusted a pillow under his head, and cradled Serena so that she lay across his chest.

"Can I ask you something, Serena?"

Serena sighed.

"You want to know why I was so abrupt with Keith when I met him." She made it into a statement.

"Yes, I do," Kyle answered, moving his hand in slow circles over her back, caressing her as he waited for her response. When she didn't answer, he spoke again.

"I care a lot about you, Serena. I hope you know that. Keith is my buddy. We've known each other since basic training. Doing the kind of work we do, you place a lot of trust in your teammates. Apart from my family, you two are the most important people to me, the ones to whom I'm closest. I'd hoped that you and he would be friends, at least."

He waited again. He felt her heart beat erratically and wondered how she couldn't know that she meant a lot to him. Hell, she had complained that he was too jealous and overprotective. Her breath washed over his chest as she sighed again, and then she made a startling statement.

"Did you know I was once engaged?"

Kyle felt a jolt of surprise. Of all the things he had expected, this was not one of them.

"No, I didn't," he said slowly. "What happened?"

She ran her hand lightly up and down his arm, her head rested on his chest. The steady cadence of his heart seemed to soothe her. She hugged him fiercely and began her story.

"Annette and I had gone away with some girlfriends for the weekend, but unfortunately, they got sick, and we decided to cut short the trip. We had borrowed his SUV, and I drove over to his place to return it and pick up my car."

Her voice was flat, emotionless. "When I got there, I saw another car, figured he had company."

"Let me guess, he was having an affair," Kyle said, disgusted.

"Yeah, you can say that. He was having an affair all right—with his *boyfriend* from the office. I caught them in bed together," she finished in a low voice. Kyle strained to hear the last few words.

"I'll never forget how I felt when I saw him all wrapped up in his lover's arms. I felt as if I would collapse. There wasn't any air to breathe. I flung his ring at him and got the hell out of there. I never saw him or spoke to him again. But you know what really tore me up? He was going to marry me so that people would think he was straight and *still* carry on with his boyfriend." She shuddered.

Kyle swore. He pulled Serena up closer to him and held her tightly in his arms.

"I'm sorry, babe, sorry you had such a horrible experience. And you still haven't got over it yet, have you?" he added with a flash of insight as he realized where Keith figured into the scenario.

"Listen to me, Serena," he said quietly, cradling her face between his hands and holding her gaze with his. He could see the pain of her memories swimming in her pretty brown eyes.

"Keith and I are nothing like that. We're good friends, is all. You're more than enough woman for me. Hell, didn't you just prove that?" He gave her a sexy smile. "I'd be more than happy to prove it again. You're *my woman*, and I don't want anyone else—no other woman and, most certainly, not a *man*." With another flash of insight, he said, "That's another reason why you felt so strongly about getting tested, wasn't it?"

She looked back at him with huge eyes, the pain of remembrance vivid and stark on her face. He hoped his telling her she was all woman, *his* woman to be precise, that she was more than enough for him—he hoped she knew he was sincere and meant what he was saying. He could see the moment the truth sunk in and she accepted it. The tears pooled in her eyes, her face crumpled, and she started to cry.

Kyle tucked her head under his chin, held her close, and crooned to her.

"That's right, baby. Let it go, let it all go. I've got you, you're safe." He ran his hand over her hair, down her back, murmured words of comfort as the cleansing tears ran down her face.

He held her close, whispered soothing words, and gently stroked her back as she cried all the anguished pain out of her system. Inside, he felt a murderous rage that someone had hurt this fine, beautiful woman, tried to crush her spirit.

Now that he knew, he recognized where her reserve came from—why, at times, she pulled back into her shell when their lovemaking had gotten intense; why she took so long before she decided to sleep with him, driving him crazy in the process; why she felt so strongly about getting tested. Trust, he thought, it was all about trust.

He was fiercely and selfishly glad he was the one she chose to let in past her guard. He knew how incredibly hard that must have been for her. She had a strong core, he realized, because even though the experience devastated her, it had not crushed her completely.

She still had that warm, compassionate spirit that he loved. She was still able to embrace the world with joy and wonder. It was only when situations and circumstances got too close for comfort emotionally that she threw up the barricades. But now she had brought her pain out, shared it with him, he hoped this could be the catharsis that helped her healing.

He would do anything to protect this woman, he vowed fiercely, keep her safe, slay all her demons. For just one moment, he felt a small twinge of guilt. She had opened up with her deepest secret, shared it with him; he hadn't.

Maybe he could persuade her to go on a double date with Keith and whoever was his woman of the month, show her men could be good friends with nothing sexual between them. He was sure she knew that intellectually, but when you were knocked off your feet unexpectedly, it tended to color your outlook.

But not quite yet. She would be feeling a little vulnerable and exposed emotionally now. For the present, he would pamper her, show her she was a unique woman, and any man who didn't recognize that was a fool. He would make her feel as special as she truly was and not only in bed.

When she had cried herself out, he got tissues for her to blow her nose, pulled the sheet up around them, turned out the light, tucked her close to his side, and tenderly held her close as she drifted off into a peaceful sleep.

Kyle held his woman close to his heart, not recognizing by his thoughts and actions that he had fallen in love with Serena, thinking only that he cared enough to ensure she wasn't hurt any more. As the caveman was the protector since the dawn of time, Kyle, too, felt the primal urge to keep Serena safe from harm.

Chapter 16

Serena came up slowly from the mists of sleep to the soft strains of classical music. She recognized the tune—*Moonlight Sonata,* Beethoven's famous piano solo and one of her favorites. She smiled sleepily, not yet fully awake.

As the music washed over her, she opened her eyes and looked around, at first disconcerted at not waking in her own bed. It took her a moment to remember that Kyle had picked her up at the airport when she got in from her flight, and they had gone straight to his place.

Her mouth curved in sensuous pleasure as she remembered their lovemaking the night before. It had been sweetly satisfying. Kyle had seemed … driven … intense, as if it was imperative he love her so that she had no thoughts for anything else. And so he had. Afterwards, they had talked.

She sighed, sitting up and scooting backward to rest against the headboard, drawing the sheet up to cover herself. It had felt so good to let go of all the pain and hurt, all the misery and loss of confidence she had carried around for so long.

Kyle had held her and soothed her, stroking her hair and whispering to her. What he said she couldn't recall; she only knew she had felt a healing peace she hadn't in too long. She had finally drifted off to sleep in Kyle's arms, feeling safe and protected.

The door opened slowly, and Kyle peered around, smiling

when he saw that she was awake. He came into the room and crossed to the bed, sitting down and drawing her into his arms. She went willingly. He placed a kiss on her forehead.

"Morning, babe. How do you feel?"

She thought a moment. "I don't quite know how to describe it. Quiet, calm. Like before I might've been a pool and even though it was calm on the surface, the water was all churned up at the bottom. But now, it's all calm *and* clear. I feel … rested, I guess."

He smiled a little. "That'll work. Thank you for opening up to me, for trusting me," he told her, softly caressing her neck. He felt that twinge of guilt again but banished it firmly by telling himself she didn't need to know. It had nothing to do with their relationship.

"No, thank you, Kyle, for being the man you are." She hugged him fiercely.

"No thanks necessary, babe. So ready for some breakfast? Or maybe I should say brunch; you slept for quite some time."

"What time is it?" she asked, startled.

"Half-eleven," was his amused reply.

"Damn," Serena said. "Did you eat already?"

"I only had some coffee. I was waiting for you to wake up, Sleeping Beauty," he teased.

"Yeah, yeah, okay. Let me use the bathroom and I'll be right there."

"Take your time, no rush," he replied, standing up and moving to the door. "C'mon out when you're ready. I'll do some eggs and bacon." He raised his brows, making it into a question.

"Sure, I'd love that."

Serena smiled at him over her shoulder as she headed for the bathroom. She heard the bedroom door close as she turned on the water and took out her toothbrush from her overnight case.

After a quick shower, Serena dressed in one of Kyle's T-shirts, which he had thoughtfully left out for her on the bed. She chuckled, remembering she had intended to ask him for one after her shower yesterday, but they had gotten sweetly and satisfyingly sidetracked. The T-shirt came to midway down her thighs and provided a modest cover for her bottom. She made her way out to the kitchen.

Kyle looked around at her approach, and she saw his eyes smolder when he took in her appearance dressed in his clothes. Her pulse rate went up a notch. He looked as if he wanted to walk her right back to the bedroom and tumble her onto her back on the bed. She was half sorry when he didn't follow through on that desire, unspoken but heard nonetheless. He swallowed and she gave him a knowing smile.

"I've got something for you," he muttered huskily. He drew her into his arms, smoothed the hair away from her face, and kissed her. Her arms encircled his neck as she looked up at him with a wicked smile on her face.

"Oh, I think you've given me quite a lot." She leaned into him suggestively.

"Stop that or else you'll be having dinner instead of breakfast," he warned. He reached behind her for something on the kitchen counter. His arm reappeared in front of her, and he was holding up a green vase containing a beautiful bouquet of flowers.

"These are for you. I'm sorry I behaved like such a jerk yesterday."

"Oh, these are beautiful, Kyle," Serena exclaimed as she took the vase from him and admired the flowers. There were roses and lilies, daisy poms, hydrangeas, minicarnations, and peonies—all combined in a stunning array. She fingered the white satin bow, which was tied around the vase. "Thank you. I love them."

She placed the vase in the middle of the small table and

smiled up at him. He answered the unspoken question in her eyes.

"I went out early this morning while you were still sleeping. I left you a note in case you woke up before I got back, but I guess you didn't see it."

He pulled out a chair for her. "Sit down and I'll get your breakfast," he urged as he turned toward the stove.

"Here you go. Bacon and eggs coming right up," he announced in a cheerful voice as he slid a plate in front of her. His plate was already on the table. He filled two cups of coffee from the coffeemaker and placed one in front of her.

Serena had already started on the eggs, and he chuckled.

"Little ravenous this morning, aren't we? I wonder why."

She looked up at him flirtatiously from under her lashes, chewed, swallowed, and retorted, "As if you didn't know."

"Oh, I do, I do," he replied softly.

She smiled at Kyle in remembrance of the evening's activities before returning her attention to breakfast. Kyle had something entirely different on his plate with a bowl of grits to the side.

"What do you have there, Kyle?" Serena asked, looking with interest at his plate.

"It's called grillades. I had this for breakfast when I was a child, and I usually try to make it on the weekend."

"Can I have a taste?"

"F'sure. I didn't know if you would like it; that's why I did bacon and eggs for you." He speared a small bit of the cooked meat on his fork and held it up for her. She leaned forward, closed her lips over the offering, and started to chew, her eyes closed as she processed the taste.

"Not bad, but I think I'll stick to bacon and eggs." She smiled to take any sting out of the words. He smiled back.

"That's awrite."

A small silence ensued, broken only by the sound of their cutlery on their plates and the classical music Kyle was playing.

Serena polished off the last of the eggs and bacon and sat back with a contented sigh.

"That was absolutely fabulous, Kyle. It certainly hit the spot."

She drew her coffee toward her, poured in some milk, added sugar, and stirred the mixture before taking a sip.

"It was my pleasure, babe. Sorry I don't have any hot chocolate for you. I forgot to get some Swiss Miss when I picked up a few things at Kroger's yesterday." He looked irritated at himself.

"Oh, it's fine, Kyle. I do like coffee. I had just felt like hot chocolate that night," she replied, referring to the first time they met and spent some time at the Atrium.

Kyle smiled, picked up his cup, and got to his feet. He held out his hand to her. "Let's sit in the living room while we finish this. We can hear the music better."

"Yeah, what's up with that? Didn't peg you as someone who listened to classical music," Serena said, turning to look at him curiously as they walked into the living room.

Kyle placed their cups on the small table beside the sofa, sat down, and settled Serena comfortably in his arms. He passed her cup back to her and picked up his own. She felt his shrug.

"I've grown up with classical music. My dad would always play the classics on weekends—Tchaikovsky, Beethoven, Chopin, Mozart—and I grew to appreciate that kind of music. I love Tchaikovsky's *Swan Lake*. It relaxes me and helps me unwind after an assignment. I thought you might enjoy listening to some classics."

It was one of the few times he had made such a long speech.

Serena twisted around slightly and looked at him, head cocked to one side in wonder.

"You're a deep one, Kyle Drummond. There are hidden depths to you."

Kyle returned her gaze steadily. "I'm not going anywhere," he said quietly.

Serena felt her heart begin to pound. Did he mean … what *did* he mean? Was he telling her he was sticking around for awhile? Was he inviting her to discover whatever she wanted about him? Was he reinforcing what he said last night when he said he cared about her, and that she was very close to him? Or was she simply hearing what she wanted to hear because she loved him so much?

She knew she was in love with him because somewhere along the line, it had stopped being mind-blowing sex and had become a trip to the stars when they made love. In her mind, they no longer had sex; they made love.

Serena twisted around without replying and lay back against his chest. His arm came around her, caressed her slowly. The music washed over them and a peaceful silence ensued. Serena closed her eyes, feeling content. Good food, good music, and the man she loved holding her in his arms like there was nothing else he'd rather be doing. What more did she need?

The music came to an end, and Kyle stirred. "Give me a moment. Let me change the CD. Want to hear anything in particular?" he asked as he knelt by the CD player, his hand on some CDs.

He had a Bose Wave music system. If nothing else, she knew those were really good. She had once contemplated buying one and was acquainted with the features. This one had a CD/MP3 player, FM/AM tuner, clock, and alarm. No wonder the music sounded so good. *No offense, Beethoven*, she thought silently. Kyle's was silver.

"*Swan Lake*, of course," Serena replied with a smile. "Can I see the one you were playing?"

"Sure." He replaced the Beethoven CD in its case, slid the one Serena requested into the player, and hit play. He walked over to the sofa and gave Serena the Beethoven CD.

Serena looked over the CD, leaning back as Kyle repositioned himself behind her and the melodious strains of *Swan Lake* began. She saw a sticker with the initials SAD at the bottom of the case.

"Who's SAD, Kyle? Your dad?"

She heard the smile in his voice as he replied, "No, that's me, yours truly."

"I'm confused. I thought your name was Kyle?" Serena asked in a puzzled tone.

"My *full* name is Sakyle Azizi Drummond. Kyle is a shortened version that everyone calls me," he replied as he resumed stroking her skin.

Serena digested that information, turning it over.

"Sakyle Azizi," she murmured softly. "I like that. Do you know what it means?"

Kyle lifted her up, turning her over so that she lay atop his chest. He stroked her hair, winding a curl around his finger before letting it go.

"To tell you the truth, I can't remember what 'Sakyle' means. I *think* it's 'warrior,' yeah. I know 'Kyle' means 'a strip of water between two islands.' 'Azizi' means 'beloved' or 'precious one.'"

Again with the long speech. He was becoming quite chatty.

He smiled at her as he stroked her cheek with the back of his fingers. He looked like he was enjoying himself. He seemed to like touching her.

"Azizi, beloved or precious one. I like that." She nodded her head in appreciation.

"Am I your precious one?" he asked softly.

He looked at her intently, and she was sure he could feel her heart race as she lay on his chest.

"Yes, you are," she whispered, looking back at him unblinkingly.

"You're precious to me too, babe," he said softly, drawing

her up and kissing her tenderly. She sighed when he broke the kiss, dropping her head back on his chest. He caressed her back slowly.

"Do you have a middle name? What does your name mean?" he asked.

"My name—Serena Helena Hopewell. 'Serena' is Latin and, of course, means 'serene or peaceful.'"

She could feel Kyle start to shake with laughter and gave him a punch on his chest.

"'Helena' is Irish and means 'torch or bright,' something like that."

Kyle was still laughing. "You know what's funny? Your parents missed the boat twice."

"What do you mean?"

"Well, Helena is okay. You have a real bright spirit about you, but calm and peaceful is stretching it a bit, and when you take your initials—SHH." He chortled out loud. "One of nature's jokes, I guess."

Serena didn't mind; she had been the butt of that joke growing up and had long since gotten used to it. The music of Tchaikovsky's *Swan Lake* rose and fell around them.

Kyle gave a sigh and said quietly, "Serena."

She looked up, alerted by his tone. "What's the matter?"

"I'm going to be gone for about three to four weeks."

Serena's eyebrows shot up and her eyes grew large. "Four weeks! Where are you going?"

"Down to Glynco. Remember I told you I had to give some instruction in basic training for recruits? The areas I'm going to be giving instruction in will take that long. I'm leaving next weekend."

Four weeks! It felt like it was a lifetime. Even though they didn't see each other every day, this would be the longest they would be apart. Serena felt the bottom dropping out of her world. How was she going to stand being apart from him so long?

He was watching her face, and she knew her emotions were flashing across her expressive features. She could never keep a secret.

He gathered her closer, saying softly, "Don't be sad, baby. The time will pass pretty quickly, and before you know it, I'll be back."

He kissed her cheek before tucking her chin into the crook of his shoulder and neck.

"I know. I wish it didn't have to be so long. I'll miss you. Can't you drive back on the weekends?" she asked wistfully, playing with his hair.

He captured her hand as it moved across his face, brought it to his mouth, and kissed the palm before he released it.

"I'll miss you too, baby. It's too far to drive back and forth. But don't worry; we'll talk every night on the phone if you're not flying. It will help to keep me going."

"It's not going to be the same as seeing you," she muttered, pouting.

"I know, I know. I feel the same way," he soothed.

His hands continued moving softly over her. Silence reigned, Serena was as busy with her own thoughts as she was sure Kyle was with his.

Kyle was feeling pretty good right now. Even though he would miss seeing Serena during the next month or so, he was also looking forward to the training sessions at Glynco with the recruits. It always made him feel good to impart his knowledge to others, to interact and get feedback.

Before he met Serena, although he missed being full time with the SOG, he had been enjoying his time in Georgia, catching up with Keith and engaging in training sessions with local law enforcement agencies more than he normally did.

Now, of course, it was even better. He enjoyed being with Serena, her feisty spirit, how she always kept him off balance when she would say or do something totally unexpected. And of course, their lovemaking was deeply passionate. He didn't think he would ever tire of making love with Serena.

Kyle was an intensely virile man and had enjoyed a lot of encounters in bed with women, but he didn't think any of those encounters ever gave him as much pleasure and contentment as he was now experiencing with Serena. In fact, he knew that they didn't. And it wasn't only the sex.

When he was with Serena, he felt like his journey was complete; he didn't need anything else. He felt ... whole. Like right now, being with her like this, enjoying the classics—it felt so right. He had never shared his love of classical music with any other woman before, but he didn't even have to think about it with Serena. It simply felt natural, like the right thing to do.

His arms tightened around Serena as he felt his lower body stirring. She was so warm and felt so good. His arm slid slowly down past the T-shirt onto her smooth, silky thigh, enjoying the feel of her skin, and then back up again before stopping abruptly on her bottom.

He loved her delectable behind. It was nice and firm and tight. It jiggled enticingly when she walked. It was the sweetest ass he had ever seen, and right now, he discovered as his hand skimmed up her leg and stopped there, it was bare. She wasn't wearing any panties.

Chapter 17

Kyle's lower body was really stirring in earnest now. His hand started to knead the smooth tight flesh of her buttocks as he pulled her higher up his chest and looked into her eyes, feeling his desire flare hotly as he saw the sultry, sexy look in hers. The one that spoke directly to his groin, no shortcuts taken. She was ready, oh boy, was she ready.

"I like your invitation," he whispered. His eyes were heavy lidded and burning with the yearning for her that was always there, ready to erupt at a moment's notice into full-fledged passion. He just got his notice.

"Going to do anything about it?" she challenged saucily.

"Oh, you better believe I am, baby," he promised before dipping his head and covering her mouth with his.

His tongue slid in eagerly, exploring her mouth. Her tongue started to play with his, catching it and sucking before releasing and starting again.

Kyle moaned into her mouth; his peaceful mood vanished as he felt his body come alive. He slid her leg over his thigh so that she was half straddling him on the couch. He broke off the kiss, pulled the T-shirt up and off her body and swiftly reclaimed her lips.

She was gloriously naked, and the scent and feel of her—not to mention seeing her naked during the day—was driving him crazy. They had only ever made love in the night, and she looked even better in the daylight.

He ran his hand through her hair, enjoying the feel of her bouncy curls and slid his hand down her back and around to the heart of her. She was already wet, moving slowly up and down his erection, which had rapidly made its presence felt. He slid his finger up inside her, and she clenched onto him eagerly, her body shuddering.

He stroked her slowly, enjoying the feel of her warm sheath squeezing and releasing him. He was about to pull his pants down when he remembered they were on the living room couch. He didn't have any protection out here in the living room; it was on the bedside table. Damn. But then again, moving might prove to be interesting.

He placed his left foot on the floor, held her firmly around the lower back, and swung around to sit up on the couch so that her legs were now around his waist. He stood up with care and started toward the bedroom.

"Why are we moving?" she murmured, slowly running her tongue along the column of his neck and nipping him on the muscle where it bulged at the crook of his neck. He almost missed a step. He certainly missed a breath.

"Ahh, we need to get some protection," he hissed out, weaving an uneven path to the bedroom door. He had not removed his other hand, and Serena was proving quite adept at keeping his finger exactly where she wanted it. His erection was pushing against the front of his pants, eager to join in the fun.

Kyle knelt on the bed, lowering Serena and reluctantly removing his hand from her inner warmth to swiftly pull his T-shirt over his head. He untied the drawstring on the lounging pants which he had changed into, pushed the pants down, and freed his eager erection from its confines.

He turned around to get a condom, took it out of the packet, and swiftly rolled it onto his thick throbbing rod. He felt two arms twine around his middle and looked over his shoulder to see Serena smiling at him, kneeling on the bed. She appeared to be in a playful mood.

"Kyle."

"Yeah, baby," he breathed, turning around and reaching out to enfold her in his arms, kissing her neck and shoulder. His erection prodded her in the stomach.

"I … uh … I liked how we were just now," she said shyly.

"You mean, like this?" he curved his right arm behind her back and lifted her, his other arm taking her right leg and hooking it around his waist. She quickly followed suit with her left leg as he held her securely in his arms.

"Yeah, like this," she moaned, leaning in and kissing him hungrily.

He returned the kiss with interest, turned around, and sat on the edge of the bed with Serena in his lap. He raised her up slightly and opened his legs a little so that her thighs were spread wider. His manhood unerringly found her hot entrance when he lowered her, like a homing pigeon knows how to find its way.

He swallowed her moan of pleasure, loving the sound, his hands tight around her, running up and down her back. She shivered; her legs crossed at the ankles at the small of his back.

"Is this good? Do you like it like this, baby?" he crooned, kissing her all over, moving to the base of her throat when she threw her head back as she held onto his shoulders. She appeared to have lost the power of speech.

"Uh-huh, uh-huh, ahhh," she moaned, riding him gently, pulling with her leg muscles which were securely anchored behind him. He placed his hands on her hips and pulled her into him as he thrust up with his hips. Oh, God, she was so tight. The sensation was blowing his mind.

He slid his hands around and held onto her bottom,

squeezing and kneading the firm flesh. His lips trailed across her collarbone and down her sternum. He brought his hands around and palmed her breasts, pushing them up and close together before taking first one and then the other into his mouth, flicking his tongue across the taut nipples.

Serena leaned away, placing her hands on his thighs so that her breasts were raised. He licked and suckled at them, pulled her into him, and worked his way up her neck until he found her lips and took them hungrily. His tongue swirled in her mouth and captured hers in their own private dance—forward and back, side to side, advance and retreat.

The tempo increased; and she leaned into him, hugging him closer, tighter, sliding her mouth from his, and resting her head on his shoulder as she hurtled toward her climax. It was always like this when he made love to her—the first time hard and fast before they slowed down and explored each other.

Kyle thrust harder as he felt her start to tremble and clench harder around his shaft. She stiffened, and he felt the shocks rippling through her. She locked her arms and legs around his back and hips, pulling him fiercely into her as she exploded with a sharp cry.

It felt as if she would pull his backbone through his body and hers to meet her own spine. He felt his own release rushing up and, with one last thrust, emptied himself into her. They collapsed on each other's shoulders, too spent to do anything else, their breathing harsh and labored.

Gently, carefully, still holding Serena tightly in his arms, Kyle let himself fall back on to the sheets. He could feel her fingers running through his hair, caressing his head, and he murmured in pleasure. He stroked her back slowly, feeling her tremble in his arms.

He felt he could stay as he was for the rest of the day, but after a few more minutes of enjoying the feel of her in his arms, he gently eased her off him and on to the bed. Pushing slowly to his feet, he went into the bathroom, discarded the condom, and cleaned himself off. He returned to the bed with a smile of satisfaction on his face.

She was drifting into sleep, her eyes closed. He eyed her with an equal mix of pleasure and possession. She was so beautiful, with her lightly muscled body and smooth, satiny skin. After gently cleaning her off, he lay down on the bed and eased her into his arms, pulling her around so they were lengthwise. He was too tall to be comfortable lying across the bed as she had been. She made a meaningless sound as her arms came around him and went back to sleep. He closed his own eyes as a feeling of lethargy came over him. Oh yeah, it didn't get any better than this.

They slept for about an hour. They remained in the bed, gently caressing each other when they woke. Serena stretched, a sight Kyle thoroughly enjoyed, and said, "I'd better give Annette a shout. She's probably wondering what happened to me."

Kyle gave a groan. "Aw, hell, sorry, babe. I forgot to tell you that your phone was ringing when you were taking a shower. It was probably Annette. You looked so sweet when you came in for breakfast that I completely forgot."

He probably looked as disgusted as he felt because she laughed.

"It's okay, Kyle. It's not a big thing. I'll call her now."

She leaned over the edge of the bed, stretching for her bag which was on the bedside table. Kyle took the opportunity she presented to run his hands over her bottom. She swatted his hands away and turned over, the phone in her hand and pressed the quick dial for Annette's number.

"Behave, you've used up your quota for the day," she teased.

Kyle raised his brows. "Oh, have I now? Says who?" he asked challengingly as he advanced on her threateningly.

She squealed with laughter as he scooped her into his arms

and turned onto his back, holding her on top of his chest. She placed a finger on his lips as Annette answered the phone.

"Hey, Annette, sorry I missed your call earlier. No, I'm fine. Kyle picked me up last night when I came in. Yes, I'm over at Kyle's right now. Well, I would've but we … ah … we … uh … were … uhm … busy."

Kyle chuckled as he listened to Serena trying to explain to Annette that they were too busy making love last night for her to call.

"Tell her you were busy this morning too," he whispered wickedly.

Serena frowned at him, flapping her hand and making shushing movements.

"Yeah, probably later. Yeah, all right, take it easy."

She disconnected the call and closed the phone.

"So, where were we?" Kyle murmured silkily. "I believe it was something about using up quotas, yeah? Let me show you exactly how mistaken you are."

"Yeah, why don't you do that?" Serena agreed as once again they started their own private dance, waltzing toward the stars.

Another hour passed, another waking. They took a shower together and now were in the kitchen, preparing something to eat. Serena only wanted a sandwich, so Kyle decided to treat her to a po-boy, Louisiana style.

He looked at Serena out the corner of his eye as he reached into the refrigerator for the ingredients. She was a bit quiet, and he figured she was thinking about his upcoming departure. He hoped she didn't let it dampen her spirits.

It was not like he was a soldier and was going off to Iraq for a tour of duty, but he guessed, to her, it was just as bad. He often wondered how wives of soldiers dealt with that—not only the long separation but also the terrifying knowledge that their husbands might not make it back.

He turned from the fridge and placed the ingredients on the breakfast table.

"When's your next flight?"

"Day after tomorrow. Going to Las Vegas." She took the buns out of the bread bin. Her face had a fixed look, as if the prospect of playing slot machines and enjoying cabaret shows was all that was on her mind. He knew it wasn't, but he didn't pick her up on it.

"Sweet. Do you need to be back tonight? I'd love it if you stayed. I'll take you back in the morning when I'm leaving for work."

He brushed a kiss on her lips. She gave him a tremulous smile.

"I'd love that, Kyle."

She asked him, "Did you get my car fixed? What was wrong with it?" She watched as he quickly and efficiently put together two po-boy sandwiches. He placed them on the plates she had put out and slid one across to her.

"Of course I got it fixed. Your water hose had burst and I replaced it. Keith gave me a hand, so it didn't take long. It's back at your apartment and I gave Annette the keys."

"Thanks, Kyle."

"I aim to please, baby."

"Yeah, you do that and then some!" she said under her breath. As quietly as she spoke, Kyle heard her, however, and smiled with male satisfaction.

They spent a lazy afternoon talking and listening to music. The classics had given way to jazz. Kyle stripped down his handguns and started cleaning them. Serena sat next to him, watching him as he worked on the Glocks, very important tools of his trade.

He had not bothered with a shirt, and when he raised his head, he caught her staring as she greedily drank in the sight of his muscles, watching his biceps bunch and flex as he worked. She gave a shudder as she looked at the raw-looking scar on his shoulder, where he had been injured. In a strange twist of fate, his current happiness was because of that scar. If he hadn't been shot, he would not have been in Georgia, and they would not have met. The thought made him flinch.

Kyle bent his head and pursed his lips in concentration, focusing on cleaning his Glocks and on not giving in to the urge to take Serena back to bed. It seemed she was thinking the same thing. Leaning over, she ran her fingers through his hair and caressed the nape of his neck. He turned to her with a smile, and she placed her lips softly, reverently over his. He felt her emotions through the kiss and kissed her back as softly. They broke apart and looked at each other silently.

I'll miss you, her eyes said.

I will, too, his eyes responded.

His phone rang, causing them both to jump and breaking the spell. Kyle wiped his hands on a rag and picked up the phone. It was Keith.

"Where y'at?" Kyle said in greeting.

"Fixing to save you from one of your boring Sundays, is all. You're listening to that god-awful music by dead people, aren't you?" Keith was decidedly not a fan of the classics.

Kyle laughed and replied, "Yeah, I am but I'm not bored."

Keith snorted in disbelief. "Yeah, well, better you than me. Anyway, I thought you might like to hang, listen to some real music. Spencer is feeling enterprising today; he's throwing some meat on the grill, and a couple of the guys are over here. Why don't you bring your sorry behind over here so I can kick it in person?"

"Sounds good, hold on a second." He covered the phone and looked at Serena. "Want to go to a barbecue? One of the guys is grilling."

"Oh, that sounds good. Sure!" she replied, looking pleased.

He held up a warning hand. "Serena, Keith is going to be there."

He looked at her carefully, full of concern. He wouldn't mind going but not if it made Serena uncomfortable. It would take her mind off thoughts of the upcoming separation hovering over their heads. He wanted to give her some more time before she saw Keith again, but maybe this way might be better, like getting right back on a horse after you've been thrown.

Her expression dimmed for a second, and then her chin came up. She looked at him with a determined expression on her face. "Well, good. I do need to apologize to him, don't I?"

A slow smile spread across Kyle's face. He leaned over and kissed her, and then lifted the phone once more to his ear. "Yeah, awrite, we'll be there in an hour or so."

Keith was nothing else if not sharp. He gave a low whistle. "Serena is coming with you? You're sure?" He gave a sudden laugh. "Now I see why today wasn't boring. I'm not even sure you were *listening* to that damn music, were you?"

Kyle didn't rise to the bait. "See you later, Milk." He disconnected the call and turned to Serena. "I'll finish up here while you get dressed."

"Okay, but I still have to go home to change. I'm not going like this."

"I know, baby," Kyle said with a smile, "I know."

Chapter 18

In a little under an hour, they were on their way to the barbecue. Kyle had placed his last two six-packs of Budweiser in the vehicle—Georgia did not sell liquor on Sundays—and they had gone over to Serena's apartment while she changed into "something more summery," she told him.

When Serena reappeared, he whistled appreciatively. She had on light green capris with a rainbow-colored blouse that seemed to have bits of cloth flying everywhere. Her pretty feet were highlighted by open-toed sandals the same color as the capris, and she wore colorful chunky bracelets on her wrist.

"You look beautiful."

She gave him a pleased smile. "Thanks, Kyle. I wanted something lightweight, as we're going to be outside. I was thinking of jeans, but I thought I'd be too hot. Aren't you going to be hot?" she asked, looking at his long legs encased in denim.

"Nah, I'm good. Don't bother me none." Kyle shrugged away her concern.

They turned into the subdivision in which Spencer lived, and after turning down two streets, pulled up at a large ranch house. Kyle parked behind two F-150 trucks.

"I thought this was just a small gathering," Serena said in amazement as she looked around at the number of vehicles.

"Me too," Kyle responded.

He frowned as he did a quick scan of the vehicles. Not counting Kyle's truck, there were three cars in the driveway—the two Ford trucks Kyle parked behind on the road and a black Mustang with tinted windows and windshield. Kyle pointed it out to her as Keith's. He said it was faster than the factory-issued Mustangs, as Keith had modified the engine for extra performance.

Collecting the Bud from the vehicle and with a hand resting lightly on the small of her back, Kyle and Serena walked up the driveway and onto the single path to the front door. The door opened as they reached it, and Spencer's wife, Samantha, appeared.

"Hey, Kyle, good to see you." She reached up and gave him a hug and then turned to look at Serena with interest.

Kyle had visited Spencer and his wife a few times, but this was the first time he had brought someone with him. He guessed she was wondering who Serena was.

"Samantha. Good to see you too. This is Serena. Serena—Spencer's wife, Samantha."

"Pleased to meet you." Serena smiled the greeting as she shook Samantha's hand.

"Honey, not as much as people are going to be to meet you," she muttered half under her breath as she shook Serena's hand. Serena looked puzzled and Kyle's brows drew together ominously.

"Take the beer through, Kyle. Paul will show you where to put it. Everyone's out on the back deck," Samantha said, moving past them and down the front steps. "I'll be back in a moment; I need to make a quick dash to the store."

Serena turned as if to ask Kyle if he knew what Samantha meant, but at that moment, Keith appeared, a Bud in hand.

"Hey, Drum, you got here, with reinforcements too." He laughed as he spotted the beer in Kyle's hand. He turned to Serena, giving her a careful look. "Serena." He dipped his head slightly, a guarded but curious look on his face as he waited for Serena's response.

She gave him a hesitant smile and turned to Kyle. "Will you give us a moment, please, Kyle?"

Kyle looked at her, concern evident on his face. He lightly ran the backs of his fingers down her cheek.

"I'll take these through to the back. If he gives you any trouble, punch him."

He gave her a wink and moved away, grinning at Keith as he started to protest against such cavalier treatment. Serena turned back to Keith.

"I owe you an apology for my behavior last time we met. Wait." She held up her hand as he would've spoken. "I had some issues I've been trying to deal with, and I'm afraid I dumped it all on you. I'm really sorry about that. Can we start over?"

She extended her hand and smiled at him. "Hi, I'm Serena. I'm really pleased to meet you, Keith."

Keith gave an answering grin and took the hand she extended. "Likewise. I've wanted to meet you for a while now."

"Really? Why is that?"

"Oh, just wanted to see the woman who put the smile on Drum's face."

Serena blushed and Keith laughed.

"It's all good. *You're* all good for him, you know. He actually talks now in conversation! More than two sentences!" Keith had a look of mock awe on his face.

Serena laughed, feeling completely relaxed with Keith.

"You've been friends for a long while, haven't you? You two are so different."

"Yeah, since basic training. I *basically* wore him down. I think he decided he was using more energy trying to shut me up, and it was less of a hassle if he just talked to me."

Keith laughed again, a carefree sound. He appeared to have not a worry in the world.

A clicking sound made Serena turn with a smile on her face, seeing Kyle coming toward them. He slipped his arm possessively around her waist.

"Everything okay? You two good?" he asked.

"Oh, it was terrible," Serena teased, smiling up at him.

"Yeah, awful," Keith chimed in. Kyle groaned and shook his head slowly.

"I knew the two of you together would be trouble. No peace in the world now for me."

Serena laughed even as Keith asked, "Say, why were you clicking your fingers like that?"

Kyle chuckled. "Serena says I move too quietly. She doesn't hear me coming, and I always make her jump, so I promised to give her advance warning when I can."

Keith chuckled as well but Serena protested good-naturedly. "Well, you do move quietly, you know."

"I know, baby, I know. Say, Keith, I thought you said it was only going to be a couple of folks." He gestured in the general area of the back deck. "And why was everyone watching me as if I had grown horns or something? Damn, I had to fight not to check to see if my zipper was down and I didn't have my business outside!"

Keith gave a snort of irritation. "When I was talking with you earlier, Spencer overhead me say you were bringing Serena, and when Duncan called him—probably asking who was here—he mentioned that you were coming with your girl. In all fairness, I don't think he expected Duncan to spread the word like that. Since Duncan heard about that scorcher you dropped on Serena at the hospital, he's been dying to see her." He gave another snort of disgust.

Serena flushed and said, "So that's what Samantha meant when she was leaving."

Kyle didn't appear to have heard; he had an ominous scowl

on his face, but Keith looked questioningly at her. Serena explained. "Samantha said people were going to be pleased to meet me."

"Well, you're not a freak show attraction like the bearded lady at the circus, yeah," Kyle growled.

"Chill, Drum. Chill, Kyle," Keith and Serena said together. They looked at each other and laughed. A slight smile tugged at Kyle's lips.

"Yeah, definitely trouble. C'mon, let's get you something to drink and face the wolves. Get this over with."

They made their way through the house and on to the back deck, Keith in front and Kyle at her side, his hand still on her waist. To Serena, it was clear as day that he was proclaiming she was his. There were six guys and two women relaxing on the deck and in the backyard.

Kyle introduced her to their host, Paul Spencer, who was busy at the grill with hamburger patties and chicken quarters. They found a seat at an umbrella-shaded table, and Kyle brought her a wine cooler. The three of them continued to chat. Kyle looked pleased with how well she and Keith were getting on. Occasionally, someone would wander over to exchange a few words with Kyle and Keith. Kyle would introduce her, but for the most part, they were left alone.

However, Serena could feel the weight of their stares riding her back. There was one guy in particular who kept looking at her. Judging by the glare on his face and the amused smirk on Keith's, she knew Kyle had noticed as well. Knowing Kyle to be so jealous and possessive, she was amazed at the restraint he was exercising, which effectively kept him in his seat. He looked like he wanted to march over there and warn the guy to put his eyes somewhere else. He also looked like he wanted to box Keith's ears too if he didn't stop smirking.

As they finished eating a plate of the barbecue chicken and some corn on the cob, both delicious, Keith told Kyle, "I got that system installed in the Mustang. Want to check it out?"

Kyle gave Keith a resigned look. "What have you done now, Thommo? You've already got a performance chip in the computer."

"Got some ethanol for some more turbo boost. Let me show you," Keith said, jumping to his feet, his ever-present grin in place. "I'm going to steal him away for a few minutes, Serena."

"Sure," said Serena with a smile. Keith was like a kid with a new toy.

"I'll take a look later, Thommo."

"Go on, Kyle. I'll be fine," Serena urged as he looked reluctant to leave her.

"Awrite, I'll be back in a few moments."

The two left quickly, Kyle pausing on the way to have a word with Spencer.

Serena, a slower eater than the two men, continued her meal. Her fingers felt extremely sticky and she decided to wash them inside. She placed her plate in the large garbage container Spencer had provided and made her way to the back door, carrying her glass of water. As she passed the man reclining in a deck chair—the one who had been staring at her and whom she felt sure was the blabbermouth, Duncan—his hand shot out and grabbed her arm, jerking her to a stop.

"Hey there, gorgeous. I'm Ted Duncan. What's your name, other than gorgeous?" He leered at her and winked.

Serena looked down at him, feeling irritated. He had definitely had a little too much to drink.

"Please take your hands off me," she told him in a calm, polite voice. Out of the corner of her eye, she could see Spencer hurrying up from the backyard.

"Ah, c'mon, sugar. Can't you see I'm hot for you?" Duncan drawled.

"Oh, you're feeling hot? Well, let me help you cool off." And she turned her glass of cold water over and emptied it onto his lap. Duncan gave a yelp and let go of her arm immediately, scrambling to get out of the low chair.

"Yes, you look very cool now," Serena told him. Behind her, she could hear Spencer's laughter. Unfortunately for Duncan, he was wearing khaki cargo pants, and the large wet stain in such a prominent place was not an attractive sight.

"You stupid bitch! Look what you did!" Duncan yelled angrily.

Serena stiffened in rage. Her first reaction was to haul off and slap his face for insulting her, but she controlled the impulse. This was the home of Kyle's friend, Spencer, and his wife, Samantha, whom she had liked immediately after that brief meeting. She wouldn't embarrass Kyle or herself by behaving like a shrew. She took a calming breath and faced Duncan. He had grabbed a handful of table napkins and was trying frantically to blot the front of his trousers. Now *that* was a lost cause.

"Are you calling me stupid? I'm not the one who looks like his mama didn't teach him how to use the toilet. Or did you forget your Depends? If those don't work for you, there are other products," she said sweetly. "And yes, I am a bitch and proud of it. I'm a *babe in total control* of *herself*." And she spun on her heel and left, to a smattering of applause from the other guests.

When Serena returned from using the facilities, she was surprised that Kyle and Keith had not yet returned. How long did it take to look at wires and stuff under the hood of a car? You pop the hood, the owner of the car proudly points out what's been modified, the observer exclaims in wonder and awe, they clap each on the back, and exchange "yeah, but guess what I did" stories before closing the hood and coming back inside. Five minutes tops. So where were they? As she sat down at the table, she heard someone call her name.

Serena turned around and saw Spencer approaching. "Oh, hi, Paul. Still grilling?"

"Yeah, almost done. Listen, Kyle and Keith had to leave in a hurry. He asked me to give you these so you can have a ride home"—he handed her the keys to the Silverado—"says he'll pick up the truck later this evening."

Paul smiled and started to turn away, but Serena stopped him.

"Why did he and Keith leave? What's going on?"

Paul looked reluctant as he turned back and explained. "Kyle got a call, some information about a fugitive he's searching for, so he left to follow up that lead. He came inside looking for you, but I guess you were in the bathroom. He couldn't wait. That's why he left the keys for you to have."

Serena felt the blood leave her face. "Parker," she said in a low trembling voice.

Spencer's brows rose but he answered gently, "Yes, it's Parker. But don't worry, Serena. Kyle is the best there is. He's not reckless. Besides, he's got Keith covering his back. He'll be okay. You're welcome to stay as long as you like. You don't have to leave right now. Oh, and don't call him. He won't answer, and a phone that's buzzing could be dangerous, depending on where he is."

"Thanks, Paul. I'll be all right."

Serena gave Paul a brave smile even though her heart felt it was going to burst through her chest; it was banging against her rib cage so hard. Forget about driving, she knew if she tried to stand right now, her knees would buckle. She took a sip from the glass of water she had replaced and tried to look as if everything was all right in her world. She was sure she failed miserably.

Serena looked at her watch for what seemed the hundredth time. Ten minutes to ten. She still had not heard from Kyle, and it was killing her, not being able to call him. Her imagination had been working overtime as she imagined both him and Keith lying somewhere in a dark alley bleeding to death.

She had left the Spencers about three hours ago, when she felt controlled enough to drive back to her apartment. Annette had gone out, for which she was thankful—less explaining to do—and had not yet returned. The doorbell pealed and she rushed to look out the peephole. It was Kyle.

Serena yanked the door open and stared at Kyle mutely. After imagining all kinds of horrific scenarios, now that he was standing in front of her unharmed, she felt as if everything had stopped. He raised his brows when she just continued to stand there, took her gently by the hand, and led her inside. He looked tired and frustrated at the same time.

"What happened? Did you catch him?" Serena asked anxiously.

Kyle shook his head, closed the door behind him, and exhaled tiredly.

"Nah, we didn't. By the time we got to the apartment where he was supposed to be hiding—some cousin of his—he was long gone."

Kyle paced a few steps forward and swung back, his manner restless.

"The police took the man in for questioning, but they couldn't hold him for aiding and abetting because there wasn't any evidence to prove that he was. Keith and I listened in on the interrogation, but we didn't get any real info. They had to let him go. Although he did seem to recognize me, but I've never seen him before."

He frowned in recollection and then dismissed the thought. At the moment, he was more concerned with alleviating Serena's fears. He stopped in front of her, grasped her shoulders, and looked into her eyes.

"I wasn't in any danger, Serena, truly."

"I didn't know that," Serena whispered, the anguish and dread she had felt only slowly dissipating. "I kept imagining you in another shootout like the one at that apartment complex, that you and Keith could be hurt, and I don't know because there's no television crew. Do you have any idea how paralyzing that is?" She trembled with the release of nervous energy.

"I know, baby, I know," Kyle murmured, pulling her into his arms and gently stroking her back, running his hands up and down her arms.

Cold, she had felt so cold. But now she was rapidly warming up, thanks to Kyle. His touch always did that to her, created a heat that penetrated her skin all the way through to the core of her. She linked her arms around his neck and held him close, her head rested on his shoulder as he leaned into her.

She knew when he changed roles from comforter to lover. His touch moved from soothing to arousing as his large hands caressed and stroked. His breathing became ragged and heavy as he pulled her closer into his body, letting her feel the steely bulge in his pants. Her hips automatically shifted to accommodate him as her body aligned with his. He groaned, and his powerful body shuddered as his arms tightened around her, pulling her closer still. He asked two questions.

"Annette?" His lips seemed to possess a heat of their own as they trailed down the side of her neck.

"Not home," Serena gasped out as she tilted her head back to allow him access to her throat. He obliged, the fiery trail of desire he left in his wake causing her to moan.

"Your room?" His hands slid under the hem of her blouse and moved up her ribcage, his thumbs coming to rest on the underside of her breasts. If he hadn't been holding her, Serena knew she would've melted into a hot puddle at his feet. Her mouth opened, but it took three tries before anything coherent emerged. All the while, Kyle caressed and stroked, his mouth heating her flesh wherever his lips landed.

"First door," she finally managed to get out.

Kyle slid his hands under her bottom and lifted; Serena slid her legs around his waist. They were like a well-rehearsed, choreographed routine. He strode through the open door, pushing it shut with his foot before moving over to the bed and placing her on it, bracing himself on one knee.

He got rid of their clothes in record time, slid on a condom, and with a powerful thrust, joined their bodies together. Their lovemaking was hot and fast and fevered, burning away all the frustration and fear and anguish of the last few hours. Then it turned to slow and caring and gentle as they explored each other's bodies and reaffirmed their commitment to each other. In time, they slept.

Kyle awoke shortly before dawn, one hand curved possessively around Serena. He had heard Annette come in around midnight, but Serena, physically and emotionally exhausted, had slept on. Kyle rose on one elbow and looked down at Serena sleeping so peacefully. The security light from the complex filtered through the drapes and was enough for him to see. One hand was tucked under her cheek, the other rested on his hand which was draped over her waist. Her lashes, thick and black, looked like little fans. Her expression was relaxed and peaceful. His woman.

As he lay there watching her, Kyle agonized over the worry he was causing her. He hated that she was fearful over his pursuit of Parker. She seemed to be okay with the rest of his work—not totally comfortable but accepting. It was just something about Parker that triggered her alarm. She had good instincts, Kyle thought. She had never met Parker—and he prayed that she never did—yet instinctively, she knew he was bad news. Well, he would just have to catch the SOB quickly, that was all. Bring the sunny smile back to her face, and erase that scared expression from her eyes.

He sighed. It seemed like he was doing everything wrong with Serena. His job was too dangerous, he was too jealous and possessive—she said he smothered her—he panicked if he thought she was leaving him. No one else had ever made him feel or act this way. It made him feel that he wasn't in control, and he didn't like that. But what was the alternative? To let her go? Just thinking about it caused his gut to clench and the sweat to pop out on his brow. He didn't have any answers. He sighed again.

The warm breath on her face caused Serena to stir. She blinked and opened her eyes, turning on to her back. Kyle smiled down at her.

"Morning, baby. Didn't mean to wake you up," he said softly. "I've got to go. I need to get in the office early. We're moving some prisoners, and I've got to deal with the paperwork."

He leaned down and kissed her gently. "I'll call you later, awrite. Go back to sleep. I'll let myself out."

He gave her another kiss, gathered her in his arms, and hugged her and then slid from the bed and started to dress. She watched him sleepily as he tugged on his loafers.

"Bathroom is across from my room." She yawned and rolled onto her stomach, hugging her pillow. "You have to push back the truck seat. Drive safely."

He chuckled and then kissed her shoulder, giving it a playful nip.

"Take care of yourself."

"You too. Just be careful."

"Always."

Kyle closed the door gently and stood for a moment with his back to it. He hadn't left yet, but a month had never seemed so long.

Chapter 19

Serena hummed a little tune to herself as she placed some underwear into a small overnight bag, a smile on her face. Kyle was going to be back this evening, and she couldn't wait to see him. It had been a very long month, even though they spoke often on the phone, but she missed being with him, seeing his wonderful smile when he looked at her.

She missed their lovemaking—truly heaven on earth—she even missed how he moved so silently she never knew he was there behind her until he spoke.

Annette had left two days ago to be in New York, taking some vacation time to help her parents with their wedding anniversary celebrations, so she was even more alone. She was glad when Kyle suggested that she wait for him over at his apartment this evening, as he would be coming in late.

She thought of how he would wake her if she happened to fall asleep—though she didn't think she would—and she shivered in anticipation. He would slide softly and quietly into bed beside her; he would take her in his arms and kiss her on her ear, sliding around to her cheek before coming to rest on her mouth. His agile little tongue would tease her lips before delving inside to explore her mouth more thoroughly.

And what would his hands be doing? Let's see, those oh-so-talented fingers of his would be stroking her breasts, winding their way down her stomach, and coming to rest on her center, where he would stroke her into a flaming frenzy. Serena felt like she was already on her way to a flaming frenzy just thinking about what she and Kyle would be doing in a few hours.

Her cell phone rang, and she jumped, abruptly jarred out of the sensuous, erotic daydream she was most thoroughly enjoying. Her first thought was that Kyle had forgotten to tell her something before she realized it was Annette's ring tone.

"Hey, Annette. How's it going?" she asked in a cheerful if somewhat husky tone.

She cleared her throat and only belatedly realized that Annette was gasping at the other end of the line.

"Annette, Annette, what's the matter? What's happened?" she asked frantically.

Annette gave a low moan.

"Oh, Serena, it's Dad. He … he … he was mugged last night on the subway. They broke his arm and pushed him down, and he cracked his head on the concrete."

"Oh my God," Serena breathed in horror. "Is he going to be all right? He's going to be all right, isn't he?" she asked, dreading the answer.

"He's in the ICU. The doctors say he's critical, that the next twenty-four hours are going to be crucial. Mom is freaking out, she's not holding up well at all, and Gerald and Tiffany are frightened too. I hate to ask you but can you come up for a day or two? Vince can't get here till day after tomorrow and I … I need …" She broke off, drawing a shuddering breath.

Serena didn't hesitate.

"Of course, I'll come, Annette, I'll come right away. Don't you worry, honey. He's going to be all right, your dad is going to be all right, Uncle Clyde is going to be all right," she reassured her friend in soothing tones. Annette sounded like she was on the verge of losing it as well.

"Oh, Serena, I really hate asking you. I know Kyle is supposed to be back soon and—"

"Don't worry about Kyle," Serena broke in, "he'll be all

right. I'll see him soon. I don't want you to worry. Just keep an eye on your mom, and I'll be there before you know it."

After some more soothing words, Serena broke the connection and immediately checked in with crew scheduling to see if there was a flight with an available crew seat she could use. It didn't matter that she would have to be in uniform and use the jump seat; she would get to reach New York tonight. Luck was with her and she made the necessary arrangements.

Her thoughts were in a whirl, and she was becoming more agitated as she empathized with how Annette was feeling. She knew how much Annette loved her dad. Serena thought he was pretty wonderful herself.

During their college days—after that terrible time when her parents had been killed in the drunk-driving car accident—she was a welcome visitor at their house and got to know Annette's family well.

Now for this to happen so close to the Benton's wedding anniversary. She prayed that Mr. Benton—Uncle Clyde as she had taken to calling him—would make a full recovery.

She realized that she was standing in the middle of her bedroom and shook her head. *Get it together, Serena. You don't need to fall apart too.* She would need more clothes than what she was taking over to Kyle's, she thought, and started across to her dresser. Then Kyle's ringtone came on her phone.

Kyle slung his bag into the truck and swung his long legs inside the vehicle. He started the engine and rolled out, impatient to get onto the interstate and head back to Atlanta. Basic training had been good, and he was pleased overall with the performance of the new recruits, but it couldn't compare with what was waiting for him in Atlanta—Serena.

They had talked often during the last month, but it was not the same as being together, not by a long shot. She had taken to calling him by his middle name, Azizi, sometimes prefacing it by saying "My Azizi."

It pleased him no end when she did that because what she was saying, in effect, was that he meant a lot to her, as his name meant "beloved or precious one." She meant a lot to him too—he had come to realize this over the past month—and where before this might have been cause for concern, now he was happy to have her in his life.

Perhaps that was why he made the suggestion he had last night.

"I'll be coming in late tomorrow night, around eleven or maybe even later. Are you flying?" he asked, hoping she said no.

"No, I'm not, but you're going to be back so late."

She sounded disappointed that she wouldn't see him right away. He surprised himself by asking her, "Would you wait over by my place for me? It'll make me feel so good to see you when I get in."

"Yes, I'd love that, Kyle. I can't wait to see you too," she said softly.

"Okay," he replied, pleased. "I asked Keith to swing by my crib a couple times to keep an eye on things. I'll call him and ask him to drop off that spare key at your apartment. He knows where you are; he picked me up when I dropped off your car the other day."

Thinking about that conversation, knowing Serena was at his place waiting for him, gave him a warm feeling all over. He took out his cell phone and speed-dialed her number. She picked up, but Kyle didn't give her a chance to even say hello; so eager was he to let her know they would see each other in a few hours.

"Hey, baby, just wanted to let you know that I'm on my way back. I managed to leave a little earlier so I might even make it back by ten. Great, huh?" he said in a satisfied tone.

There was silence on the other end, broken by what sounded like a stifled sob.

"Serena?" he asked with a feeling of concern. "What's the matter, baby? What's wrong?"

There was a sudden panicked feeling in his gut—he was so far away from her.

"Kyle … I have to go … Annette … her father … she asked me … " Serena was talking in disjointed sentences and not making any sense.

"Calm down, baby. What about Annette and her father?" he asked.

"He was going home from work and he got mugged on the subway. They broke his arm and hit him in the head with a gun and shoved him down. He cracked his head on the concrete steps."

She was breathing jerkily. He knew how close she and Annette were—how she thought of them as her second family—and tried to comfort her.

"It's going to be okay, baby. Hang on. I'll be there in a few hours. It's going to be all right."

"That's what I'm telling you, Kyle. I'm not going to be here. I have to go to New York."

"What do you mean you have to go to New York? I'm on my way back to Atlanta now!"

He couldn't believe this was happening, not now when he had been looking forward to seeing her all day.

"I'm sorry, Kyle. Annette is freaking out, her mother fell apart, her brother and sister are scared their dad is going to die. It's all just a mess. She needs me. I have to go."

"Well, can't she need you tomorrow? I need you tonight, baby."

He was so frustrated he didn't think about what he was saying. He heard a shocked gasp at the other end.

"Kyle, how can you be so selfish? Annette is my best friend and she *needs* me! Do you understand? They were there for me when I needed them. I can't not go. I *have* to go."

Kyle swore silently. "Well, couldn't you at least wait until I get there before you leave? I want to see you too, you know."

Serena let out a tremulous gasp. "I know, Kyle. I want to see you too, but I can get a flight now if I hurry, and Annette sounds as if she's really losing it. I want to get there as quickly as possible. I want to see Uncle Clyde too. Why is that so hard to understand?"

Kyle let out a breath slowly, fighting for control against the huge disappointment and irrational anger that threatened to swallow him.

Not now, not this *now.*

"Why is it so hard for *you* to understand that I want to see you too? I thought the feeling was mutual—on the phone you certainly sounded like you missed me—or was I wrong, was all that just chat?"

He could hear his voice turn biting and angry and once again fought for control. It wouldn't do to make Serena angry; there was no telling what she would say or do.

"Kyle, please!" Serena sounded like she was at the end of her tether. "Don't do this now. I have to go to New York. I'll see you in a few days. Please try to understand, *please!*"

"A few days! A few days! It's already been a few days! It's been a month, in case you hadn't noticed!"

"Well, a few more won't matter, will it?" she snarled back, beginning to sound angry now. "Suck it up!"

"Can't you even wait until I get there?" he snapped back. "We can go up together. I don't like to think of you being in New York, even with Annette. It's not safe."

Serena made a strangled sound. "Arrgh! Kyle, would you *please* stop telling me what to do! I know you're accustomed to taking charge with your team and all, but I can look after myself! I'm capable of making my own decisions, you know."

Kyle was so angry he didn't care Serena was mad as hell. He was too.

"Do you seriously expect me not to worry about you?" he

roared. "I'm sorry if I'm coming across as a jailer, but you *are* special to me. I'm accustomed to looking after the women in my family, and I'm just trying to look out for you, too, if you would let me!"

He clenched the steering wheel tightly, his heart beating fast, but before he could continue, she jumped right back in.

"Well, you don't need to hover over me quite so much. I've managed to reach the grand old age of twenty-eight without too much going wrong, and I'm sure I can make it a while longer. Stop trying to run my life like it's a special ops assignment!" She exhaled loudly, angrily.

Kyle let loose a pithy expletive under his breath but apparently not low enough. Serena gasped.

"What did you say? Did you just swear at me, Sakyle Drummond? Because if you did, you had better do that to yourself 'cause you won't be doing it to me! And don't call me *baby* either!" she yelled irrationally. "I'm a grown woman!"

Kyle listened to the sudden, unexpected silence in his ears—all the more deafening coming so suddenly when he and Serena had just been yelling at each other—turned the phone over, looked at her picture on his phone in stunned disbelief, and realized she had hung up on him.

How did it all deteriorate so fast? One minute he was full of pleasurable anticipation that he was finally going to see Serena after an extremely long tension-filled month—he would be with her, make love to her, drown himself in her sweetness—and the next, it had all gone to hell in a handbasket.

Okay, so he could've been a little more patient and understanding about her friend's dad—hell, he should've been a *lot* more sympathetic—but surely Serena could understand that he loved her and missed her.

And hearing the thought running through his mind—one that had been bubbling just below the surface for the longest while—Kyle realized at that moment that he did indeed love Serena. He was staggered by the revelation, which hit him with the force of a bomb blast, draining away the anger and frustration he was feeling.

She was never far from his thoughts, even when he was working—which was not really a good thing, as he needed all his focus. He loved how she was so warm and caring, how she was always going out of her way to help others; in fact, wasn't that what she was doing right now? Offering love and support to her best friend?

He loved her smile, the way she teased him, made fun of him, how she was so passionate and giving in bed. He realized he had been looking forward to have her smile at him in that special way she did when they were together, like he was the focus of her world, but right now he might be lucky if she didn't beat him over the head with a baseball bat. He also realized it was because he loved her that he was always so jealous whenever any man so much as smiled at her too hard or touched her, however friendly.

He took a deep breath and willed himself to calm down. Getting upset and retaliating sure didn't help anything, but the woman had him so tied up in knots he didn't know if he was coming or going.

He'd let her calm down, he decided, before he called to apologize. No sense getting her more riled up than she already was. He was sure if he had been standing in front of her this very moment, thunderbolts would've been shooting out of her eyes and smoke pouring out of her ears.

And she had every right to be mad, he acknowledged with a wry grimace. Her best friend's dad had been grievously injured—a man she considered a second father—and he was being all kinds of an insensitive jerk. Hell, he would crawl on his knees over hot coals on a bed of nails if that's what it took for her to forgive him. But he'd do that later when she'd calmed down.

And he'd tell her he loved her, he decided suddenly. Tell her he loved her so much it was driving him insane. Acknowledging the love he felt caused it to blossom in his heart, suffusing his whole being, filling him with a sense of peace and wonder. Once again, he couldn't wait to see Serena, but this time, it was for a different reason.

He wouldn't wait either, he decided, making another split-second decision. He would go to New York, see her in person, beg her to forgive him, and tell her he loved her.

Now that he had decided on a course of action, he felt impatient to put it into motion. He'd check flights; hopefully, he might be able to catch a flight going to New York and be there early tomorrow morning.

The long lonely miles churned under his wheels, carrying him closer to Atlanta but not to Serena.

Serena couldn't understand why she was crying. She felt so furious with Kyle. How could he be so heartless? Her hands clenched and opened, clenched and opened. If he had been standing in front of her, she didn't know what she might have done.

Annette was her best friend; did he expect her to abandon Annette when she needed her the most? And to actually swear at her like that? How could he? Did she mean nothing to him? That hurt her a lot.

She loved him so much, but he didn't seem to feel the same way. Why did everyone she loved hurt her and break her heart? She felt battered by her emotions—worry over Annette, anger at Kyle for his hard-heartedness, and heartsick because he didn't appear to care for her.

Maybe she was fighting a losing battle, thinking she and Kyle could make it work. She had been so sure their relationship had been improving. They had reached a compromise concerning his dogged determination to track down and arrest Parker; he had given her that beautiful bouquet of flowers after apologizing for throwing that hissy fit when Somerset had his arm around her. And he had eased up on his heavy-handed ways after hearing of the incident at Spencer's barbecue when she had put that lecher, Duncan, in his place so effectively. When he had come by for his truck later that night, he mentioned that Spencer had told him what had happened.

But now, this. She couldn't seem to think, didn't know what to do, which way to turn. She still worried about him and the dangers of his job, but as he had so succinctly pointed out, hers was a high-risk job, too, in these days of air terrorism.

The tears poured down her face, blinding her as she dumped clothes into an overnight bag. She was fortunate to get one of the late flights into La Guardia, one of the benefits of working with an airline. If there was a seat, you could hitch a ride when you needed it.

Thank goodness she had some time off. She had planned to use it to be with Kyle when he returned from Glynco. These three days would come in handy now to be with Annette in New York. She was too upset and angry right now to worry about Kyle. One heartache at a time was enough, thank you very much, and this one was Annette's. She would concentrate on being there for Annette, to focus on her friend and think about Kyle later. Right now, it hurt too much. To Serena, it was a case of *que sera, sera*—whatever will be, will be.

Chapter 20

Serena opened her eyes as the first light of dawn crept through the drapes in Annette's room. They had set up an air mattress on the floor of her bedroom. Annette wanted Serena to take the bed, but Serena put her foot down and insisted she was fine on the air bed.

It was comfortable but she had not slept much. Her eyes were closed, yes, but she wasn't at rest. Her mind kept replaying the quarrel with Kyle, and she felt heartsick.

Her Azizi. Her beloved. Her precious one. How could he have been so unfeeling? Surely he could see she had no choice? That as much as she ached to be with him after having not seen him for so long, she had to offer support and solace to her friend. Annette's needs were greater than his at the moment, and if he couldn't appreciate that, he wasn't the man she thought he was.

That was what was really bothering her, making her so upset. She had put him on a pedestal, imbued him with godlike traits, and now it turned out he had feet of clay. Her heart felt heavy in her chest. On top of all that was her worry over Annette.

She could see the toll the attack on her father was taking on her best friend, the fear she was keeping in check. Annette's nerves were stretched tight as a drum as she put on a brave face for her mother and younger siblings.

Her mother was falling apart, seeing her husband of thirty-five years battling for his life in the intensive care unit. It was all the more heart-rending, as they had been looking forward to celebrating their thirty-fifth wedding anniversary.

Serena knew Annette had not slept well either; she heard her tossing and turning before she dropped off into an uneasy doze, which was broken by moans.

Toward dawn, the tossing and moaning ceased, and Annette appeared to have drifted into a more relaxed sleep. She sighed in compassion for her friend, thankful that she was finally able to get a few hours of sound rest.

After lying on her back for a few moments in sorrowful contemplation of recent events, Serena turned over slowly and quietly, not wanting to disturb Annette now that she was sleeping at last.

She reached for her phone to check the time. The voice-mail icon was displayed, and she flipped open the phone, checking to see whose call she had missed. It was from Kyle.

Her heart skipped a beat and then started to race. She sat there for long moments, not doing anything, tempted to close the phone and not listen to the message. She was still upset. At last, she pressed the button and keyed in her password.

She put the phone to her ear, lying back on the mattress, listening to the automated voice: "You have one unheard message. First unheard message, sent yesterday, at 10:15 pm."

He tried to call me last night, she thought, and a little of the ache she felt lifted. She heard his beloved voice, smoky and soft but sounding a little bit sad. Her heart beat faster.

"Serena. I'm sorry, bab … I'm sorry. Uh … I behaved like a real asshole, and you've got every right to be angry with me. Forgive me, please. You know I would never hurt you. I was … it's just that … I've been looking forward to seeing you so much. That's no excuse, I know, but I was really frustrated that I wouldn't see you tonight. And I wasn't swearing at you, bab … Serena, I promise. I was just upset. I'm sorry about

Annette's dad. Please tell her for me that I hope he makes a full recovery. And I'm ...I'm really, really sorry for hurting you. I didn't mean to. You're my Azizi, too. Uh ... I'll see you soon." There was the light sound of a kiss being blown into the phone, and the message ended.

Serena sat with the phone clasped to her ear, unaware that she was crying until she felt the tears sliding down her cheeks.

"Oh, Kyle, sweetie, of course I forgive you. I was upset too," she whispered aloud, feeling the sun coming out in her world again. She replayed the message, listening eagerly to his words, drinking them in like she was dying of thirst.

He sounded so sad for causing her pain and so humble, she thought, her heart overflowing with love.

"My Azizi," she repeated softly. She smiled when she remembered him stumbling over his words in his agitation, how he had started to call her *babe* and stopped. "Well, I did yell at him that I was a grown woman," she mused, feeling the smile widen on her face.

She was at the point of dialing his number, eager to talk with him, when she heard the bed creak as Annette woke up and moved. She closed the phone and hurriedly wiped her cheeks before getting up. She smiled at Annette.

"Hi, how are you feeling?" she asked softly.

"Like hell," Annette replied. "I don't think I slept a wink last night. I hope I didn't keep you up," she added anxiously.

"No, no, you didn't," Serena reassured her.

It was true; she had kept herself awake with her own worries.

"What time are we going over to the hospital?"

"Well, actually I have to go to the bank first and get some funds. My dad and I have a joint account so that if anything happened to them, I would be able to have access to funds for whatever needs to be done."

"Mom is in really no condition to do anything like that. Besides, I don't want her worrying about anything like that right now. She's got enough on her plate with Dad at the moment to worry about anything else."

"Okay," Serena said, "we'll have some breakfast, get dressed, and head out to the bank. What time are your uncle and aunt going to get here?"

Annette's Uncle Harold and Aunt Edna, her father's brother and his wife, were flying in from Washington DC. They had originally planned to drive to New York next week for the anniversary celebrations, but following the attack on his brother Clyde and his serious condition, they changed their plans and were flying instead, arriving early to offer support. Annette's older brother, Vincent, and his wife, Paula, managed to get an earlier flight and were also expected to arrive today, hence the need to visit the bank. Funds were running low.

"They're all coming in tonight. Uncle Harold and Aunt Edna get in at eight, and Vince and Paula get in at eight thirty. I'm going to pick up Uncle Harold and Aunt Edna so they don't have to wait around for Vince and Paula. Who knows if they might be delayed. Vince says he'll rent a car from the airport when he gets in."

Annette ran a hand over her face. She looked tired and frazzled. Serena's heart ached for her friend.

"Okay, honey, here's what we're going to do. After we have some breakfast, I'll clean up while you shower and change. After I get dressed, we'll be on our way."

"Oh, Serena, I don't know what I would do without you," Annette exclaimed tearfully.

"That's what friends are for, honey," Serena replied, hugging her friend. "Now, c'mon, let's have some breakfast so we can get a move on."

Serena folded the sheets she had used on the air bed and made up Annette's bed while she used the bathroom. She longed to call Kyle but decided to wait until she had more privacy and had more time. She washed her face and brushed her teeth, and arm in arm, the two friends went downstairs for breakfast.

Chapter 21

The Southern Air flight touched down smoothly on the runway. Kyle thought it poetic justice that the first available flight he was able to get was on the airline Serena worked for, but in another sense, it made him feel connected to her. Luckily, the attendants did not recognize his name—he didn't know if they were aware of his connection to one of their own—but he was glad nonetheless.

Kyle was anxious to get going on his mission of redemption. It had not been an easy flight for him. His mind refused to give him any respite, constantly swirling around a lot of *coulda, woulda, shouldas* as he replayed the argument with Serena in his head.

He already accepted that his behavior was far from commendable, and he was impatient to set things right, hopefully. No, not hopefully. He *had* to set things right with Serena. He would lose it if he lost her; it was as simple as that.

He couldn't believe how blind he was before, not to see why she was so important to him, why he thought about her constantly. It wasn't just lust, he acknowledged wryly, although there was a very healthy dose of that. It was love.

Kyle was one of the first to deplane. He bought a business class ticket specifically so he could be first off the plane, and now he quickly made his way to the car rental area and secured a vehicle. Not quite how he imagined spending the first of his three days off after Glynco, Kyle thought as he swung out of the airport complex.

It was still dark enough that headlights were a necessity, but over to the east, the first rays of light were rising over the horizon as the sun got ready to proclaim another new day.

His mouth opened suddenly in a yawn, catching him unaware. He needed some sleep and decided to take an hour's nap after he booked into a hotel. He *had* hoped to spend the day in bed, sure, not because he needed to but because he *wanted* to do so.

A day in bed with the most beautiful, the most important person in the world, *his world*, rediscovering the delights of her luscious body, stroking the satiny texture of her skin, running his hands over firmly muscled flesh, inhaling the flowery, fresh fragrance combined with the unique scent that was hers and hers alone, kissing those honey-drenched lips, sliding into her moist warmth, hearing the little kittenish cries she made as she got more and more excited and her legs tightened around him.

Kyle's body shuddered, and a small moan escaped him in a hiss of breath as beads of sweat popped up on his forehead.

Recalling an earlier conversation with Serena about Annette's parents, he remembered she had mentioned their names—Clyde and Sheila Benton—and where they had moved to in New York. It was near the Belmont Racetrack.

Using that as a guide, Kyle drove to Queens and booked into a Marriott. He crawled into the bed and set his internal alarm clock for one hour.

The sun was really coming up when he awoke after an hour, and the day looked fresh and inviting, eager for new experiences. He needed a shower and a shave and also to use the Internet to locate the precise address of Annette's parents.

After freshening up, he left his room in search of some breakfast. He checked his weapon, which was on a foot holster.

As a deputy US marshal, he was able to take it with him on the flight. Picking up the keys to the rental car and sliding the hotel room key card into his pocket, he turned off the light and left the room.

Feeling much better after his meal, he went to the business area to use the computer. He could have used the Internet connection on his iPhone but preferred to use the hotel's facilities. The monitor was bigger than his phone's and would be more comfortable for prolonged use. Even though it was convenient—unless it was absolutely necessary—he hated using the Internet connection on the phone.

After about fifteen minutes, he had narrowed the search down to about five possibilities. They were all within reasonable distance of each other and not too far from where he was currently, he noted with pleased satisfaction. That was extremely convenient.

He decided he would visit each location in person. He didn't want to risk another phone hang up from Serena or, worse, Annette. He knew the two women would've talked; they were that close. After all, Serena was here in New York if he needed any further proof of how close they were.

Besides, Annette would probably have dragged it out of Serena once she took one look at her. His baby was not good at maintaining a poker face, and she was pretty upset when she had hung up the phone. Mad as hell, yes, but upset as well.

He copied the relevant information on a pad provided by the motel, ripped the sheet off, folded the paper, and stuffed it into his pocket. He had one other search to make.

After clearing the screen, he spent another ten minutes on the computer before again jotting down some information on another sheet of paper, also securing this one in his pocket. His face had a somewhat nervous but hopeful look.

His phone rang and his heart accelerated in response. *Serena!* was his first thought as he whipped the phone off his hip before his mind registered that Marvin Gaye didn't want any "Sexual Healing." Disappointment coursed through him as he spoke into the phone. "Drummond."

"What's the matter, PT? You sound upset."

It was his sister, Akilah. She had nicknamed him PT because when she was a small child, she thought he was as tall as a palm tree. As she got older, she shortened it to PT, and the name had stuck.

His face softened into an involuntary smile. He was fond of his little sister and knew she adored him. They had always been extremely close. Even though she was nearer to his brother, Junior, in age, she had bonded more with Kyle. Now that she was a grown woman, she was not as fulsome in her affections, but he knew the strength of their tie remained just as strong as it was when she was younger.

"Hey, small fry," he answered, his disappointment easing slightly. "What's up with you?"

"No, what's up with *you*?" she insisted. "What's wrong, PT?"

"Nothing, Aki," Kyle said calmly, knowing she was like a terrier with a bone, and he would do well to nullify her concern immediately. "You're up early, what's going on?"

There was a small pause, as if she was debating whether to push him for an answer, before she rushed into speech, explaining the purpose of her call.

"Momma and I want to know if you're coming home for Thanksgiving and if you're going to bring Serena. Please, please, please say yes, Kyle. We can't wait to meet her."

Kyle was unable to prevent an involuntary sigh from escaping. He remembered the first time he had told them about Serena—no, the first time they had *dragged* it out of him.

"Kyle, honey, are you eating regularly? Do you get enough sleep?"

His mother was on the other end of the line, and her maternal concern washed over him. He always had a feeling of guilt whenever she fussed over him. After years of worrying over his father, Steve Senior, when he was on assignment, her focus had shifted to her two sons, Kyle and Steve Junior.

Like Kyle, Junior had a very dangerous job; he was a firefighter and first responder, answering calls for rescue under hazardous conditions. Junior was among the first wave of rescue personnel during Operation Katrina and also one of the volunteer firefighters in New York during 9/11.

When Kyle was shot and initially went home to recuperate, Jean Drummond swung into full "mother hen" mode, clucking over him and fussing as she looked after his needs, shooing everyone else away.

In a strange way, his being shot helped her. After years of nameless fears, finally something tangible happened, and her dread coalesced into something that could be focused on and dealt with in an efficient manner. Now that she was past that crisis, she reached a place of calm acceptance. She worried about him, to be sure, but not with the same edgy, frenetic fear. Nonetheless, Kyle still felt guilty for causing her to worry at all.

"Oh, I'm fine, Momma, never better," Kyle answered cheerfully. His mother picked up on his tone immediately. Kyle was not known for being effusive. Her tone became interested.

"Oh, what's happened? Is it a girl? Did you meet someone?"

"Momma, can't I be fine without it having to be a woman?" he protested.

"You can't fool me, Kyle, I'm your mother. Now, out with it. What's her name? How long have you known her? Where did you meet? When are we going to meet her?"

The questions rolled off his mother's tongue in rapid fire, faster than he could fire his Glock, he was sure. In the background, he could hear Akilah questioning their mother. There was a click as she picked up the extension in the kitchen. Kyle sighed. He might have been able to stall his mother but not both of them together and especially not Akilah.

"Hey, small fry, what's up?"

"You tell me. What's Momma going on about?"

"Quiet, Aki. Kyle's about to tell us all about his new girlfriend."

Kyle closed his eyes and groaned as Akilah squealed delightedly. He was doomed.

"PT! You've got a girlfriend! And you didn't tell me! What's her name? When did you meet her? When are we going to meet her?" Unknowingly, she repeated her mother's questions.

"He's now about to tell us," his mother said drily. "Go ahead, Kyle, we're all ears."

Kyle sighed again in defeat, knowing he was well and truly trapped. He could never say no to his mother and sister when they ganged up on him.

"Her name is Serena ..."

An excited squeal interrupted him. "Ooh, Serena, pretty."

"Quiet, Aki," his mother ordered peremptorily. "Go on, Kyle."

"We met when I was coming back to Atlanta from Las Vegas about two months ago. She's a flight attendant. I don't know when you're going to meet her, and yes, I like her very much."

He forestalled the inevitable question as he summed up the important points succinctly.

There was another excited gasp from Akilah at this bold admission, but his mother ignored that delicious bait and went straight for the jugular.

"Is she the reason you haven't come back to Louisiana, Kyle? I thought you would've been recovered by now. Your wound wasn't that serious."

There was a loaded silence as they all waited for his reply.

"Yes," Kyle finally replied softly, knowing in his heart that it was true. Thinking about leaving Serena and going back to Louisiana was an unpalatable thought.

"Oh, Kyle," his mother breathed.

Akilah uncharacteristically seemed to have lost the power of speech and was reduced to gasping again.

"Now, Momma," Kyle said warningly, "don't get ideas, okay?"

"I don't have to," his mother replied enigmatically. "I'm happy that you're happy, dear, and I hope we get to meet her soon."

"Yeah, well, we'll see," Kyle said, frowning at this sudden capitulation on his mother's part.

Kyle was jerked out of his musings by Akilah's sharp voice in his ear.

"Kyle! Are you there?"

"Sorry, Aki. I was thinking of something else. What did you say?" he said, knowing full well what she asked but gaining a few seconds to focus his thoughts from his woolgathering.

"I asked if you're bringing Serena for Thanksgiving."

"I don't know, Aki, we just had a quarrel," he admitted.

"Kyle! You didn't! You'd better apologize right now!"

"Hey, that's not fair. How do you know it's my fault?" Kyle protested.

"Oh, it's always the man's fault," Aki said in a tone of supreme authority. "And even if it isn't, still apologize. I want to meet this woman," she said grimly. "I've never heard you sound as happy as when you talk about her, and I'm not going to let you ruin your happiness because you're being a pigheaded, stubborn man. So you apologize right away."

"I intend to," Kyle assured her. "But Aki, I don't even know if she'll talk to me. I hurt her pretty badly," he admitted in an anguished tone.

"Oh, Kyle," Aki said, her heart breaking at the pain in her beloved big brother's voice. "She will. If she loves you half as much as you love her, she will," she assured him.

There was a short stunned silence. "How do you know I love her?" Kyle asked wonderingly. Damn, did everyone know he loved Serena? Was he that obvious? He remembered Keith asking him the same thing a while back when they had finished a workout session.

Akilah gave an exasperated sigh.

"PT, Momma and I have known you love Serena ages ago. It's so obvious every time you talk about her. So don't screw this up, okay? We really want to meet her."

"Okay, small fry. Listen, I gotta go. Say hi to Momma and Dad and Junior for me. Thanks for the pep talk. Love you."

"Love you too, PT. Call me."

"Will do."

He hung up, feeling marginally better and got up off the chair, preparing to leave. He had turned off the computer and gone into the lobby while he was on the phone with Akilah. He left the hotel on his mission of redemption.

Chapter 22

Serena pushed the bank door open, holding it to allow Annette to enter and followed her inside. A middle-aged guard stood by the front door, looking slightly bored and not quite awake. At this hour of the morning, even though they had left later than planned, there were still only a few people inside. She guessed it was because it was not yet lunch hour, when workers might make a quick stop at their bank to conduct their business. Besides, life was so fast paced these days that almost everyone she knew—herself included—used the ATM machines or the convenience of the drive-thru. Not so Annette. She was real old school.

"I still don't see why we couldn't use the drive-thru or the ATM," she grumbled good-naturedly but mildly to her friend. Annette snorted.

"ATM, ha! More likely than not, someone's waiting round the corner to relieve you of the money you just withdrew. Or standing right behind you to do so. They really should call those machines *Alright, Thanks for the Mugging.*"

Serena let out a low laugh. "Annette, girl, you are such a trip."

A reluctant smile crossed Annette's face, a change from the worried expression which now seemed to be permanently etched there.

"And what's wrong with the drive-thru?" Serena continued,

curious now to hear the reasoning for the avoidance of this time-saver.

"I always feel flustered, especially if there's a car behind me. I can never seem to find my bank card or a withdrawal slip." Annette pursed her lips and shook her head in disgust. "Somehow it always happens that I'm never close enough to the tube thing and have to stretch. It's a nightmare. Besides, in case you haven't noticed, this bank doesn't have a drive-thru."

Serena grinned again, highly amused.

"So it doesn't, but don't you ever use ATMs or the drive-thru?"

"Oh, sure, if I haven't any other choice, like after hours, you know. But I'd much rather go into the bank and have a face-to-face with the teller. Well, as much as you can these days with the *bandit barriers* in some of the banks," she said, speaking of the clear plexiglass found in quite a number of banks. Stretching from counter to ceiling, it isolated the tellers from the customers, affording them a layer of security against a robbery.

"I see this one doesn't have any though. Besides, as this is a joint account and I've never used it before, I thought it might be best to come inside in case there're any problems."

She finished filling out the withdrawal slip and took her place at the end of the relatively short line. There were only three persons ahead of her. Two tellers were at the counter, and about a dozen customers were in the bank. Serena stood behind Annette and slightly to the side, idly looking around.

Piped music streamed softly from speakers hidden in the ceiling, and two flat-screened televisions were tuned to CNN, volume turned low. The atmosphere was quiet, peaceful, like a stream flowing gently on, winding its way to the sea. Then the doors opened and the gentle stream turned into a flash flood.

Serena turned around when she heard the doors opening, and her glance took in the three men who entered. One was tall, about five ten to eleven inches, while the other two were of average height. The tall one was also the only one wearing dark sunglasses. All three had caps pulled low over their faces, and their hands were in the pockets of their cavernous jeans.

They made their way to the counter with the withdrawal slips but didn't take any out, merely leaned over, heads together, and started to converse in low tones, their eyes darting around the bank.

Serena felt a frisson of awareness brush across her back. She didn't know if it was from being around Kyle, seeing how he would stand still and observe everyone around him. No matter where he was or what he was doing, he was always aware of people and what was happening around him.

She felt her danger antenna go on alert. Something wasn't quite right about these three men.

"Annette," she whispered softly, moving closer to her friend, "I don't like the look of those men who just came in."

"Huh? Who? What do you mean you don't like the look of them?" Annette queried, swiveling her head to get a look at the three men.

"Don't look at them!" Serena hissed in alarm, feeling extremely agitated. Annette swung her head back. Her eyes grew wide at the look of tension on Serena's face.

"What's wrong? What is it?"

"I think, and I pray God that I'm wrong, but I think they might be here to rob the bank."

"Oh my God," Annette breathed in horror. Almost of its own volition, her head turned—as did Serena's—to check out the three would-be robbers.

They had split up, one ambling back toward the front door—no, toward the guard, Serena realized with horrified dread—one toward the open office where a manager could be seen working, and one toward the two tellers.

Acting on some unseen signal, they all sprang into action at the same time. Whipping a gun out of his pocket, Bandit

No. 1—the tallest guy, the one with the sunshades—stepped behind the guard, put the gun to the back of his neck, and wrenched the guard's gun from its holster.

At the same time, Bandit No. 2 was in the office, his weapon pointed at the manager, and yelling at him to put his hands in the air. The third crook was waving the two tellers away from the counter, warning them not to press the security buttons. The shouted commands of the robbers along with the screams of the customers were creating havoc.

The chaos was instant and frightening in its suddenness. One minute, everyone was going about their business normally; the next, the world had turned upside down in a sudden, terrifying blink.

"Get down, get down! Put your hands in the air!"

Bandit No. 1 yelled at the customers, who were still screaming hysterically. He gave the elderly guard a shove in their direction and laughed as the man stumbled and fell, sprawling on the ground. He came down close to Annette, and she gave him a worried look, hearing his head hit the floor as he fell.

"Shut up, shut the hell up!" the robber yelled, waving his weapon at them. There was an instant silence, broken only by gasping heaves from an elderly woman as she fought for breath.

The second robber pushed the manager, hands clasped over his head, toward the group on the floor. The first robber, who appeared to be in charge, strode over to the counter and beckoned one of the tellers forward. He took a black nylon bag out of his pocket.

"Miss, I'd like to make a withdrawal. If you'd be so kind as to assist me?" he said in a sneering tone. The girl remained frozen in place in shock and terror.

He turned his weapon on the other teller, who whimpered in fear, and asked the first one, "Would you like to be the only teller on duty today? Get your butt over here and fill this bag!"

Trembling, ashen faced, the girl moved forward shakily and took the bag.

"Hurry up, hurry up. I haven't got all damn day!"

The teller quickly emptied her cash drawer and started to hand the bag back.

"That drawer too. Are you trying to be smart with me?"

"I have to get her key," the girl stuttered.

"Well, get it and hurry up!"

The man was extremely agitated, moving from side to side, his eyes roaming over the customers huddled together. For a moment, Serena felt as if his eyes locked on hers, but she quickly averted her head. Meanwhile, the teller had returned with the key to the second drawer and swiftly emptied that one of its cash as well. She thrust the bag at the robber and stepped back quickly toward the other teller. The two clutched at each other in fear.

"Get them around here," he ordered the second robber. "You"—he gestured with his weapon at the huddled group on the floor—"on your feet. Take them into that manager's office," he told his two cohorts.

"Rip out the phone and take their cell phones. We don't want any calls going out now, do we?" He smiled evilly at the customers as they were herded toward the small office.

One robber stepped into the office, moved to the phone, ripped the cord out of the jack on the wall, and removed the other end from the phone. The other one collected the cell phones as they went in. The dazed guard was being helped along by a male customer.

"As a matter of fact," the first robber said thoughtfully as he surveyed the frightened group crammed into the office, "I think we'll take out a little insurance policy."

"Huh?" one of the others asked, looking puzzled.

The leader sighed. "We'll take one of them with us. You never know if they managed to get a signal out, you know how sneaky they are in banks. They take your money from right under your nose."

The other two laughed in glee. "They'll think twice about shooting us if we've got a pretty girl with us."

Serena saw his eyes roam over the group and lock on her face, definitely. She stared back defiantly, her heart beating wildly in its chest.

"Yes," the robber breathed, "you'll do, my pretty. She looks familiar. Get her."

"No!" Annette shrieked in alarm and terror.

Serena turned to her swiftly. "It's okay, Annette. I'll be okay. They just want to get out of here, and then they'll let me go." She prayed to God it was so.

She felt as scared as Annette looked and wished desperately that Kyle was there, knowing that he would've done something to try and save them. *Now* would've been a fantastic time for him to pull some of that overprotective crap that he was yelling about yesterday. She would've loved to have seen him show up right now. But you know, if wishes were horses, beggars would certainly ride.

He was all the way back in Georgia, and the likelihood of him showing up was about as good as her winning the Miss USA title—highly improbable. Their recent quarrel was completely forgotten, vanished in a puff of smoke, and she prayed she lived long enough to see him again, to tell him how much she loved him.

Now more than ever, she wished Annette had been modern enough to use the ATM or that her bank had a drive-thru.

Annette continued to scream hysterically, restrained now by two of the women as Serena was marched out, the two robbers in front and the leader at her back, slightly to her left. He had his gun tucked under his shirt, and there was no need for him to say anything. She had got the message—no funny business.

Serena tamped down the fear she felt as she was forcibly

led out of the office and across the floor to the entrance. She tried to remain calm, but that was proving difficult when her heart was racing in her chest and the fear threatened to overwhelm her.

Think of something! she urged herself fiercely. She tried to imagine what Kyle would do if he were in this situation, and it brought to mind a recent conversation. It had been before he left for Glynco.

She had spent the night at his place, and they were relaxing the next day after a most enjoyable evening and morning making love. He had been cleaning his handguns, and the conversation had led to what to do if you were being threatened by someone with a gun.

"The thing to remember," Kyle said as he competently stripped the Glock down, "is don't try to be a hero. Someone points a gun in your face and says give me your purse or your car keys or whatever, give it over. There's nothing in your purse that you can't replace, and you can always get another car, but you only have one life."

"You have to wait for your opportunity and seize it, like I'm doing now." He smiled wickedly, leaned forward and kissed her sweetly, slowly.

"How do you do that? How do you know?" Serena asked, looking slightly dazed.

"Well," Kyle said, looking thoughtful, "it all depends, but you try and talk to the person. That's what negotiators do in hostage situations. The more you know about someone, the more information you have, the better decisions you can make. Talking can also serve as a distraction, take their mind away from concentrating fully on you, and that can cause you to create an opportunity to escape."

He looked at her and smiled seductively. "Would you like me to hold you hostage and see if you can talk your way out?"

She smiled back, looping her arms around his neck.

"But I don't think I want to escape," she whispered as she

leaned into him and kissed him, flicking her tongue across his lips.

His hands snaked around her back and he said, "That's good because I don't think I'm going to be distracted from this mission."

The conversation played back in Serena's mind as they opened the door and stepped out into the sunlight. *Talk to him,* she said to herself, *distract him.*

"Why are you doing this? I'm not a threat to you. You're outside now and there are no cops around. You're safe. You can let me go."

"Shut up, bitch," the thief snarled. He yelled at his two cohorts to slow down, but they continued to forge ahead.

Suddenly, so quickly that Serena gasped, four men in flak vests bobbed up from behind a car and pointed guns at them, yelling for them to put their hands in the air.

Chapter 23

Kyle pulled his rental car into the curb at the third location on his list and parked. It was after ten, but his other errand had taken a little longer than he expected. However, he had wanted to take his time and get it right, and there was nothing he could have done to hurry the process along.

The temperature had risen, and it was now around eighty-two degrees. Thankfully, a light breeze stirred the air every now and then, so it was not as unpleasant as it could've been.

He shut off the engine and studied the house for a few seconds. A neat, well-trimmed lawn lay spread out from the front steps to the curb. A hedge of rose plants separated the property from the neighbor on one side while a chain-link fence performed the same service on the other side. He could see two dogs, the reason for the fence, playing in the neighboring front yard.

Kyle eased his long legs out of the Impala and started up the walkway, hurrying up the four steps and pressing the doorbell. He took a step back so he wouldn't be menacingly close when the door was opened. He knew his size was often intimidating if someone came upon him unexpectedly. An asset in his profession, to be sure, but not the effect he wanted to create now.

Footsteps sounded coming closer; there was the click of a lock, and the door swung partially open. An attractive young woman—she appeared to be in her late teens or early twenties—looked at him curiously, half hidden behind the door.

"Yes? Can I help you?" she inquired politely, her eyes widening as she took a good look at him.

"Good morning, miss," Kyle responded, equally politely. "My name is Kyle Drummond. Is this the residence of Clyde and Sheila Benton? And Annette Benton?"

"It is," the girl answered cautiously. "Who're you?"

Kyle closed his eyes in relief. Thank goodness. He opened them to find that the young woman had been joined by a young man, who seemed to be a few years older. He assumed they were Annette's younger brother and sister. They both had a worried, tense air about them, which was understandable, considering their father's present condition.

"I'm a friend of Annette's good friend, Serena. But first, I'd like to say I'm sorry to hear about your dad. How is he doing?"

The young man opened the screen door, which had been locked and waved him in.

"I'm Gerald and this is Tiffany," he said, shaking Kyle's hand as he stepped into the room. "Dad's still the same. Mom's at the hospital and we're about to go over there. Did you want a ride over or maybe directions?" he asked, spotting Kyle's rental parked at the curb.

"Well, actually, I was hoping to speak with Serena, if that's okay?" Kyle responded.

"Wait a minute. Did you say your name was *Kyle?*" Tiffany asked suddenly, as if now making a connection. Kyle nodded.

"Oh, boy, are you going to get it. I overheard them talking last night. You're in the doghouse!"

Kyle winced, but it was nothing more than he had expected.

"She's not here," Tiffany continued. "She and Annette

went out early this morning. They're going to the hospital later."

Damn, Kyle thought, *so near and yet still so far.* "Do you know where they went?" he asked Tiffany, who was grinning at him, apparently enjoying the thought of all the trouble he was in and how he was going to "get it."

"They went to the bank over on Merrick, but I doubt they'll still be there now. Maybe you should go straight to the hospital. You can follow us, if you like."

"Thanks, but I think I'll check the bank first, and if they've left already as you suspect, I'll swing by the hospital. Which facility is it?"

After getting the names of both the bank and the hospital and directions to both, Kyle took his leave. The younger Bentons followed him out the door and walked toward a Honda Accord parked in the driveway.

Kyle swung out onto the street and headed for the bank. It was actually on a side street off Merrick Boulevard, and he turned down the street, pulling into a parking spot a few cars down from the entrance of the bank.

He swung his legs out of the vehicle, eager to get into the bank and yet reluctant at the same time. He thought he was more afraid of Annette's reaction than Serena's. He remembered the intense look she had given him when he had gone to their apartment to pick up Serena for their first date.

It was a look that had silently said, *Don't mess with my friend or you'll answer to me.* He was unhappily aware that the day of reckoning was now here. He would have to answer.

He pressed the remote button as he turned away, hearing the *beep beep* as the locks automatically engaged, securing the vehicle. At the same time, two men exited a vehicle three cars up on the other side of the street, with guns drawn and darted across to take up defensive positions behind a large SUV, a Ford Expedition. They were wearing bulletproof vests and, as they ducked behind the vehicle, he read "US Marshals" on the back.

Kyle's eyebrows rose, and his antenna kicked in as he automatically, seamlessly, shifted into operational mode. *What the hell was going on here?*

He started to approach the two deputies swiftly but cautiously. One of the men swung his head around, doing a visual sweep of the area and saw Kyle approaching. His eyes widened as he saw the US Marshals ID badge that Kyle had the foresight to flip open and was holding in front of him as he approached.

The deputy marshal beckoned Kyle closer with a short, snappy flick of the wrist. Two strides later, Kyle was hunkered down slightly behind the man.

"Who're you?" the guy hissed, his eyes scanning the front and side of the bank as his partner in front of him did the same.

"Kyle Drummond, from Louisiana. Currently on TDY in Georgia. What's going on here?"

"I'm Todd Simpson, and he's Antonio Rodriguez, Tony," the deputy replied as he introduced himself and his partner. "Did you say Louisiana? Iceman from SOG?" he queried, looking up at Kyle with interest. Kyle nodded briefly.

Simpson continued, "How the hell did you get up here so fast? We only sent that e-mail early this morning. Did you get word?"

Kyle frowned. "What e-mail? Damn, I forgot to check that on my phone. I've been down at FLETC."

"That request you made a while back for any leads on your fugitive, Parker. Word was out that he was in Queens. We got some info that he's planning on hitting this bank. He should be in there with two others." He stopped when Kyle gave a stifled exclamation.

"Damn. I've tangled with him twice, but he got lucky. He must be Irish."

"Then I'm sure you won't mind giving us a hand?" Simpson raised an eyebrow, but Kyle knew Simpson realized it was a done deal. No way would a deputy with that kind of history between himself and the fugitive leave the scene.

"Couldn't drag me away," Kyle responded grimly.

Kyle couldn't believe his luck. What were the odds that over a six-month span, he would tangle with the same criminal, not once, not twice, but *three* times and in two different states? Parker had eluded him twice—first in the judicial courtroom in New York when he got wounded saving the life of the key witness, and then in Georgia, Parker fled into the shopping complex when Kyle responded to the call for assistance. Now here they both were, again back in New York and about to tangle once more. This time, Kyle vowed, it would be third-time lucky for him and unlucky for Parker.

"How do you want to play it?" he asked Simpson.

"We need someone to get inside and recon the situation, but we're all in gear." He indicated his flak vest. "We've got four more deputies on the other side, waiting for them to show. You look like an ordinary citizen, but Parker will recognize you."

He grinned humorlessly.

"Actually, I *was* going into the bank," Kyle answered. "Parker recognizing me can work in our favor. Once he sees me, he won't stick around. He'll get the hell out of there and straight into your waiting arms." He smiled tightly, also humorlessly.

"Okay, Drummond," Simpson replied. "You carrying anything?" Kyle nodded in the affirmative, pulling up the leg of his jeans to show him the holstered Glock. Simpson gave Kyle a description of what Parker was last reported to be wearing.

Kyle was about to stand and approach the bank when a low whistle and comment from Tony alerted them.

"Stand by, Todd. They've picked up company."

Three men had come out of the bank along with a woman. They scanned the sidewalk and started to move swiftly away from the door, the third man slightly behind and to the side of the woman and moving slower than the other two.

Kyle swore vehemently, his heart almost stopping in his chest. The woman was Serena.

"That's not company. That's a hostage," he growled.

Simpson swore. "You're sure? How do you know?" Simpson asked.

"Because that's my woman. So help me, God, if he so much as harms one hair on her head, I'll kill him," Kyle snarled through gritted teeth.

Simpson cursed again but with real feeling this time. The two men in front were moving so quickly they were well ahead of the last man, who was yelling at them to slow down and wait. They didn't heed his advice. Before Simpson could alert the other agents that the woman was a hostage, they had already made their move. The two men had reached a green Malibu when the other agents surrounded them, guns drawn.

"Hands in the air! Let me see those hands! Let me see those hands!" the agents yelled.

Unfortunately for Kyle and the other deputies, this action now put Serena in immediate jeopardy. Moving swiftly, the fugitive—Dave Parker, the third man—grabbed Serena around the neck with one arm and whipped out a gun with the other. He jabbed it into her temple. Kyle swore again, even more viciously, his heart pounding in his chest.

Parker pulled Serena back into the small recess into which the front door of the bank opened. He had lost his sunshades and was yelling at the marshals; they were yelling back. It was a standoff.

Kyle noticed that Parker was facing the other four agents. The area on his right was his blind side, and so he was vulnerable in that area. An idea sprang into his mind. He would only get one chance to do this right and save Serena, but it would take all his courage because one false move and she would be dead.

He whispered to Simpson, "I'm going to come up on him on his blind side. Let the other guys know before they give away my location. Call NYPD for backup."

"Tony already did," Simpson replied. He didn't try to talk Kyle out of his plan. One look at his face and Simpson could see it would have no effect. Still, he gave it a try, not caring that Kyle was an SOG operative.

"Sure you don't want to wait for NYPD and ESU?"

Kyle shook his head, already starting to inch away.

"It's a safe bet that we've also got hostages in the bank, don't forget. We don't know what condition they're in; they might be injured. The quicker this is over, the better."

He angled away from the vehicle and moved up onto the sidewalk. He heard Simpson on the handheld radio, alerting the other agents that he was a deputy US marshal as well and to hold their fire and not alert the fugitive to his position. Taking a deep breath and steadying his nerves, Kyle began the most difficult assignment of his career.

Chapter 24

He inched along the front of the building, right arm holding his Glock extended, his body facing in toward the building so that when he reached the recess, he would not have to bring his right arm, his gun hand, across his body.

Every nerve, every sense, was finely tuned and honed in on the recess where Dave Parker was holding Serena trapped. He moved with extreme caution, knowing he would only have one chance at bringing Parker down and keeping Serena safe.

As he crept slowly closer, he could hear Parker yelling at the deputy marshals to move away or he would shoot. Parker was not a fool; he would know that once he shot the hostage, he would no longer have an advantage, and they would take him down. But he knew they didn't want to take that chance, and so it was a standoff.

Kyle felt like it was the longest five yards he had ever crossed. About three feet before the edge of the recess was a short decorative ledge two feet from the ground in which the window of the bank was set. He stepped up onto the ledge and worked his way to the end.

It would give him an added advantage, as he would now be higher than Parker. If Parker swung his gaze to his right, Kyle would not be on a level with Parker's eyesight or peripheral vision. Gripping the bottom of the metal abutment for the flagpole at the front of the bank with his left hand, he cautiously leaned forward and looked around the edge of the recess.

The deputy marshal in charge, Simpson, was monitoring his progress. Seeing that he was about to look around, Simpson increased the urgency of action engaging the fugitive so that Parker's attention was wholly focused on the deputy marshals facing him.

Kyle looked around and down. Parker and Serena were right below him and about one foot in from the edge. The low bill of the baseball cap hindered Parker's peripheral vision. Kyle lowered his right arm and placed the gun barrel right up on Parker's face, the cold muzzle of the gun on his temple. His voice, as wintry as an arctic breeze, whispered in Parker's ear, "Let her go, Parker."

The deputy marshals rushed in closer, yelling at Parker, "Put the gun down! Let her go and put the gun down!"

He heard Simpson's voice saying urgently, "Don't do it, Drummond, you hear me? Don't do it."

Parker turned his head slowly to the right and looked at Kyle. He smiled.

"Well, well, if it isn't Drummond," Parker sneered. "Come for your little woman? You've only got yourself to blame for this, Drummond. If you hadn't interfered back then, if I had popped that witness, none of this would be happening. I had a big payday coming with that job but you screwed that up for me. Now you can watch your woman die." Parker was shaking with rage.

Kyle's lips moved in mocking imitation of a smile. "You think if you were holding my woman, you'd still be standing? Nah, Parker, I've come for *you*."

Kyle's voice was soft but steely, even as the fine hairs on the back of his neck stood up. *How the hell did Parker know Serena was his woman?* He would have to be very careful; the stakes had just gone up, and there was too much to lose.

"You trying to tell me if I shoot this woman I got here, it don't matter to you?" Parker asked disbelievingly.

"Collateral damage. Lots more fish in the sea. You shoot her, then I shoot you." He closed his mind to Serena's gasp of disbelief, which was tinged with pain, the shock on her face. He didn't doubt for a minute that she would be feeling betrayed, given her history.

Kyle's stomach roiled. It went against the grain, against everything he believed in, to put her in a position like this, but it was the only way to save her. Never, in any of the highly dangerous assignments he had undertaken with the SOG, did he feel the extreme terror he was now going through, seeing Serena held at gunpoint at the mercy of a career criminal like Parker. The breakfast he had consumed a few hours ago threatened to leave his body the same way it went in.

But none of this showed on his face or in his stance. His grip on his Glock was firm and unwavering; his eyes were fixed unblinkingly on Parker, his jaw clenched tight. He was putting all his experience on the line—putting the woman he loved at mortal risk—gambling that Parker would not shoot because he had a highly developed sense of self-preservation. Parker knew if he shot the hostage, he would resemble Swiss cheese the next second, riddled full of holes. Looking at Kyle at this moment, it was easy to see how he got the nickname Iceman.

"You're both here in New York, aren't you?" Parker wasn't buying it. Kyle knew he needed to be more convincing.

"Didn't know *she* was. I got a call that you were spotted this way. You've got a choice, Parker. You can walk out of here under your own steam or you can be carried out. You shoot if you've got the balls. I promise you, they'll be scraping your brains off that door."

The truth of his words was right there in Kyle's eyes—eyes which were cold, implacable, and showed no sign of wavering. He had seen Serena's eyes open wide when he said he didn't know she was in New York. He could almost see her mind working, sifting through what he said.

Parker looked into Kyle's face and saw death staring back at him. His eyes bulged, and a look of uncertainty, underscored with a hint of panic, appeared on his face.

Then Serena burst out, "You bastard! I trusted you!"

She twisted in Parker's arms, as if to lunge forward and attack Kyle. The sudden movement caught Parker off guard, and he stumbled slightly and took his eye off Kyle. The gun at Serena's temple wavered even as he tightened his grip on Serena's neck. It was the smallest of openings but it was enough for Kyle. Moving swiftly, he wrenched Parker's gun hand away from Serena and up in the air, pressing on the pressure point on Parker's wrist. The deputy marshal, who had circled around Kyle and Parker, caught the weapon as it dropped from Parker's nerveless grasp. Before Parker could even blink, deputy marshals had swarmed all over him, two pulling Serena away and two others wrestling him to the ground.

Simpson approached. "You two"—he motioned to the two deputies holding Parker—"get this piece of garbage out of here. Good job, Drummond, but easy now. It's over. Lower your weapon, man," he said to Kyle who had not holstered his weapon.

Kyle still felt a murderous rage directed toward the man. Parker was yanked to his feet, hands cuffed behind his back. He looked into Kyle's face, at the gun still pointing at him, and started to shake and scream.

"Get him away from me! This man's crazy! Get him away from me!"

Kyle heard Serena's voice coming from somewhere to his right.

"Kyle Drummond, if you shoot that man, I'm going to be very upset," Serena warned him.

"Why?" he asked, still in that calm, remote, emotionless voice.

She stepped closer to him and pitched her voice low so that it was audible only to him and to Simpson, who was right by his side.

"Because you'll go to jail, and if you go to jail, who's going to keep me warm at night?"

Kyle felt his jaw drop. At his side, he could hear Simpson give a choked snort. It sounded like a cross between laughter and disbelief. Of all the reasons he expected to hear why he shouldn't shoot the fugitive, this one was completely unexpected. But then, that was Serena. He should have realized by now to expect the unexpected where she was concerned.

An unexpected quirk tugged at the corner of his mouth, and he could feel his rage begin to dissipate.

"I swear I'll never understand you. Are you okay? Did he hurt you?" he asked anxiously, quickly holstering his weapon and gripping her shoulders. He looked her over quickly.

She had two deep bruises on her upper arms, where she had been roughly grabbed, and her throat looked sore, but other than that and some rumpled clothing, she appeared to be fine.

Kyle stared at Serena, unable to comprehend for a moment that she was safe, it was over, and she was unharmed. He hauled her into his arms, crushing her against his chest, uncaring at that moment that they were out on the street, surrounded by deputy marshals and police officers, who had arrived on the scene.

Curious spectators had gathered at safe vantage points across the street and were looking on with avid interest. More police officers swarmed up to the door and into the bank to free the hostages, who were locked in the manager's office.

Kyle's whole body was shaking as he murmured brokenly to Serena, his hands moving unceasingly as he stroked her hair, her arms, sweeping across her back.

"Oh, God, Serena, ba … are you sure you're okay? I was so terrified. I kept thinking he would call my bluff and shoot you before I could get you safely away. Are you sure you're all right?" he asked again, anxiously running his hands over her.

Kyle held onto Serena tightly, and he could feel her trembling in his arms. He knew she had to have been scared out of her wits, being held hostage by a maniac like Parker. Added to that, to hear him say she was just collateral damage had to have hurt her. Even though she might have some idea of what had gone on, he would have to explain that stunning statement.

"I thought you cared about me. How … how could you make a decision like that, with my life? Who gave you the right?" she asked in a trembling voice, a pained look on her face.

He winced and swallowed hard. "I know and I'm sorry, but I had to downplay your importance to me, had to make him believe you meant nothing to me. Holding a hostage gave him an edge. Holding *you*—believing you meant a lot to me—that was his ace. I had to make him believe that what was important to *me*—above anything else—was capturing him because he had got the better of me twice. I had to make him doubt himself, believe that his ace was worthless. You know I would *never* willingly put you in danger. If there was any other way, I would've taken it, but he had already grabbed you hostage. If we had let him walk with you, he would've killed you as soon as he no longer needed you. That's how he is. I had to work with what I had, play the hand I was dealt. But, oh, Serena, I was shaking inside. You'll never know how terrified I was." He shuddered again and drew her back into his arms. Definitely the longest he had ever talked at one time.

"He's right," Simpson said. He had been standing close by and heard what Kyle said. "I don't know if I could've pulled it off as well as he did. No wonder they call you *the Iceman.* I was damn glad to have you here today, Drummond, I can tell you that."

"I'm all right, Kyle, I'm all right," Serena assured him as he continued to hold her tightly in his arms. He had let his guard down totally, and the naked fear and pain—now that it was over—was plain on his face for anyone to see.

"Kyle," she said tremulously.

"Yes, ba … Serena," he whispered into her hair.

She smiled, "You can call me babe or baby, I don't care. What *are* you doing in New York?"

He raised his head and looked down at her, such an expression of tenderness coming over his face that she swallowed, unable to say a word.

"I came up to New York to look for you, to apologize for being such an ass about you coming up here to support your friend. I'm really sorry, baby, sorry that we quarreled."

He placed his finger over her lips when she would've spoken. "And to tell you"—he paused, his eyes seemed to take on an extra fire—"to tell you that I love you, that you mean everything to me."

Bending forward, he kissed her forehead and repeated softly, "I love you, Serena Hopewell, so very much, and I was too blind to see it before. When I saw Parker come through that door and saw that the hostage was you,"—he shuddered in remembered terror and clutched her close to him again—"I about lost my freaking mind. I was never so scared, baby. I died a thousand deaths."

Serena's breathing became erratic, her eyes growing larger as he spoke of his love for her. She hugged him fiercely, looking up at him with all her love shining out of her eyes. "Oh, Kyle, I love you too and it was so hard. I thought you didn't love me. But I thought there was a lot more fish in the sea, hmm?" she teased lightly, in an attempt to get him to lose that haunted look in his eyes.

Before Kyle could respond, Annette came barreling out of the bank, her eyes wild and staring.

"Serena, Serena! Oh my God, Serena. Are you okay? Are you hurt?"

She seemed not to notice that Serena was clutching onto Kyle as she grabbed her friend, practically wrenching her from Kyle's arms, and enveloped her in a crushing hug. Serena hugged her in return, giving her soothing pats on her back.

"It's okay, Annette. I'm okay, I'm okay. Kyle came to New York to see me, and he joined up with some other marshals, who were hunting the bank robbers. Kyle's been looking for the one who grabbed me for some time now."

"Kyle!" Annette exclaimed as she finally noticed him standing at Serena's side with one arm at her waist. He couldn't bear not to be connected to her. Kyle's heart sank as he noted Annette's aggressive stance and the way her mouth started to set in a grim line. It looked like he was about to find out the consequences of not heeding the silent warning Annette had given him, find out in spades.

"You!" she snarled. "What are you doing here? Don't you think you've done enough damage? Or have you come now to deliver it in person?"

Two years older than Serena, Annette's attitude toward the younger girl had always been protective and mothering. He assumed it had come from consoling Serena after her parents died. She stepped in front of Serena in a clearly defensive posture, placed her hands on her hips, and continued to berate him.

"I really misjudged you. I thought you were different, but noooo"—she dragged out the word sarcastically—"you're just the same."

"Annette!" Serena exclaimed. She looked horrified at her friend's outburst.

"Shut up, Serena," Annette said without missing a beat, glaring at Kyle. Kyle's face had a stunned look and he was temporarily lost for words. Annette resumed her attack.

"I thought you cared for her. You certainly *acted* like you cared, but you men, as soon as something happens that clashes with your agenda, that's it, isn't it? It's always about what you want and to hell with everybody else."

Her chest was heaving, rising and falling rapidly in her agitation. She looked like a mother hen defending her chick—no, nothing so tame. More like an enraged lioness protecting her cub.

Judging from her words, Kyle realized Serena had not told Annette he had called and apologized, and he wondered suddenly if *Serena* knew he'd done that.

She seemed to have taken his appearance in stride, but maybe he only imagined that to be the case because it was the lesser of two evils, he thought bleakly. If you had to choose between being held hostage at gunpoint and seeing the person with whom you had recently quarreled, he guessed he would go with the latter option. After all, the likelihood that you could be shot and killed with the second option was extremely negligent.

He wisely kept his mouth shut, thinking he'd let Annette work off the fear she had felt for her friend. If channeling it onto him was the way to do it, he'd gladly stand here and take it. And in all honesty, it was not like he didn't deserve to get chewed out either. He'd let Annette get everything she wanted to off her chest, and it was obvious she had a lot on her chest, no pun intended.

Serena had other ideas, however. She whipped around in front of Annette, standing between her and Kyle.

"Annette, stop it! It wasn't entirely Kyle's fault. I said some pretty stupid things too."

She had? Kyle wondered. *I don't remember that.*

"Besides, Kyle already called me and apologized. That's why he's here. He came to New York to see me and tell me in person."

"He has? He did?" Annette asked uncertainly.

She deflated like a pricked balloon, all the antagonism draining out of her.

"Oh my God. I'm sorry, Kyle. I didn't mean to … I didn't know …," she babbled incoherently.

Kyle reached over Serena's shoulder, one hand wrapped securely around her waist, pulling her into him, and laid his other hand on Annette's shoulder.

"It's okay, Annette. Calm down, I understand. I deserve to get yelled at anyhow. I was an asshole. I'm really sorry to hear about your dad. I hope he's doing better?"

"He's still in intensive care but thanks for asking. My uncle and my brother are coming in tonight, that's why we were in the bank … the bank! Oh my God, Serena, what happened? How did they get you away from that man? I was so terrified!" she exclaimed. The remembered horror of the past hour was starkly etched on her face.

"That's what I was telling you," Serena explained patiently. "Kyle got me; he came up on the side and put his gun to that man's face. He also did some pretty fast talking."

She shuddered in remembered terror.

"But Kyle," she said, turning to him with a puzzled expression, "how did you know where I was, where we were?"

"Yeah," Annette echoed, "how did you find us?"

Kyle had both arms around Serena. He was worried at how calm she was, too calm, he thought. She was in shock, but that state of calm was probably going to shatter soon. He wanted her somewhere private when that happened, not to mention that *he* also needed to unwind and just hold her, hold her for a long time and give thanks that she was alive and unharmed.

"I caught a Southern Air flight that was coming up this way. I went to Annette's house, but her sister told me you two had left early to go to the bank. When I got over here, the other deputies were already here, and Simpson, the guy in charge, briefed me when I identified myself. Then the four of you came out, and the deputies took down the other two. Parker had grabbed hold of you."

Kyle's voice stopped, and he closed his eyes in anguish, unable to go on as he remembered that first sharp moment of terror when he had realized the hostage was Serena.

There was a short silence, with each of them lost in their own thoughts. Kyle opened his eyes and looked at Annette.

"Annette, I hope you don't get mad at me again, but I need to be with Serena right now"—he glanced down at her face; it was still unnaturally calm and composed—"so we'll go now, but we'll be back over at your place in a few hours or maybe meet you at the hospital, yeah."

Although he was phrasing it as a request, he could see Annette had sense enough to know he was telling her this was what was going to happen right now and to hell with anyone who didn't like that plan.

Watching Annette look at Serena's face, even though there were no physical injuries except for a few bruises and what looked like a sore throat, Kyle knew she realized Serena was having a delayed reaction to the traumatic events of the morning.

"Yes, go," she said, shooing them with her hands. "I think I'll do the same. I'm in no condition to conduct any business today. Call me later or whatever," she finished vaguely.

"We'll do that," Kyle promised. "C'mon, Serena, let's go."

He held her tightly into his side as they walked down the block to where he had parked the rental car. Kyle pressed the remote to unlock the doors, ushered Serena into the passenger seat, and strode swiftly around the car. He pulled out into the street and headed for the Marriott. He could feel himself coming slightly unglued, and if it was that bad for him, a seasoned operative, he was sure it was a thousand times worse for Serena.

Chapter 25

Kyle swiped his key card with one hand, the other firmly attached to Serena's side. He swung open the door and ushered her inside, followed her in, and let the door swing close behind him. He took her in his arms at once, his hands touching her all over—her face, running over her back, caressing her head—all the while murmuring her name over and over. "Serena, baby, I love you so much."

Serena clung to him, her arms wrapped securely around his neck, her body trembling as the shock of the attack started to set in. Kyle started to strip off her clothes and his own with frantic haste. Serena could feel the urgency in his movements, an urgency that was transferred to her, and suddenly she also needed to touch him, only him, no clothes barring her way. She needed him to touch her the same way.

He made short work of their wardrobe, and still wrapped up in each other's arms, they fell onto the bed. Serena buried her face into the crook of his shoulder, shaking with delayed reaction.

"Oh, Kyle, you don't know how glad I was to see you. I was so scared when he grabbed me in the bank and put that gun to my head. I thought I'd never see you again, never get to tell you how much I love you. And I do love you, Kyle."

She was trembling as she clung to him.

"Shh, baby, it's over. You're safe now. I'll never let anyone hurt you," Kyle murmured as he stroked Serena's hair and held her tight, his big body shuddering with emotion.

They held on to each other, at the moment just needing to feel close, skin on skin, no clothing, stroking, and touching each other. They stayed that way for a long, long time. As her terror faded, other emotions came into play.

Serena felt her heart brimming over with love for Kyle. She had to show Kyle how much she loved him.

Serena rose up, giving Kyle a slight push so that he rolled onto his back. He looked at her, eyebrows raised in silent question. She smiled at him, placing her hand on his head lightly.

"I love your hair." She ran her fingers through it, caressing his scalp. "It's beautiful and strong, just like you."

She cradled his face between her hands and gazed into his eyes.

"I love your eyes. They show me all the love and desire you feel for me."

She ran her finger lightly over his lips before bending down and kissing him. Just when she could feel he was getting ready to take it further, she broke off and continued.

"I love your mouth and lips. You tell me you love me and you show me too."

Straddling his body, she ran her fingers lightly over his ripped chest, tweaking one of his nipples, and causing him to draw in a sharp breath.

"I love your chest. It's where I lay my head when you comfort me and hold me close to your heart."

Kyle looked quite caught up now in her ministrations, lying on his back with a humble look as she displayed her love for him in her own unique fashion. She leaned forward slightly, slipped her fingers beneath his shoulder blades, and ran them down his back.

"I love your back because when I see it, it means you're protecting me from harm."

She trailed her fingers from the top of his shoulders along his arms, running her fingers over the scar from his recent gunshot wound.

"I love your arms. They keep me safe and protect me."

She took his hands in hers, slowly licking between the base of his fingers and along the back of his hand. Kyle drew in a shuddering breath, the pleasure that simple action produced showing on his face.

She smiled sexily at him and continued, "I love your hands. They do so much for me; they soothe me when I'm in pain, comfort me when I'm sad, and caress me until I'm on fire."

She continued her sensuous journey down his body, moving to the end of the bed and holding his feet in her hands.

"I love your feet. They would kick down barriers separating us."

She kissed his instep and slowly licked it, repeating the action on the next foot.

Serena felt an explosion of feminine power when she saw the pleasure on Kyle's face as she poured out all her love. He was probably wondering if she was reading the Kama Sutra on the sly. In all the time they had been together, she had never initiated their sexual encounters. Every time they made love, he always made the first move, but she eagerly responded as her sensuality became rampant, ensuring her complete and wholehearted participation, which gave both of them a great deal of pleasure.

But this was different. This time, she had initiated their lovemaking, and it was because she had seen the naked fear and pain on his face, how terrified he had been when Parker had her hostage. She believed he truly loved her, would not hurt her as her ex-fiancé had done, and the knowledge overcame her fear of rejection, finally and totally. It added a deeper meaning, a sweeter flavor to their lovemaking.

Kyle drew in another shuddering breath as he watched and

waited to see what she would do next. He was enjoying the sexy but serious game she was playing as much as she was.

"I love your legs because they would travel miles to get to me."

She worked her way slowly up his legs, alternately nipping him with her teeth and stroking the small bite with her tongue, working first one leg and then the other.

She wondered how much more of her sexy teasing he could take. He was an extremely virile man, and he was getting very turned on by her potent words and actions. Oh yeah, he was definitely rising to the occasion.

"And last but certainly not least," she whispered, gently taking his manhood in her hand.

"I love your chocolate bar," she said as she caressed him slowly up and down.

His manhood felt thick and heavy and pulsed and twitched in her hand like a trapped bird. Kyle moaned softly.

"You've turned it over to me."

She slid her tongue from the base to the tip on one side.

"Exclusively."

She repeated the motion on the other side.

"For my pleasure."

She took him in her mouth, sliding her lips gently and sensuously along his length, slowly withdrawing to kiss him on the tip. Kyle's breath hissed through his teeth, erratic and choppy. She got on to her knees and straddled his body again, guiding him to her entrance, holding herself open with her other hand.

Kyle swiped a foil packet off the bedside table, fumbling in his haste to get it open when Serena leaned forward, plucked it out of his hand, calmly and uncaringly tossing it aside.

"We don't need these anymore," she whispered against his lips before repositioning herself.

"I love how."

She slid her body up along his shaft and back down with a sigh of pleasure, one immediately echoed by Kyle.

She rose up slightly and continued, "You take me."

She slid down onto his proudly erect shaft with a blissful moan, taking him into her warm, welcoming heat.

"To heaven."

Another moan of pleasure as she raised her hips and sank back down on him.

Kyle seared her with his gaze, raw desire blazing out of his eyes. She smiled slowly, seductively, an answering promise in her own eyes as she slowly, tantalizingly eased her hips up. She was totally in control; he was hers to do with as she pleased, and she loved the feeling of power it gave her.

She sank down again on his hot thick shaft, gathering him in inch by beautiful inch, prolonging the sweet sensation. She moaned in pleasure, "Ahhh, sweetie, this feels so good, you don't know."

Kyle shuddered in response as Serena moved slowly, sensuously, up and down on him.

Her face wore a rapturous look of extreme ecstasy as she let her sensual nature take over, holding nothing back in giving and receiving pleasure.

Her movements began to increase in tempo, rising and falling. Kyle gripped her buttocks and thrust up each time she sank down.

Serena moaned in ecstasy, savoring each exquisite feeling as she rode him—how she rode him! Everything else faded away until there was just the two of them and the incredible feel of him beneath her, between her legs. His large hands on her hips urged her on; his eyes, hot and blazing, held her fast. Their breathing grew jerky and frantic as they came closer and closer to reaching paradise. God, how she loved this man! She had just told him, but sometimes words were not enough, could never be enough. Besides, the showing was so much better than the telling.

She leaned forward, gripping his shoulders and attacked his mouth in a sudden, savage burst of passion. This is what it meant to be alive and to love and know that you were loved in return. Their moans were punctuated by the sound of slapping flesh as her buttocks bounced against his groin. She pumped up and down on his body. Her inner muscles clenched and released his hot rod. His voice urged her on to more and more pleasure.

Serena could feel molten lava beginning to bubble in her pelvic area, feel the coil of fire getting hotter and hotter, winding its way upward, tighter and tighter. Her movements became more urgent, more frantic as she rode him faster and harder.

She was pounding down the home stretch now, could almost taste victory, lunging toward the finish line; and with a long guttural cry, her body convulsed, her neck arched, and the volcano erupted, exploding out of her. Again and again, she convulsed, milking the very essence of him as the tremors raced through her body.

She collapsed on Kyle's chest, her breath coming in short gasps, hearing the accelerated beating of his heart moments before he turned her over. He was shaking, striving for control as he steadily drove into her.

The feel of him, unfettered, moving in and out of her, flesh on flesh, was the ultimate in sensuality; and she reveled in it. The sweat dripped off of him and on to her skin, dotting her face and neck and shoulders.

Incredibly, she could feel the fire beginning to roar in her again. She clamped her legs around his waist, urging him on, lifting her hips to meet every thrust, welcoming his possession, needing it.

Kyle's buttocks clenched, his hips tilted forward as he plunged into Serena's welcome warmth, feeling her muscles close tightly around him. He loved the feel of her inner warmth without the protective barrier of the condom; it heightened his senses and increased his pleasure.

He could feel his scrotum tightening as, with a fierce cry and one last plunge, he was over the edge, spilling his seed into this woman, whom he loved so much. Serena's arms tightened around his back as she held him fiercely, pulling him into her body with the same frantic urgency he felt as she once again soared up into the heavens, bucking under him, her body exploding as another orgasm made her quiver.

Kyle felt boneless as he lay panting on the bed, Serena entwined in his arms, so close it felt like they were melded together. Neither of them spoke but lay gazing at each other, gently stroking each other's face with trembling hands as their heartbeats slowly returned to normal.

Kyle remembered something Serena had said while they were making love, and a dazed look came onto his face.

"What's the matter?"

"I was remembering something you said earlier and it's … I was a little surprised at what you said, that's all."

She looked mystified. "What did I say?"

Kyle reached out and stroked her hair, looking into her eyes as he replied, "In all the time we've been together, you've only ever called me by my name, either Kyle or Azizi. This is the first time"—he swallowed—"this is the first time you've called me *sweetie.*"

She gave him that slow sexy smile that set him on fire.

"It seemed like the right time. Don't you like it?"

He reached up and kissed her throat. "I love it, babe. You can call me *sweetie* any time."

He nuzzled her neck, feeling that all was right with his world. His woman was safe, he loved her, she loved him. What more could a man want?

He still felt some of the horror and rage he had experienced when he had seen Parker with the gun at Serena's temple. He had come perilously close to killing Parker, and if Serena had not distracted him, who knows what might have happened. Making love as they had done went a long way toward alleviating some of that fear.

He felt Serena shiver and thought that she, too, might be reliving the horror of her abduction. He held her closer still, stroking her back gently and murmuring soothing words.

"It's okay, you're safe now; he can't hurt you."

Serena lay still for a moment, not replying, and then said, "I *am* scared, Kyle, but not of him. After I got your message on the phone, I knew you'd come, even though I yelled at you and hung up the phone. I'm sorry about that," she apologized again.

"Forget it, babe. You had every right. I behaved like a real ass," Kyle quickly dismissed. "But if it's not being held hostage at gunpoint, what else has you scared?" he asked, somewhat mystified.

Serena was quiet for a moment before she spoke, her words slightly muffled against his chest. "Forget it, it's nothing; it doesn't matter."

Kyle raised her face to his and looked down on her with a serious expression.

"No, it does matter. Tell me, Serena. It doesn't matter what it is. You can tell me anything, anytime."

She looked straight back at him, deep into his eyes as if gauging his sincerity.

"All right. It's … I'm scared for us, Kyle. I love you so much, it scares me. It makes me feel … vulnerable, exposed. Because if you ever left me, I don't know what I'd do. It would kill me, worse than what Danny did," she whispered.

Kyle was stunned and humbled by her stark, no-holds-barred confession. Almost of their own volition, the words tumbled haltingly out of his mouth, softly, slowly, spoken straight from his heart.

"I'm scared too, Serena baby. Hell, I'm probably just as scared as you are. I've never loved anyone the way I love you, and frankly, I'm petrified. I'm a protector, Serena, and that includes my own feelings. And loving you, well … it makes me feel pretty vulnerable too. It's not a feeling I'm accustomed to having."

He paused for a moment, gathering his thoughts and continued, holding her gaze with his.

"I've never been down this road before. It's uncharted territory for me, but if we can face it together and look after one another, well, maybe, we won't have to be scared."

He paused again and then gave a shrug and a wry smile. He looked down at her, all the love he felt blazing out of his eyes. Serena's breath caught in her throat.

"I was planning to do this properly, take you out for a nice romantic dinner at Chanterelle, but it seems as if the moment has chosen me. Nothing with you ever follows procedure, does it?"

He leaned over, swiping his pants off the floor, and fumbling around in the pocket. He turned back to her, bracing himself on one elbow. He took her hand and turned it palm up, placing a small black velvet box in the center.

This was his first errand. He had spent close to two hours looking for the contents earlier in the morning before heading for Annette's house. Serena's eyes opened wide. He smiled at her. "Open it," he told her softly. Serena popped the lid and a gasp escaped her.

The ring was beautiful. The diamond was embedded into the band, slightly raised above the surface and surrounded by sapphires. He liked it the instant he saw it, and apparently, Serena did too. Tears welled in her eyes and her lips formed an O in surprise and wonder.

Kyle sat up, took Serena in his arms and placed her so she was sitting at the edge of the bed, slid off the bed, and knelt in front of her. He held her hands in his and looked into her eyes, his face serious.

"Serena Helena Hopewell, I love you. I want to spend the

rest of my life with you, have children with you, and grow old together. Will you marry me?"

Serena looked at him, speechless with emotion. A nice romantic dinner at Chanterelle followed by a proposal would have been the traditional way to go, every girl's dream, he supposed. But that would have been following procedure, and the two of them had always blazed their own trails. He hoped he hadn't made a big gaffe by not waiting to propose as he had originally planned to do.

Proposing to her now, when they were both naked, having affirmed their love and the most basic of all rights, the right to live—*this* was what was right for them. They could always go to Chanterelle for a celebratory dinner.

She smiled tremulously at him as he waited patiently for her answer, the open velvet box on her right hand covered by Kyle's left palm. The tears were sliding down her face, her throat was all choked up, and, for a moment, she couldn't speak.

"Yes," she finally replied. "Yes, Sakyle Azizi Drummond. I will marry you."

Kyle smiled, taking the ring from the box and sliding it on her ring finger. He leaned forward and gathered Serena gently into his arms.

"I love you, baby," he whispered softly into her hair before bending to kiss her tenderly.

"I love you too, Kyle," Serena managed to respond before Kyle's lips touched hers, and they sealed their mutual declarations fittingly with a kiss. He kissed her tenderly and then rested his forehead against hers as he cupped the back of her neck and massaged it gently. A fleeting thought crossed his mind and he grinned—*what would she tell people when they asked how he proposed?*

His heart felt like it was too big for his chest; he was bursting with such joy and happiness. Pouring out his heart out to Serena, having her accept his proposal, agree to be his wife, he couldn't think of anything that had given him greater pleasure. He would never hurt her or cause her harm, would always protect her and keep her safe because that's what he was—a protector. After all, he was her own private US marshal, at her service. He wrapped his arms tightly around her, and they drifted into a contented sleep, emotionally and physically exhausted.

Kyle bolted upright, his heart slamming so hard in his chest it felt like it was going to burst forth. His skin was slick with the sweat, which poured off him and soaked the sheet, soaked Serena lying next to him. He sensed her moving scant seconds before her soft arms curved around his waist from behind, and she murmured soothing words. He gave a tortured moan.

It had been four days since Serena was taken hostage and he tricked Parker into releasing her by means of a colossal bluff, capturing Parker in the process. It had also been four nights of hell.

The nightmare was always the same: Parker pulled the trigger and Serena's head exploded. Over and over, the vivid images played in his mind. Kyle moaned again, wracked by overwhelming guilt at placing Serena's life in danger.

At the time, he made what seemed to him the best decision based on his analysis of the situation. But looking back, he was horrified at what he had done. Parker could easily have decided to kill Serena, knowing that it would make Kyle suffer. Of course, Parker most likely, would've been shot and killed by the deputy marshals, but Kyle didn't care about that. Serena could've been dead, and it would've been all his fault. Oh yes, he would've suffered. He shuddered again.

"Oh, Kyle, sweetie, it's all right. *I'm* all right. I'm right here," she murmured, her arms tight around him. He turned in her arms and she lay back down, cradling his head against her breasts as her right hand stroked his head. He concentrated on his breathing, getting his heart rate back to normal.

Serena was also sleeping badly—moaning and thrashing in her sleep—but she seemed to be comforted when Kyle held her in his arms and murmured soothing words, drifting into a more relaxed slumber. Not so Kyle.

The numbers on the clock on Serena's nightstand glowed brightly in red neon: 4:32. They had flown back to Georgia after Annette's family had shown up. They had not slept apart since that day, staying either at her place or his. Neither had returned to work as yet, although Kyle had gone into the office upon his return to file his report and speak with his chief. He had also requested and received additional time off.

He felt her twist and push against his shoulders, and he rolled onto his back, his hands automatically coming up to hold her as she lay half sprawled on his chest. He looked into her eyes—eyes which, for the past four days, were clouded with worry but now held a tinge of determination—and waited for her to speak. His own eyes were bright with the sheen of unshed tears. Serena cradled his face between her palms.

"Listen to me, Kyle," she said fiercely. "You have to stop torturing yourself like this. You made the best decision in the circumstances, the only decision. You heard what Simpson said. *You* said it yourself. He would've killed me once he was away. Don't you think I know how much courage it took to make a decision like that, when you were afraid for my life?"

"He could've killed you *then,*" Kyle whispered brokenly. "So easily he could've pulled the trigger, and you would've been lost to me forever."

He closed his eyes in anguish, and a tear leaked from beneath his lids and trickled down into his temple. Serena tapped his cheek lightly with one hand.

"But he didn't and I'm not dead. I'm right here and we're together." She wiped away the tear from the corner of his eye. "I could go on a flight tomorrow and anything could happen.

Remember that flock of birds that hit the engine of that plane and it had to land in the Hudson River? I might not be so lucky. Nothing is promised to anyone, Kyle. Let's enjoy what we have now and not borrow trouble, okay? Trouble finds you soon enough."

Kyle looked into her anxious but determined face even as her words penetrated the fog clouding his brain. She was right. She was alive and warm and in his arms, where he always wanted her to be. They had to take each day as it came and give thanks.

In a sudden, swift movement that caught her by surprise, he pulled her more fully on to his chest, raised his head, and kissed her.

"I hear what you're saying and I know you're right. I can't promise that it'll get better, but I promise to try, okay?" He smiled at her and she smiled back, looking relieved. He knew he would still have bad moments about the whole incident, but the numbing fear that jerked him awake each night was easing its tight hold on his mind.

"How many more days off have you got?" Southern Air had given her some more time in addition to her days off to recover from her traumatic experience, but he wasn't sure how much of that was left.

"I have another four days," she replied. "What are you thinking?"

"Good. How would you like to go to New Orleans, meet your future in-laws? Momma and Akilah have been bugging me to bring you for a visit. I was going to ask you if you wanted to go for Thanksgiving, but I need to talk to my dad about this, get some perspective. What do you say?"

"I'd love to meet your family, Kyle," Serena answered with a happy smile. She dipped her head and ran her tongue over his nipple. His body shuddered, and his hands tightened around her waist.

"Okay, that's settled. We'll leave tomorrow," he said

raggedly. He had something else he needed to tell her, and this was probably as good a time as any. He had given it a lot of thought, more since admitting to himself that he loved her. On second thought, make that since the truth had slapped him in the face.

"Serena," he said softly, his warm hand moving up to caress the nape of her neck.

She looked up at him with a devilish smile, which faded when she saw how serious he was.

"What's the matter, Kyle? You're not worrying again, are you?" she asked, looking a little worried herself.

"No, I'm not," he assured her quickly. "This is just something different."

"What do you mean?" She frowned, not understanding.

His hand moved from the nape of her neck, almost as if it had a will of its own, and his fingers stroked her cheek. He held her gaze with his.

"I'm leaving the SOG," he said baldly.

Her eyes popped wide and a gasp escaped her.

"Kyle! No! Why? You love the SOG! You were looking forward to going back." She looked astonished, staring at him in total disbelief.

He gave her a small smile and said, "I do and I was but I love you more."

He placed a finger against her lips when she would have spoken.

"Hear me out. I do love the SOG, but I'm going to be a married man soon, yeah. Being in the SOG is a dangerous occupation; it's best suited for someone who is single, not someone with the responsibility of a wife and a family, which I'm hoping we're going to be blessed with." His smile widened as she blushed.

"I've given this some serious thought, Serena. I've seen how hard it's been on my mother when my dad was on assignments. *You* try to hide it from me, but I know you worry about me, that I'll be shot or worse. And I never want you to be put at risk again."

He shuddered, his hand squeezing her shoulder as the horrific image of Parker with the gun to her head flashed across his eyes.

Serena listened to him without interruption, a strange half smile on her face. He wondered what she was thinking.

"Where are we going to live, Kyle? Here in Georgia or in Louisiana?"

Kyle blinked in surprise. *Where did that come from?*

"I wouldn't mind moving back there, but if you want to stay in Georgia, we can do that. Why'd you ask that?" He looked at her curiously. She linked her fingers behind his neck and chuckled.

"On my last flight, the senior attendant mentioned that she was taking up a position in administration. I thought that might be something to think about—ground operations. Then *you* wouldn't have to worry about me when I'm flying. Guess where she's going?"

Kyle laughed. "Uhh … Louisiana?" He laughed again when she nodded, a bright smile on her face.

"Baby, you don't have to do that. I know how much flying means to you, how much you love it, yeah. I can handle it."

He was touched that she was willing to give up a job she was passionate about, all because he mentioned that he was a little fearful when she was up in the air. She still looked troubled though.

"Oh, Kyle, I don't want you doing something that will make you unhappy either. I know how much the SOG means to you. When you hear your buddies talking about the different cases, you'll start to feel resentful you're not doing that anymore. You've only ever wanted to be a US marshal, that's what you told me."

"I still will be a deputy marshal, just not in the SOG. I know what my priorities are and you're at the top of my list. If you're not happy, then I'm not going to be, and I can't bear to think of you worrying because I'm on assignment. I certainly don't want you put at risk again because of me."

Serena sighed, still looking doubtful and uncertain. She loved that he thought of what would make her happy above his own desires. That's what love meant, putting the needs of your partner above your own. For that same reason, she was also prepared to stop flying and take an administrative job in one of the offices. She'd still be in the airline industry, just grounded voluntarily. But he was very stubborn when he made up his mind, and right now he was very determined this was what he wanted.

Kyle looked at her thoughtfully, his mind working. He hated to see her unhappy, but he had to admit he was surprised. He had been so sure she would've welcomed his decision, that her not agreeing was totally unexpected. Again. Really, he would've thought he'd be accustomed to that by now.

His brow puckered and then he said, "Okay, how about this? I stay with the SOG but in a volunteer capacity, not full time. That any better?"

She mulled that over and then smiled happily. "Yeah, that's better, but let's talk more about it later. Seeing we're awake, why don't we put the rest of the night to good use?"

One of her hands was already caressing his face, trailing onto his chest, and down to his rock-flat stomach.

His smile returned. His gaze got heated, eyes started to turn black as he became aroused again.

"Love that plan."

She dipped her head and kissed him, one hand cradling his head, the other running urgently over his well-muscled body. There was no more conversation for a long time.

Chapter 26

Kyle pulled the rental car onto the driveway of a charming two-storied brick house and parked behind a fire-engine red Nissan Titan pickup truck. They had flown to Louisiana, as they didn't want to spend too much of their limited time off driving. The warm bronze color of the bricks gave the house a welcoming air, not to mention the rose bushes blooming in profusion at the side of the steps and along the front of the house. The front steps led onto a wide porch, which was dotted with a few outdoor chairs and a swing seat.

Tall shady trees on either side of the house cut the sun's rays from heating the porch. It was a cool, shady spot in the late afternoon and early evening and was a favorite quiet-time area at the end of the day for Kyle's parents.

Kyle turned off the ignition and shifted in his seat, his hand caressing her hair and rubbing the back of her neck softly.

"Well, this is it, baby. My parents' place. Welcome to Louisiana."

He gave her a warm smile, love and tenderness shining out of his face and enveloping her in its warmth.

It was almost a week since Serena had been held hostage in the foiled bank robbery, and she and Kyle had forged even tighter bonds of commitment to each other as the strength of their feelings had been forcibly brought home to them when each had thought they would lose the other.

Annette had finally gotten the support she needed, surrounded by family members who had flown in—her brother and his wife plus her uncle and aunt. Her father had regained consciousness, and his prognosis for a full recovery went a long way toward easing Annette's state of mind and improving her well-being.

Kyle asked Serena to come to Louisiana with him. He mentioned that he had planned to invite her for Thanksgiving to meet his family, but in light of recent events—especially the difficulty he was having coming to grips with the decision he had made—he wanted to visit sooner rather than later. They would still be coming back for Thanksgiving, but he was impatient for Serena to meet his family now. They also had an initial discussion about his decision to leave the SOG. Serena, surprisingly, was against his decision; but he was determined she was never going to have another moment of worry because of his job. She had already had too many.

"It's so beautiful here, Kyle," Serena said, looking around with wonder.

"Just so you know, this is a surprise visit. Only Junior knows we're coming," Kyle informed her.

His smile widened as he took in her look of dismay.

"Oh no, Kyle, why did you do that?"

"Well, Momma and Akilah have been bugging me so much about meeting you, I decided I might as well; but it would be on my terms."

He didn't add that he wanted both of them in the bosom of his family so that they could be surrounded with love—especially from his mother—and hopefully ease some of the horror of the nightmarish episode. Her sleep since the incident had been punctuated with moans, only ceasing when he stroked her and murmured soothingly to allay her fears. He was in even worse shape.

"So only Junior knows. No sense letting Dad in on the plans. He could never keep a secret from Momma. C'mon, let's go."

He chuckled at Serena's face, coming around to the passenger side and taking her hand as she stepped out of the truck. Junior was waiting for them by the front door, a broad smile on his face. He embraced his brother warmly, and they pounded each other on the back.

"Great timing, Kyle. We're now about to have dinner. I told Momma I forgot something in my truck."

He laughed and turned an interested gaze on Serena. "So this is Serena, huh? Pleased to meet you at last. I'm Steve but everyone calls me Junior."

Serena extended her hand but only got as far as "I'm pleased to meet …" before Junior enveloped her in a warm hug.

"None of that here. You're Kyle's lady. You're part of the family. Welcome."

Serena smiled, looking a little less troubled with Junior's affectionate greeting.

Kyle placed his arm lightly on her waist and urged her forward through the door behind Junior. They could hear the clink of cutlery on plates and dishes and the murmur of voices. Junior stepped down a short hallway, and they could hear his voice as he went around the corner. "Hey, guess what the cat dragged in?" he asked just as Kyle, his arm now firmly around Serena's waist, came into view with Serena.

"Hey, y'all! Where y'at?"

He drew Serena forward and then stood behind her with his arms locked around her waist, his head dipping as he rubbed her cheek with his own.

"I'd like you to meet my fiancée, Serena."

Pandemonium. There was a shocked gasp from his mother as her hands flew up and crossed each other as they came to rest on her bosom and her mouth dropped open, an excited squeal from Akilah as she pushed back her chair, and raised eyebrows from his father as he took it all in calmly. It was easy to see from where Kyle got his cool, calm demeanor. His father didn't bat an eyelash, taking it all in stride.

"Good to see you, son," he greeted Kyle. "So this is your fiancée, eh?"

He got up and moved forward, as his wife seemed temporarily stunned into immobility. Akilah was too excited to sit still and wait until her father greeted Serena. Quick as a flash, she was around the side of the table and gave Serena an almighty hug, her mouth going nonstop.

"Ooh, Serena! You're finally here! Way to go, PT! That's what I'm talking about. But I can't believe you didn't tell us you were bringing Serena! And you two are engaged, that is so fabulous! You're so pretty. Your hair is gorgeous. I'm so glad Junior told me to come by this evening. I can't believe this! I'm finally meeting you, wow! I'm Akilah, by the way."

Serena felt as if she had been caught in a whirlwind. Before she could catch her breath, however, Mrs. Drummond had regained hers. She pushed to her feet and went forward to meet Serena.

"Shh, Aki, I do declare you're going to have Serena thinking we're one mad, crazy family. How do you do, m'dear? I'm Kyle's mom and I'm so happy to meet you at last."

She gave Serena a gentle hug and kiss on the cheek; Kyle's father smiled warmly at her and hugged her too.

"I'm happy to meet you all too," Serena stammered, feeling a little overwhelmed. She instinctively looked for the comfort and solidity of Kyle's presence. He stood behind her and enfolded her once again in his arms, crossing them in front at her waist, bringing a soft smile to his mother's face. She turned to Akilah.

"Set two more places, Aki. I'm sure Kyle and Serena are hungry. Show Serena where to wash up, Kyle. And y'all hurry back now. We've got a lot to talk about."

"Yes, ma'am," Kyle answered smilingly.

It had started; his family was welcoming Serena into the fold—as he had known they would—a little exuberantly perhaps, but that was Akilah. And if he wasn't mistaken, he'd swear that his mother was already thinking of grandchildren.

He had a sudden vision of Serena pregnant, her belly swollen with his child, and he swallowed, suddenly feeling fiercely possessive. He knew instinctively that she'd make a wonderful mother.

He saw their future unfold before his eyes, he and Serena and two or three kids. He didn't know how many she wanted, but that was all right with him. However many babies his baby wanted, he'd do his best to oblige, and they'd have fun trying too. A powerful feeling of contentment flowed through him, and he tightened his arm around her, dropped a kiss on the top of her head.

She looked up at him with a smile on her face.

"What was that for? Not that I'm complaining, mind you," she chuckled as she wrapped her arms around his waist.

"Did I ever tell you that you make me very happy?" His smile was tender and full of the love overflowing his heart.

Serena swallowed and answered softly, "No, but it makes me feel good, you know why?"

He cocked an eyebrow questioningly, his hand running over her hair. With a mischievous twinkle, she replied, "I aim to please."

The End